SNARES OF THE DEVIL

James K. Zavez

Get In Line Publishing

SNARES OF THE DEVIL

Book 2

Get In Line Publishing
getinlinepub@gmail.com
New Hampshire, USA
James K. Zavez

Cover Art by James K. Zavez
Design and Layout by James K. Zavez

Printed in the United States of America

This book is dedicated to my wife, Marsha Zavez, who helped me more than anyone in bringing Snares of the Devil to its publication. She is an exceptional teacher and brilliant artist who brings much joy to those who hang her paintings in their homes.

Acknowledgements

First and foremost, I would like to thank my wife Marsha who stood by me while writing this novel. She read my manuscript many times helping me work out the story both in my mind and on paper.

Thank you Betsy Thorpe at Betsy Thorpe Literary Services for editing this novel. I am very grateful for her edits that helped me pull the story together in a more logical and meaningful way. (www.betsythorpe.com)

And finally, I want to acknowledge the fiction genre. Fiction is defined as a class of literature comprising of works of imaginative narration. Something that is feigned, invented or imagined; a made up story. It is the lasting impressions of fiction that make us who we are.

Jaws reminds us that a bigger boat would be needed to get us back into the water.

Mission Impossible proves that no mission is ever really impossible.

Carrie showed us that bullying others is not a good idea and will have consequences.

Titanic demonstrated that even though we knew the ending, we'd be on the edge of our seats up until the final credits.

A Few Good Men made us feel good about ourselves because we could handle the truth.

Just Say No

"Life can be great, but not when you can't see it. So, open your eyes to life: to see it in vivid colors that God gave us as a precious gift to His children, to enjoy life to the fullest, and make it count. Say yes to life. And when it comes to drugs and alcohol, just say no."

Joint Address to the Nation
September 14, 1986
President Reagan and Mrs. Reagan

"The evidence is clear that the D.A.R.E. Programs, Fear Based Advertising , and Just Say No campaigns of the 1980s had no benefits at all." Said Keith Humphreys, a psychiatrist at Stanford University who served as a drug policy advisor under President Barack Obama.

Heroin from Mexico accounted for 93 percent of the heroin seized and analyzed by the Drug Enforcement Agency in 2015, according to the agency. The remaining 6 percent came from South America or Asia. The agency can determine the source of heroin through chemical testing.
(Associated Press, October 27, 2017)

PROLOGUE
Tuesday, February 2, 1999 / 3:30 PM
Virgen de la Candelaria Festival
Puno, Peru

The twenty-seven foot wooden 1958 Chris Craft Continental skims over the clear, smooth waters of Lake Titicaca at a comfortable cruising speed of 38 miles per hour. Its 175 horsepower dual carburetor six-cylinder flat head engine has a throaty sound similar to a Harley Davidson motorcycle. The boat's driver, Alvaro Morales, owns and operates a small marina in Puerto Acosta on the Peruvian Bolivia border. When out on charters, his wife Leandra helps with answering the phone and selling bait. He's forty-two years old and has lived along the banks of Lake Titicaca all his life.

Alvaro believes he draws life from its crystalline waters. Leandra often hears her husband boasting about never being sick due to his daily swim in "Rock Puma." Unfortunately, their son and two daughters weren't interested in the fish business and moved away to the cities of Lima and La Paz. Because Leandra almost drowned as a child, she only wades in the shallows wearing her bright orange lifejacket. Alvaro believes her cancer would be cured if she'd join him on his morning swimming ritual. But sadly, the near death experience makes her more afraid of water than the disease. He's made up his mind that if this cancer takes his wife, he will move away and never again touch the healing waters of Titicaca. Follow his beautiful Leandra into heaven. For now, he hopes that her splashing along the shoreline will be enough to heal her body.

Alvaro's only passenger to Puno Peru is a white female from the United States. She arrived at his dock at exactly 1:00 PM in a yellow and white Grumman G-44 Widgeon Seaplane. The woman is about five feet

i

seven inches tall, with long brown hair and light green eyes. She's wearing faded jeans, a button down blue sweater and a Washington Redskins Cap. Playing tour guide, Alvaro can't help but notice her bright smile every time he says something mildly interesting. She's brought with her a green backpack, and a small box wrapped with red twine, with black writing on the side. He thinks it may be a name, but his English skills have been practiced in speaking, not reading. Since she didn't offer her name and paid in cash, he addresses her as "Señorita."

Approaching the city of Puno, they can hear music echoing off the tight fitting buildings that line the shore. Puno is considered the folkloric capital of Peru and is celebrating the *Virgen de la Candelaria* festivities that honor the Virgin Mary. The streets are filled with faithful Christians dressed in colorful outfits. Alvaro's favorite part of the celebrations is the dance of the demons – diablada. This is when brightly costumed devils try and tempt the crowds to join their side with chants that promise power and everlasting life. The joyous event lasts for two weeks, swelling the local population to three times its normal size.

Slowing the boat as it nears the public dock; the lone passenger stands and grabs her personal belongings. A young Indian girl standing on the dock, dressed in a red and black devil costume walks over to the boat, takes the line from Alvaro and ties it off. Once secured, the visitor climbs onto the slanting, rickety pier and leans into the boat to discuss her return.

"Señor Morales, please don't forget to pick me up here, noon tomorrow for the trip back to Bolivia. Any problems please ring me at the Hostal Los Uros where I'll be staying. Gracias for the very pleasant boat ride and please tell your wife that it was nice meeting her and I hope she feels better soon. You have my mobile phone number?"

"Si, you're very welcome Señorita. I will tell my Leandra that you wish her good health. Please enjoy the city and celebrations. Who knows, you may want to stay longer. If so, call me. And Señorita, you must be careful – you know, traveling alone and all."

"I will," she says tossing the bow line into the boat. "Can't stay longer - see you tomorrow at twelve," she shouts over the engine noise. "Gracias, thanks again!"

Watching the glossy wooden boat pull slowly away from the dock, she feels a tug on her sweater. The little girl in the devil outfit begins speaking rapidly in Spanish with only a few words discernible to the stranger - "follow me."

Walking up white, chalky cement stairs that lead to the heart of the city, the woman becomes winded and light headed, probably due to Puno's elevation of twelve thousand feet above sea level. In comparison, the altitude back home in D.C. is about five hundred feet. She slows down and watches her pint sized guide disappear behind a faded yellow stucco building. The festival music vibrating in her eardrums provides the inspiration needed to pick up her gear and finish the walk to the hotel. Grateful for the beautiful sunny day and warm temperatures, she approaches the front of the hotel. She comes to an abrupt stop when hearing a voice call out her name.

"Caroline, Caroline Dustan, wait," yells a man with a familiar sounding English accent. "We must speak – right away, Ms. Dustan."

Not expecting to meet anyone, she turns thinking she'll see Bond, James Bond. Sadly, it's just a tall thin man dressed in a dark, three-piece suit using an umbrella as a walking stick. As he approaches, his eyes widen at the sounds of sirens and he opens the red umbrella over his balding pale head. With no clouds in the sky to indicate rain, Caroline remembers an untraceable email she got yesterday warning of open umbrellas on sunny days. She moves quickly away from the hotel entrance and crosses the street, but loses sight of the man with the umbrella. Within minutes, three police cars pull up to the front of the hotel. Five officers go inside. On a hunch, she turns around, begins walking briskly from the area. She runs into the little girl, saying "Ven conmigo – come with me." This time the girl waits for her as they run through the backstreets of Puno towards the lake's shore. The festival music is now laced with the sounds of sirens, as she stands with the girl near the water, catching her breath. Then she sees the man in the three-piece suit, paddling a rowboat in her direction.

"Yes, me again Ms. Dustan – hello," he shouts. "Welcome to Peru, we've been expecting you."

Caroline realizes her personal mission to Peru is no longer a secret. It feels more like a trap.

"You possess a stone of great value, Ms. Dustan. It must be returned home - Machu Picchu. Powerful people will do anything to get it."

"Who are you? And how do you know my name?" Caroline says. "What do you know about the stone?"

"Who I am is not important, Ms. Dustan. But you knew to run when I opened my umbrella, so you must you have some idea of my employer," he replies.

"The stone came to my home several weeks ago, an anonymous birthday present for my son on his sixteenth birthday. I'm here by formal invitation from the Peruvian government to personally return it, try to determine who sent it and why. I was promised full protection – safe from prosecution!"

"Ms. Dustan, please, I know who you are, and tell me you're not that bloody naïve. Do you really think you spoke to someone in the government? If so, why would they meet you here in Puno, and not Lima? You're in great danger and we're wasting precious time. You need to come with me so we can meet an incoming helicopter."

With the rowboat approaching, she turns to see the girl is gone. A spray of bullets whiz over her head and thoughts of protection by the Peruvian government quickly fade. She spots someone in dark clothing running down the beach towards her, shouting in Spanish. The man in the rowboat moves rapidly in the opposite direction away from her. As Caroline begins to sit on the ground and raise her arms in surrender, she hears a familiar sound coming from a thick island of reeds located off shore.

She sees the wooden boat piloted by Alvaro Morales heading in her direction and starts to run into the water. It quickly deepens and she begins to swim - the green pack over her shoulders and box strung through her left arm. Something grazes her right ear as the vessel slows to her position in the water.

"We need to get out of here right away." The boat drifts to a stop and Alvaro helps Caroline out of the water. "Who is the fool in the rowboat wearing a suit?"

"Don't know Señor Morales!" Caroline screams, as she falls onto the boat's floor. "Don't know!"

iv

Alvaro plops into the driver seat and applies full power moving quickly away from land. Caroline watches men running along the shore as they pass the rowboat. Their wake is too much for the rowboat's inexperienced captain and it quickly gets swamped. Huddled down on the bench seat along the back of the boat, Caroline sees a helicopter off in the distance. She figures it must be the pick-up for the Englishman, now sitting on the keel of his overturned boat, red umbrella fully extended.

When Caroline feels assured they're not being followed, she stands and walks to the front of the boat.

"Señor Morales thanks for saving my life," she says. She looks down at his right hand and notices it is deformed. "My name is Caroline Dustan."

"I know who you are Señorita Dustan, and I'm quite sure what's in the box," Alvaro says over the engine noise. "It was easy to figure out once I saw those people shooting at you. I heard from a fishing buddy, an ex-security guy, that a woman from the U.S. was coming to the Andes carrying an ancient stone, face carved into the front of it. Stolen from Machu Picchu!"

Stunned, Caroline sits as the boat slows against the waves pounding across the hull. The sky begins filling with dark clouds and thunder rumbling off in the distance. The winds pick up and a light rain begins to fall.

"Señorita, do you know the history of the stone you carry? Are you aware of its power? Are you? Tell me, what do you know about the snares of the devil?" Alvaro waits for an answer, pulls his grey Bolivian cowboy hat down to the rim of his thick, black eyeglasses, sealing out the torrential rain now falling.

A bolt of lightning hits Alvaro's upper body, knocking them to the floor. A burning smell lingers inside the boat. Lying on the boat's floor, with his shirt smoldering, he begs her to return the stone. "Don't give to anyone – no one, please. You must return it, trust no one. Tell my wife Leandra I love her," he stammers then passes out.

Crawling unsteadily along the floor, she reaches into her backpack and pulls out a satellite phone. Caroline touches several numbers on the lit keyboard, hoping someone in Washington D.C. can track her location. Finding life preservers stored under the seats, she puts one on Alvaro and then herself. Looking out over the front of the boat, she sees an outcropping of rocks directly in the path of the moving boat. She pulls back the throttle and tries to steer the boat away from the sharp boulders at the last minute, but it's too late. The wooden boat smashes on to the rocks and Caroline feels herself flying through the air.

Caroline opens her eyes to the sound of a loud rhythmic thumping noise overhead. Someone in the water wearing a wetsuit is attaching a yellow rope around her waist, talking loudly in Spanish. The gloved thumb goes up and within seconds, her body starts to rise out of the water towards the rotating blades above. Caroline feels weight on her arm and sees the string of the waterlogged box still wrapped around her elbow. As she's being pulled inside the helicopter, someone removes the rope from around her. She tries to speak, but begins to cough, throwing up water. A familiar voice is shouting over the engine noise.

"Please Ms. Dustan, relax, you almost drowned. You have been through a terrible ordeal. Lie back, stay calm," he says, sitting across from her wearing a rumpled suit and clutching an umbrella.

Caroline's mind begins to drift, thinking about her son's high school awards ceremony on Friday, being held at the Library of Congress. She's never missed anything in his life and won't let this incident in South America be the first. Through watery eyes, she recognizes Alvaro being pulled inside the helicopter, hears him speaking rapidly in Spanish before going quiet. The only two words she understands are "gafas" – spectacles, and "diablo" - devil. She wipes her eyes and sees a red object cutting through the twine that was securing the box to her arm. As the package is removed, she remembers where she saw that red object before. Her son Joseph showed her a picture of it in a catalogue. Said it was a prize given to the top Eagle Scout in each district. "Look Mom, it even has a corkscrew!" Joseph said something about the Swiss Army Knife and why Switzerland never went to war. "Every man, woman and child carries one in their pocket."

She is snapped back to reality by a commotion in the cabin, followed by the Englishman yelling, "Off to our bloody left you fool, we're being hunted! Incoming – nine o'clock – nine o'clock! Looks like one, no two Peruvian Mirage fighter jets closing in! They fired; hold on tight!"

An explosion is felt overhead as powerful streams of air pour inside the cabin. Hearing various alarms beeping throughout the compartment, Caroline feels the floor of the helicopter drop out beneath her. She grabs Alvaro's deformed hand as the chopper starts spinning wildly – going down with such force they are thrown towards the ceiling. The helicopter lands hard on its left side, forcing the rotor blades to chop through the vegetation, filling the cabin with debris before rolling on its side.

When Caroline opens her eyes, she sees a gouged hole in the cabin and two men outside standing in a dense, tropical forest. They're yelling at each other in Spanish, arms flailing and pointing. One of the men seems to be wearing a mask of some sort, covering half of his face. Caroline moves slowly with throbbing pain emanating from her right shoulder. She finds her green backpack near the opposite door. On her hands and knees, she crawls outside, unnoticed, into the jungle. Then she sees her unopened box lying on the ground next to a mangled rotor blade. She hears the men still arguing on the other side of the helicopter, and creeps slowly out into the open, snags the box and moves quickly back into the woods.

Sensing someone's behind her, she forgets her pain and runs down a muddy trail. Glancing over her shoulder, Caroline is surprised to find the pursuers wearing blue running shorts, Cinnamon Rainbow Surf Company t-shirts and carrying spears – indigenous people. She loses her footing and stumbles down a dry ravine, wrenching her ankle. Minutes later, she is carried on a makeshift reed stretcher through the jungle by this group of indigenous people, whistling and singing a Frank Sinatra song - badly.

Exhausted and sore, located somewhere along the Peruvian – Bolivian border, Caroline finally realizes that she may not make it to her son's award ceremony two days from now. She travels a lot for work – he'll understand. Maybe this once. Seeing that her back pack and box are being carried by the man behind them, she finally starts to relax. Not sure if she's hallucinating or not, Caroline spots a double winged antique airplane flying low overhead. Realizing there's only one thing left to do, she closes her eyes and joins in for the big finish. "I grew tall through it all, and did it – MY WAY."

"Saint Michael the Archangel defend us in battle;
be our protection against the wickedness and
snares of the devil.
May God rebuke him, we humbly pray:
And do thou, O Prince of the heavenly host,
by the power of God thrust into Hell Satan
and all the evil spirits who prowl about the
world seeking the ruins of souls.
Amen."

Prayer to Saint Michael

CHAPTER 1

Present Day
Monday / 11:40 AM
Holy Spirit Mission
Outside Acayucan Mexico

Hiking up the small, rocky knoll on my way back to Holy Spirit Mission, I hear a familiar sound emanating from behind me. A feeling of déjà vu forces me to sprint towards the stone overhangs in the courtyard for shelter. Unpleasant memories jolt me back to the Middle East, running for cover from the distinct sound produced by a Tumansky turbojet engine. Experience tells me the engine is attached to a Soviet MIG 21 Fishbed Jet Fighter. My suspicions are confirmed when I see the single engine inlet nose of the camo green MIG rocketing towards me, a few hundred feet above ground. I pull the Colt 1911 from its holster and point it at the incoming jet, just as the air to ground armaments are launched from under the wing's hard points. "Oh boy – not good!"

I wake up on my back, pinned down by stones laid 500 hundred years ago. The rocks lying over my left arm are sixty pounds heavier since Fina the wonder dog has decided to take a siesta on top of them. The good news is that the Mission's owner, Clare Atwater, along with Uncle Diego, left early this morning to drop our visitors off at the Mexico City airport. Better to be alone when the old Soviet MIG flew overhead launching its air-to-ground bombs. The bad news is, from my limited vantage point, it looks like the explosives left a series of craters, some over thirty feet deep where Holy Spirit Mission once stood. I remember being near the courtyard when the raid started, but not quick enough to get beyond the fallout. Nothing feels broken, but it's hard to move with pieces of timber and stone lying across my chest weighed down by the cast iron mission bell.

1

Knowing Houdini couldn't free himself from this predicament, I decide to save my strength and come up with a plan. My immediate hope revolves around being rescued by someone in the local village less than a mile away. That might be my only way out of this. While looking for something to help free me, the phone in my pocket starts to vibrate. Even with one arm free, I'm unable to reach it through the debris. It's close to 1:00 in the afternoon and Clare won't be back till 5:00 or 6:00.

"Señor Joe, you okay?" yells a small boy up on the crater's ridge. ·

I recognize him as an orphan who was picked up outside Missing Acres Farm after the United States Navy blew it to smithereens in efforts to shut down their illegal drug operations. My girlfriend Clare and I have taken care of him ever since and have become quite attached. Fina starts barking and wagging her tail when she sees the boy.

"Pedro! Can you get help? Ayuda? Ayuda!"

He disappears from sight with the dog on his heels. Twenty minutes later, I count four adults cautiously walking down the sides of the ridge in single file. The one wearing a cowboy hat using binoculars begins pointing in my direction, causing the group to move towards me. As they get closer, I decide to stay quiet after observing they're carrying handguns and wearing masks. Here we go again.

CHAPTER 2

The ground begins shaking as the four masked strangers approach. I see a large yellow bulldozer speeding towards us. The front blade of the Caterpillar is raised to protect the driver as it easily climbs over the remnants of the mission. As it turns towards me, I'm pleasantly surprised to see a small group of men in the Cat's rear bucket. They give me a quick wave and begin throwing rocks at the masked strangers, who then run in the opposite direction. The yellow Cat stops near me. The driver shuts down its diesel engine, blanketing the area in absolute silence. I feel a small hand grab my thumb and turn to see Pedro staring into my eyes.

"Señor Joe, they get you out! You see."

"Gracias Pedro, gracias," I whisper as Fina licks the dust off my face.

I hear men yelling in Spanish followed by chains rattling as the bulldozer is fired up. They fasten one end of the rust colored chain to the mission bell, and the other to the bucket of the Cat. The loud purr of the hydraulic motor lifts the bucket into the air taking the bell with it. Within seconds, several men rush over and take a position around the largest chunk of debris lying over me. The man closest to me with brilliant white teeth and dark black hair turns and says, "Señor Joe, no worry, we strong men." Too tired to speak, I nod my head before going black.

They must have been strong because when I wake up, I find myself on flat ground sitting against one of the Mission's outbuildings with Fina lying against me. I hear my watch beep and notice its 5:00 in the afternoon. Deciding to test the strength in my legs, I stand to see the mission bus pull into the driveway, causing Fina to go into a barking frenzy. The bus stops directly across from me on the other side of the hole where Holy Spirit Mission used to be. I see Clare rush out of the bus, stand near the edge of the crater looking in all directions.

At that very moment, I can't help but think back to when Clare picked me up at the airport in Mexico City three months ago. Her file told me she

3

was an American nun helping the poor living around Holy Spirit Mission. Since my arrival, she's been tortured, shot at and almost killed, not once, but on several occasions. Due to the previous Mission's caretaker dying, Clare took full ownership of Holy Spirit Mission about a month ago. When she left early this morning, she left me in charge. Now, she returns ten hours later to find that Holy Spirit Mission no longer exists. What stood for over five centuries is destroyed in ten minutes – my fault. The recent bombings by the United States of illegal drug manufacturing sites in Mexico, Central and South America have led to promises of revenge. Being ex-military and one of the catalysts of the bombings, I think we woke the sleeping dogs.

Clare spots me. As I lift my arm in a feeble wave, the sound of the single engine turbojet Tumansky engine fills my ears. I begin running in Clare's direction yelling for them to run and take cover.

CHAPTER 3

The MIG 21 flies close to the ground over what's left of the Mission strafing the area with its 23 mm cannon. With not much left to shoot at, the pilot stops firing and swings around in a wide arc moving closer to the ground. Circumventing the large crater to get to Clare, I see her dashing for the tree line as Diego moves the bus into the woods. Realizing that I'm the only idiot out in the open, I spot the MIG turning in my direction. Seeing the Mission's bell is lying on its side in front of me, I scramble inside, hoping the iron's thick enough to repel extremely large bullets. Once inside, the bell begins ringing loudly. Thankful that the only holes are in my eardrums, I peek and see the jet making a wide turn heading back in my direction. The pilot must be feeling cocky since the MIG is coming at me at a relatively slow speed and about 25 feet off the ground. I observe a large crack along the side of the bell. When I push on the bell's wall to check the damage, it splits in two, leaving me totally exposed.

I hear several single shots being fired from the tree line. Focusing my eyes on the yellow bus, I see Diego standing on its roof, firing what looks like a single action hunting rifle. Just as I'm about to get my bell rung, the Tumansky engine goes to full power and the jet attempts vertical flight, causing it to tilt closely towards the ground. The pilot's slow reaction and control stick overcompensation forces the right wing tip to scrape the ground. The right wing comes clean off, and I get an instant spiritual message from the Wright Brothers that this bird won't fly. As the crippled jet wobbles in my direction, I quickly climb under one of the bell's halves just as pieces of the MIG 21 rain down all around me. Watching the jet go by sliding along the ground upside down, I see the tail's gone and the cockpit flattened. What catches my eye is a symbol of a white tiger with black feet and stripes painted along the side. The jet goes over the edge of the crater and explodes. Thick black smoke bellows up from the pit, followed by a series of small explosions.

I suddenly feel a hand on the back of my head.

"Señor Joe, are you okay? I get help again?"

"Gracias Pedro! I'm okay."

"Me happy Señor Joe okay," says Pedro with a huge smile as he hugs me.

CHAPTER 4

Feeling dizzy, I manage to stand. Holding Pedro's hand, I'm able to steady myself and walk crookedly towards Clare. Struggling to think of an explanation for what happened, I look down at Pedro who throws me a big smile and squeezes my hand for comfort. Thoughts of losing Clare become a real possibility due to my stupidity.

"Joe, please tell me you're alright," she yells as she runs toward us. "Pedro, are you okay?"

"Pedro fine," he replies, letting go of my hand and taking Clare's. "Señor Joe, maybe not good. Airplane tried to hit him."

"I've had a busy afternoon," I say, beginning to ramble. "I did replace the propane gas line in the kitchen. Fixed the broken vent in the ceiling of the storage closet. Oh, and I repaired those seven broken benches in the chapel. They will now take the full weight of anyone. Pedro here will vouch for me that I did a pretty good job, although you can't verify that now."

Pedro looks at me and giggles. He's five years old and doesn't understand English very well, but he's smart enough to know that my rant is total nonsense. Clare looks over at Pedro, and bursts out laughing.

"You know something Joe, no one has ever made me laugh and cry as much as you have," she says. "I love you Joe Dustan, and you too Pedro," kneeling down to give him a big hug. "I'm so happy you're both alright."

Stunned that she's not mad, I decide to keep my mouth shut hearing footsteps behind me.

"Joseph, tell me, what happened here?"

"Diego, I was minding my own business working through a list of chores when the MIG showed up," I reply, winking at Pedro and Clare. "I can't imagine why anybody would want to level this place and try to kill me. Or, maybe I do. My best guess is the drug cartels are not wasting any time seeking revenge."

7

My smartphone begins to vibrate, and pulling it from my pocket, I read a text from Jim Carlone, Washington DC DEA Deputy Director, my good friend and part-time boss. "Flight out of Mexico City your mother was on crashed. Urgent! Call!"

I tap the contact on my iPhone. As I listen to the beeps, I think of the visitors Clare and Diego had just dropped at the airport this morning. I flashback to Mike and Joanne Lenoce eating breakfast this morning, laughing and joking about our college days together. I think of Stella Rinker, my mother's best friend who'd promised me she'll look after Mom when they get back to DC. When I hear Jim's voice on the line, I hand the phone to Clare, stand up and walk away in no particular direction. I will not accept that my mother and friends died in that plane crash. I desperately try to push those thoughts away.

CHAPTER 5

Clare grabs my hands, looks into my eyes and begins to smile.

"Everyone's okay - still in Mexico City. There was some sort of delay during check in and they missed their plane. Did you hear me Joe," she says, looking into my eyes, "they missed the plane! Carlone told me your mother's name was flagged in the computer system. Needless to say, they stayed together and all missed the flight. The flight they were supposed to be on crashed into the Gulf."

Clare hands the phone to Diego and joins me walking in a large circle around where the broken bell laid. Diego's voice breaks the silence.

"151 people are missing and presumed dead," Diego says, shaking his head. "I told Mr. Carlone what happened to the Mission and the mysterious MIG. He's sending in an American team to scour the area to see who might be responsible. I think we know who did it and why, but let's wait to be sure. Also, Mr. Carlone told me a private jet has picked up your mother, Stella, Joanne and Mike, and they're on their way to D.C."

"Señor Joe, you okay?" smiles Pedro as he hugs my leg.

"I'm good Pedro, gracias."

I think of those poor souls who died in the plane crash, and worry my mother was probably the real target. There are some very powerful people focused on revenge for us bringing the drug cartels to their knees. Holy Spirit Mission is gone and a passenger plane mysteriously crashes into the Gulf of Mexico. What's next?

"Hey Diego," I say, focusing on the here and now, "I forgot to thank you for saving my life - again. This might be the first time a man using a hunting rifle has shot down a MIG 21. You are my hero!"

"Diego, you never cease to amaze me," says Clare. "You probably could take the MIG down using a pea shooter."

"Señor Diego, you my hero," yells Pedro. "What's 'hero?'"

Clare gets in a body builder's stance, flexing her biceps. "Uncle Diego is Superman!"

"Yeah Diego Superman!" Pedro cries. "Yeah, I be Batman!"

Diego walks over to Pedro, puts his hands over his ears and says, "I told you both on many occasions that I'm too old for this crazy shit. This needs to stop!"

Clare and I look at each other and start laughing. Hearing the commotion, Fina stops camping out by a rabbit hole and begins sprinting in our direction. It's gotta be close to dinner time. Looking into the hole where the mission once was, I see black smoke coming from what's left of the smoldering MIG. I then notice a large crowd of people moving in our direction. They're carrying baskets, coolers and start unfolding blankets under a large tree. The nearby villagers must have heard what happened and decided we needed a friendly distraction. How I love the Mexican people.

CHAPTER 6

The meal ends after sunset with hugs, tears, and invites to stay in the village, which we gracefully decline – at least for now. I finally catch up with Carlone who tells me that our group just landed at Andrews Air Force Base. Jim lets me know he made contact with my mother during the flight, telling her we knew they were safe. I ramble on with additional details concerning the attack at the mission. In a hushed voice, he confirms the airliner that crashed into the Gulf of Mexico was shot down. Still no word if the missiles came from sea, land, or air. No survivors. We both agree that revenge is the motive and make plans to talk again tomorrow. Carlone reminds me that a team will be landing in the morning to comb through the Mission ruins and retrieve the pilot's remains.

I see Clare heading towards one of the two outbuildings that survived the attack. One is a storage shed, and the other houses the shower and bathroom facilities. Because of our recent visitors, most of our stuff, including clean clothes, was stored in the shed. Clare sees me watching her, and gives a quick wave.

I'm startled by a hand touching my shoulder.

"Hey Joe, sure you're alright?" Diego says, concerned.

"Yeah, thanks for asking. Spoke to Jim – he's sure that the Mission bombing and jetliner crash are related. He's saying it's revenge from the cartels bosses. I think he's right. Oh, and he said Mom and the others landed safely in DC and are on their way home."

"So what now, Joseph? Holy Spirit Mission is gone and I fear the cartels will not stop the attacks. They've had several months to regroup - refocus on their enemy – the United States. They have little to lose and everything to gain. Not to mention thousands of foot soldiers scattered throughout the Americas that will do anything they say. Heaven help us."

"You're right. But I'll tell you one thing. You can't keep poking the

11

U. S. with a stick believing we'll roll over and play dead. Look at the poll numbers that came out recently. Eighty-seven percent of Americans' agree the number one ongoing threat to their security is the drug cartels in Mexico, Central and South America."

Our conversation ends when Diego takes a call from Darnell, his business partner. I decide to head over to the storage shed to look for Clare along with a flashlight, since it's getting dark. Approaching the building, I hear Clare singing a song I haven't heard for years. Mom loves Fleetwood Mac and "Landslide" is one of her favorites. Clare sings it beautifully and reminds me "the landslide will bring you down." In our case, let's hope not.

CHAPTER 7

Stepping through the door of the shed, Clare shines a bright light in my eyes that causes me to trip over something on the floor.

"Oops, sorry Joe – you okay?"

"Yeah, still feel a little dizzy – my ears are still ringing."

"Maybe you should sit down."

"Good idea." I slide down the wall to the ground.

"Maybe now you'll finally open that box that you just tripped over. Good thing we put it here, and not in the Mission," says Clare, with a pained look on her face. "You wanted to open it on your Birthday – said it was a tradition."

"You know Clare; I remember the day that package was dropped off - about a month ago. Diego just arrived from the airport with mom, Stella, Joanne, and Mike. You laid down the Mission rules for our guests and even then, nobody decided to leave. We had our weekly baseball game with the local children. Mike was showing off and his first pitch went wild. I went to shag the ball before Fina got it. Saw that box lying at the end of the driveway, forgot about the ball." Realizing I'm talking too loud and fast, I force myself to slow down, begin again.

"My experience with opening these boxes on my birthdays usually leads to more questions than answers. But, you're right; it's time to open it. Anyway, it's been several months past my birthday."

Clare looks for something sharp to open the box, and Diego interrupts us with a grim look on his face.

"Just got off the phone with Darnell - told me all three of our Desperados Restaurants were burned to the ground early this evening. The good news is that nobody was killed or even injured. If you don't mind Clare, I'm gonna take the Jeep and meet up with Darnell about an hour north of here. Is that okay? He has my car and we'll bring the Jeep back in the morning."

"Of course! I'm so sorry about the restaurants Diego," Clare says softly. "Take it, the Jeep, as long as you need it. Anything we can do - let us know - please."

"Diego, we'll go with you," I say. "Not much holding us here at the moment."

"Thanks, but no – I need to do this alone," Diego says walking away. Then he stops and turns to us, his face barely visible in the evening shadows.

"I love you both very much, you know," Diego says in a cracking voice. "You're my family – no one could ask for better. We've been to hell and made it back – together. Thanks for letting me stay at the Mission these last few months. But it's time to go home and get back to work."

His words bowl us over. Clare runs over to him and gives him a hug that almost brings him to his knees. Clare helps him steady his feet and they walk together, arm in arm towards the Jeep. I linger off to the side, thinking about what he just said and can't help but feel there's something he's not telling me. Less than a few months ago I found out he was my uncle. But our connection seems to run deeper.

Watching the Jeep pull away, I see Clare's flashlight moving inside the bus – she must be checking on Pedro. He fell asleep under a pile of blankets with Fina almost an hour ago. The temperature can still get into the lower forties even during early Spring. Standing in total darkness, I'm reminded that when the sun rises, Holy Spirit Mission will not be in the place it stood for over five hundred years. The place where I fell in love with Clare. For that, I am so grateful. On the other hand, I'm deeply disturbed by the fact that the Mission and Diego's restaurants are probably gone because of me. Sent to Mexico to investigate a family heavily involved in the illegal drug trade. Unleashing a tiger, I find difficult to put in a cage that's bent on revenge prepared to go to war to keep us hooked.

CHAPTER 8

Wanting not to disturb Pedro sleeping in the bus, I go into the outbuilding, park myself on the dirt floor and stare at the wall. A noise jars me back to reality. I see Clare walk through the door holding a large knife. Thinking it finally hit her that I destroyed her life, I stand up against the wall and move slowly away.

"Sorry I woke you," Clare whispers. "I got a knife for when you're ready to open that package. You okay?"

"Yeah, fine," I say smoothly. "It's just that I was having a bad dream and you walk in with a knife."

"Sorry," she says, putting the knife on a shelf.

"Okay, now that I'm wide awake, I guess it is finally time to open the box." Cutting through the tape, I can't help but think that it must be from the same person who's been wrapping these things for years. Growing up, I use to get one box, wrapped in brown paper, on my birthdays. I still have the soccer ball signed by the great Pele sitting on a shelf at my apartment in Key West. To this day, I still don't know who sent them, possibly my father. I know the item or items will be rolled in newspaper from Mexico City. I pull open the lid and peer down in the box with my flashlight. Sure enough, there's newspaper written in Spanish. I reach in; pull the wrapped item out of the box. Clare moves closer, watching me peel away the paper from the object. Both flashlights begin dimming as I hold the item in shaking hands. I don't need light to know what it is. My brain travels back to my sixteenth birthday in the kitchen of our house on the Maryland shore.

"Clare," I whisper. "When I was sixteen, a package exactly like this was dropped off at our house. Mom and I opened it and found a rock about the size of a softball with a man's face carved into it. Mom did some research – told me it was stolen from an ancient burial site at Machu Picchu in Peru. This is the same stone," I say as I hand it to her.

15

I smooth out the yellowing newspaper and see that it came from Mexico City. The thing that makes my head spin is that it's dated November 1st, my sixteenth birthday.

"Hey Joe, look there's words, an inscription on the bottom."

"There's writing?"

"I think so, under what looks like a beard."

"I know for a fact that when this stone showed up at our home years ago, it did not have any writing on it. This is something new. Mom and I always looked closely for any clues that might lead us to where it came from. Never found any messages, notes – anything. The only common thread was the newspaper, Mexico City, always Mexico City. I assumed that the connection to Mexico City was due to my mom living there with her family in the U.S. Embassy when she was a teenager. As you know Clare, mom had me when she was sixteen. My father was supposedly in the Mexican army. But, enough of that, you've heard it all before."

I shake my flashlight hoping to increase its brightness as Clare brings the stone close to her face, squinting, trying to read what it says.

"The writing is in Spanish. Give me a second. Okay, okay, I think I know. It reads "Trampas del Diablo.""

"Diablo means devil, but I don't know the rest," I say.

"Hold on a sec Joe, let me think. It's something for, no, of the devil. Catch of the devil – no. Trap the devil. Wait, maybe it's "Snares of the devil." Something like that. Diego will know what it means. But, I do remember hearing prayers that included the phrase snares of the devil. Something about temptation, maybe?"

"I don't know either," I say. "Temptation sounds right though – familiar."

"Joe, are you sure this box wasn't opened before today?"

"Not that I'm aware of, why do you ask?"

"I may be wrong, but isn't this Diego's Swiss Army Knife?" Clare says pulling her hand out of the box.

She hands me the knife.

"Diego's? No, it can't be. It looks similar though, anyway, millions have been made – could have come from anyone." Certainly identical to the one that saved my butt recently, on several occasions. Pulling out the corkscrew, I look closely at the circular rings, too dark – see nothing. My flashlight goes out completely, and the other's barely lit. I find new batteries on the shelf behind us. Now with both lights fully functional and bright, I place the rock back in the box.

Clare and I walk back to the bus to check on Pedro. Clare grabs my hand, senses I'm a million miles away.

"Joe, we'll talk to Diego tomorrow – you know, mention the stone, the knife. Also, talk to your mom about the stone you got on your sixteenth birthday, how it showed up again. Maybe she knows something. At least discuss it with her – please?"

"I will. I'm just really sorry again about Holy Spirit – your mission. I'd like to think that my presence here wasn't the cause of the MIG attack, but I'd be lying."

"Imagine how I felt Joe! We get back from the airport, and drive down our dirt road and see nothing – nothing – but this big smoldering hole in the ground, and you and Pedro - nowhere in sight. I was completely panicked that you'd both been killed. So even though the Mission's gone, I'm just so happy everyone is safe. It could have been so much worse if there'd been more people here."

Clare goes into the bus to check on Pedro and the wonder dog. The night is unusually warm and I'm quite surprised when she comes back out holding a bottle of wine and two paper cups, wrapped in a colorful blanket. She hands me the wine, cups and leads me down a small grassy hill under the cover of some thick trees. Following her with my flashlight, I see Clare unwrap herself from the blanket and lay it on the ground. My pulse begins racing when I realize she's not wearing anything except the simple silver cross around her neck. Faint moonlight washes in behind her, lights her physical beauty in a way I've never seen before. I stop dead in my tracks, "Clare, don't move," I say, and just stare at her. Then I join her on the blanket and take her in my arms. Our love for each other helps fuel our passion into the early morning hours.

With Clare asleep wrapped in the blanket, I get up to check on Pedro. He's sleeping soundly, arms wrapped around Fina. Even though it's warm, I throw a sheet over them as my watch beeps letting me know its 3:00 AM. I've never been a good sleeper. Even in the military when I was dog tired, I had trouble keeping my eyes closed through the night. And, once awake, it's difficult for me to fall back asleep.

Back down under the trees on the blanket with Clare, I hold her hand and listen to her soft breathing, hoping she's finding some peace in her dreams. She's been through a lot being kidnapped, betrayed by the man who used to run this mission, tortured, and almost dying. I'd like to say that I was the one who helped her get through it, but it was the time she spent with my mother that helped mend her soul. Mom has been through a lot and knows how to deal with stress and painful memories. It's hard not to feel that more bad days are ahead with tensions ramping up between the US and the cartels.

My thoughts drift to my mysterious father. I wonder where he is. Dead or alive? Is he involved in this latest war? Getting tired, I lie down against Clare and slip into my recurring dream about being in a black helicopter going over Niagara Falls. The person next to me is wearing a devil's mask, taunting me with tales of death and destruction. He says that he's the only one who can save me from dying. "Join me," he shouts over the rushing water. "I am the only one who can save the world, so join me. No one cares about you, only me!"

I feel a weight on my stomach and open my eyes to find Fina sitting on my chest and Pedro bent over looking into my eyes.

"Señor Joe, you scream join me. I join you" says Pedro. "I join you."

The details of my nightmare fade while watching Pedro disappear into the woods chasing Fina. My watch says its 6:18 AM and I feel exhausted. I walk up the path and wave to Clare who's standing by the bus wearing that blanket. Only a blanket? All of a sudden, I have a burst of energy that finds me jogging towards Clare, kicking up stones and dust. I grab her hand and lead her inside the bus making sure the coast is clear. She has a wild and sexy look in her eyes and the only two words I hear are "okay" and "quick." I pull the blanket away from her body, and bring her close, my hands roaming over her body. She feels my iPhone vibrating in my front pants pocket and breaks out into a giggle. I pull the phone from my pocket and read the incoming text – "Call me at 8:00AM... Top Priority...Carlone."

My brain shifts back to reality and the spontaneous moment with Clare hits a wall. I apologize, tell her about the message and need to leave

18

for a quick shower, a very cold one. Clare, naked and wrapped around me, whispers in my ear.

"Can you please check on Pedro on your way to the showers? Oh, and Joe, can I use your phone while you're gone?" she asks with a big smile on her face. "I don't think mine works as well as yours."

I smile, hand her the phone. "Don't forget the US government is paying the bill."

CHAPTER 9

On my way to the shower, I spot Pedro and Fina playing fetch in what's left of the Mission's courtyard. The thing is, Fina refuses to understand the game of fetch. Once the wonder dog has the ball, the game is to chase her, since she won't drop it. It's infuriating. I stop to look down into the hole where the mission last stood, and see a man picking through the wreckage of the MIG 21. The person is dressed like a local, but when he starts unfolding what looks like a map, I get the feeling that something else is going on.

"Pedro – back to the bus!" I shout. "Go now!"

I tuck the Colt 1911 away and head down into the crater. Clare hears me yelling, runs out of the bus and grabs Pedro's hand. She looks over, sees the gun in my hand and moves in the opposite direction. Unfortunately, she knows the drill.

I walk past the broken bell when the man turns, sees me and begins running. I kick it into high gear and pursue the guy out of the pit into a wooded area. After a few minutes, I lose him in the thick brush and run back towards the bus to make sure Clare and Pedro are safe. Approaching the dirt road, I see thick dust filling the air - we have company driving towards us. Hoping it might be the good guys sent by Carlone to scour the crime scene, I'm quickly proven wrong as the bus becomes surrounded by a group of people carrying weapons. One of the men approaches me. He is tall and lanky with dark skin, wearing a cowboy hat and very thick eyeglasses. He puts his pistol into one of the many zippered pockets on his pant leg. I notice his right hand is slightly deformed. He smiles, stops five feet away from me and begins to speak in English.

"Señor, my friends and I are here for something that belongs to the citizens of Peru," the stranger says. "It's a holy rock stolen over fourteen years ago from Machu Picchu. It was a gift given to the Inca people in 1512 from a Spaniard named Francisco Pizarro, sent by King Charles V of Spain and Pope Pius III. You want to hear story?"

"No! Sounds fascinating, but we're expecting company any time now."

"It's all right Señor, I tell you anyway. As legend goes, it was a gift from the Catholic Church, believed to hold great spiritual power. It is said, though I have not seen it myself, to have the image of Christ burned into the face of the rock. Ancient writings say the stone was used as a powerful symbol to convert the Incan pagans to Catholicism," the man says, speaking slowly. "You see Señor, the rock stolen from us is told to be one of the stones used by the devil to tempt Jesus as he fasted fifty, no forty days in the desert."

"And of course, you believe all that," I say in a calm voice. "Do you really think there's any truth in what you just said? You're talking about a rock used to scare people into changing sides, nothing more."

"Whether I believe it is not important," the stranger says in a whisper. "I am not a Catholic, nor very religious. What is important to me, us, is that this rock is part of a number of sacred Intihuatana stones found in an ancient temple on Picchu. While maybe this is not important to you, many feel it represents a split - a break in the world that will only bring destruction. I've been hired by a number of wealthy people who want me to find the stone at any cost."

"Why you?" I ask.

"Because Señor, I have a connection to it – I was the last to see it on my boat, in 1999. The sacred stone was in a box, carried by an American woman. I think you may know her, Señor Dustan," the stranger says, his voice competing over Fina's recent barking and howling.

As I'm about to ask for a clue concerning the woman, the familiar sounds of Sikorsky Seahawk helicopters fill the air. Within seconds, three choppers are in clear view, moving quickly in our direction. I'm thankful that a U.S. Carrier Group is still anchored off Veracruz. The stranger yells out a quick command and turns back to me.

"Señor Dustan, you may have the upper hand now, but this will not always be. You have something that belongs to us and we'll get it back," he shouts over the noise of the landing helicopters. "The American woman, talk to your mother, Señor - she knows."

21

The men get back into their vehicles and drive away as the rotors on the Sikorskys come to a stop. Naval personnel hit the ground running, running in our direction with weapons drawn. Go Navy!

CHAPTER 10

We just finished talking with the Naval Officer in Charge. It's a team of eight who will search the grounds for clues of who and why. I think I know the answer to why, but it's the who that bothers me the most. Meeting the man with the deformed hand and thick glasses only adds to the complexity of the situation. How did he know of Mom's involvement with the stone? Did he know I got the rock for my sixteenth birthday? And, that Mom sent it back to Peru? I do know that when I got it many years ago, there wasn't an inscription. I'll call Mom this morning, tell her about the rock and our visitors. How does "snares of the devil" fit into all this? I need to jump on the web and do some research.

"Joe. Hey you sitting on the ground over there - can you hear me?" yells Clare, leaning out the bus's window. "I need to talk to you!"

"Sorry Clare, lost in thought," I mumble, standing up and heading for the bus.

Clare meets me halfway with a strange look on her face.

"I just got off the phone with John Hammond, from Saint Jerome's Children's Home. John and his wife Sharon run the orfanato, the orphanage for Mexican children in Brownsville Texas," she says stopping abruptly. "I'm sorry; I hate that word orphanage. Well anyway, based on the conversation we had a few weeks ago, John says they have an American family from Austin Texas who are very interested in adopting Pedro. They claim a possible family connection. What do you think?"

"Oh…," I say, hesitating. "You know; I've become kind of attached to that little boy. Don't forget he saved my life yesterday."

"So does that mean you want to adopt him?" she says, smiling. "If so, I want to be around when they conduct your background check. He'll fit right in with your life style – running from country to country, in danger at all times"

"There's a background check? That's it, I can't adopt him. Unless, unless I put you down as a character witness on the application. Weren't you a nun when we first met?" I teased her.

"No, I was not a nun. People called me Sister Clare and you just made that assumption. Anyway, you gotta have character to adopt a child. I'd have to lie – a lot. Do us both a favor and don't put my name anywhere on the application."

"Listen Clare, you of all people know how pathetic I am. I can barely take care of myself. I'd make a better uncle anyway. What about you?"

"Look, I've grown to love him - it'll be difficult to let him go, but we've gotta do what's best for him," Clare says. "I've known John and Sharon for several years. Holy Spirit Mission has sent many children to them to be placed with good families. At last count, I think they were foster parents to some thirty-three children. Understand Joe, the kids that don't get placed become almost permanent at Jerome's and stay as long as they need to."

"Tell me Clare, do you trust them?"

"Yeah, I'd trust them with my life."

"After all we've been through; let's hope it doesn't come to that," I reply. "Anyway, I find trust is beholden to the person defining it."

"Don't worry – you'll love em."

"Then let's pack what's left and head to Brownsville. I'll tell Carlone our plans. We can spend time together and meet the family who wants to adopt Pedro. Look around, there's nothing keeping us here."

"I'll call John to let him know our plan. With a few stops along the way, we'll be there by the weekend."

CHAPTER 11

We map our route to Brownsville, knowing I might get sidetracked along the way. I get a few additional handguns from a Naval Officer after she speaks to Carlone. Walking back to the bus, I see Clare sitting on a large rock at the edge of the crater with Pedro on her lap. Getting closer, I think she's crying. This had been her home for over two years. A place she loved. Working with people she loved. All that's left are memories – both happy and painful ones. Unfortunately, many of the painful ones started the day I arrived. She sees me approaching and starts wiping her eyes.

"Sorry for crying - can't help it. It's just, just that I loved being part of this old mission. This place is where I fell in love with the Mexican people. I never felt like an outsider, or a stranger. They adopted me, took me into their lives, and shared everything they had. Truth is, they gave me much more than I ever gave them. Now, I'm leaving because the building's gone, but the people are still here. Something feels wrong. Please promise me, after Pedro's adopted by his extended family in Brownsville, we'll come back here - to visit. Maybe stay for a time," Clare says with a smile. "Alright?"

"I would love nothing more than to come back here," I say grabbing her hand and squeezing it tight. "I loved being here too. Between us, I think some of the locals even started to like me. Especially once they knew for sure I was with you."

"I back to," says Pedro with a large grin on his face. "I come too!"

Clare looks at me and begins to get teary eyed again. She snuggles with Pedro on her lap and closes her eyes. I walk away in silence towards the bus to stow our gear. Once inside, I go to the back and pull my surf bag out from under the seat. Reaching in, I find the box and open it. My fingers trace the rock's jagged edges. I go back to what the stranger said. Something about the rock - used by the devil to tempt Jesus in the desert. A gift from the pope to convert the Incans to Christianity. The face of Christ carved

25

into the stone. Miracle? No, he didn't use that word. Even if I believe any of that, who etched "Trampas Del Diablo" - snares of the devil, and why? But most importantly, how did the man with the thick glasses and mangled hand know my mother?

My ringing cell interrupts my thought process. As I'm about to tap the talk button, a small explosion rips a hole in the front of the bus. I jump out the emergency door in the back. I hear a plane overhead and see a small white single engine Cessna disappear into a bank of white, puffy clouds. Before I know it, Naval Officer Rob Morin is at my side, asking if I'm alright. I nod my head yes, while watching several Navy guys extinguishing a small fire near the bus's engine compartment. I mention to Officer Morin the small plane I saw - how it may be connected to the bus explosion. He agrees to investigate and within five minutes a Naval Super Hornet screams over our heads just above the tree line. Go Navy!

Needless to say, we'll need a different mode of transportation to get to Brownsville. First Clare's Mission and now her bus. I'd say I pretty much wiped out all her assets.

CHAPTER 12

Clare is nearly speechless and visibly shaken by what just happened. It doesn't take a genius to see that something came through the side window and exploded where the driver would normally sit. This bus has seen its last fieldtrip. Diego has the only other vehicle that can get us out of here. I call Carlone to brief him on what happened, and he asks Officer Morin to give us a ride to Veracruz where a vehicle will be waiting. Jim's getting nervous about the overall situation and our security. He manages to pull some strings that leaves the Naval Carrier Group anchored off Veracruz for at least another ten days. Waiting for our ride from the Navy, Clare and I get into a serious discussion.

"Joe, why is all this starting up again?" Clare asks in a steady voice, presumably so as not to scare Pedro.

"I didn't see this coming. I want you to leave Mexico until things settle down – till it's safe. We'll fly you and Pedro out of Veracruz directly to Brownsville. Then, I'll catch up with Diego, and I'll meet you there."

"No way!" Clare shouts while holding Pedro's hand. "It's okay Pedro; sorry." She turns to me, "Now you listen to me! Together, we'll drive to the border and meet up with the Hammonds. I don't want us to split up. Can't we stay below their radar?"

"Well because it's become very clear that they're trying to kill me, and anybody else who happens to be with me. Flying under their radar is impossible. Their intricate network stretches across Mexico, and doesn't stop at the borders - they'll keep looking for us. Clare, if," I pause, "if we're to stay together, somehow we need to be a step ahead of them. That means telling nobody where we're going. I know you want to make some stops along the way, but you can't give any prior notice. We'll do the pop in," I say thinking about one of my favorite old Seinfeld episodes.

"Okay, makes sense."

"One more thing Clare." I say staring into her blue eyes. "I can't lose you - we gotta be smart about this."

"Yes – smart, gotta be smart. Right, you're right Joe."

"I need you to promise me, if we meet any resistance on our way to Texas you'll fly to Brownsville – you know, meet us there."

"Okay – it's a plan. That stuff that happened to us, all of us, a few months ago, put me in a scary place in my mind that I'm having a hard time pulling myself out of." Clare says. "I have nightmares, and even some daydreams scare me. You know I thought daydreams were supposed to be pleasant – swirling happy memories about the past or future. So yeah, if the going gets tough – I'll fly back with Pedro. Sorry but, nightmares during the day scare me," she says as Fina the wonder dog starts howling.

Painful silence is broken by our incoming ride to Veracruz. The Sikorsky Seahawk helicopter circles around our position scoping out a place to land. Pedro gets all excited and starts yelling, "Airplane, airplane." Clare scoops him up in her arms as it touches down, and says, "No, sweetie, this is a helicopter." Several men jump out of the helicopter and start loading our gear as I go looking for Fina, who seemed to disappear the moment the helicopter landed. Not seeing her anywhere, I run to the outbuildings, find her hiding in one of the bathroom stalls. At times like these, Fina the wonder dog is not so brave. I gather her up in my arms and carry her towards the waiting Sikorsky. I can feel her body get tense the closer we get to the bird. Thinking she might try to get away, I pull out her leash and snap it on her collar. I feel Fina's body relax when she sees Clare and Pedro in the chopper. I hand Fina to Clare, and pull myself inside.

Pedro's strapped into a seat too large for him, but the huge smile on his face says it all. The doors close and our makeshift family is on our way to Veracruz, about a fifteen-minute flight northeast. Music overcomes the engine noise inside the cabin and the powerful voice of Freddie Mercury reminds us that "The Show Must Go On." At this point, I don't think I have a choice. "I have to find the will to carry on."

CHAPTER 13

Tuesday / 12:45 PM
General Heriberto Jara International Airport
Veracruz, Mexico

We circle over what looks like an old colonial fort and land between two crumbling buildings on the edge of the airport. A windowless black van pulls up closely to the helicopter, its side door slides open before coming to a stop. The driver and passenger jump out, urging us to move quickly. The pilot tells us, "Move your asses" so they can get back into the air immediately. In 90 seconds our gear is loaded and we're riding down a dirt access road that dumps us into heavy traffic. The Seahawk buzzes overhead, dropping anti-missile flares as it heads for open water, flanked by two Navy Super Hornets.

Clare seems to understand the situation we're in and brandishes an awkward smile. Staring at her, I say the first thing that comes to mind. "We're not in Kansas anymore." Few words are spoken as the vehicle navigates the streets at high speeds, weaving in and out around cars and obstacles. Pedro is laughing loudly enjoying his first trip to the big city. In less than ten minutes, we pull into the heavily guarded US Consulate office complex, and are directed into a large underground garage. Clare shoots me a nervous look as the van comes to an abrupt halt and the door opens with a voice booming from the outside.

"Welcome to Veracruz Mr. and Mrs. Dustan. My name's Dave Shea and I work for the United States Government here in Mexico. I received a high priority call from a Mr. James Carlone attached to the Washington DEA office," he says reading off a clipboard. "He gave me specific instructions - told me to get whatever you requested. I understand you'll be staying here tonight and leaving in the morning."

29

"Thanks Dave. And yes, out in the morning. There's supposed to be a vehicle for us," I say. "Do you know anything about this?"

"Let me check into your transportation requisition, Mr. Dustan. Oh, and just so you know, we have three other children staying here. Plus, a small dog and two cats – kittens any day now, I hear. Anyway, we're equipped to handle families like yours due to the recent events – you know, the cartels and such," he pauses. "Even though we're on official lockdown, this consulate has almost become a safe house for friendlies passing through on their way out of Mexico."

"Dave, Mr. Shea, my name is Clare and he's Joe and the little boy's name is Pedro. We truly appreciate you having us stay here on such little notice. Thank you."

"It's my pleasure Mrs. Dustan, I mean Clare. If you guys can grab your stuff, I'll take you to your room."

"Dave, are you the person in charge? I seem to remember hearing about someone named Lisa or Linda Somersworth at this location," I say, hesitantly.

Our conversation comes to a dead stop as he stops, and then leans against the wall next to him. His shoulders slump forward and his eyes start to water.

"I'm sorry, it's still hitting me hard," he inhales, and then looks as though he's trying to pull himself together. "Linda was killed in a carjacking last week," he says with his voice cracking. "Her car was surrounded by two big semis – someone got out and shot her – close range. Her husband and fourteen-year-old daughter were taken. We've not heard a thing – no contact concerning ransom demands, anything. We're going crazy trying to track them down. Just another killing – murder - drug war collateral damage I guess."

"Sorry Dave," Clare says, pulling Pedro close to her. "That's very sad, tragic."

"Thanks, thank you Clare."

Before I have a chance to say something, three men come through the door and begin picking up our gear. We walk in silence through the heavily air conditioned halls to a bank of elevators. Dave shows us to our room on the third floor that has only two windows that are tinted and look recently barred.

"You have the entire floor to yourself," Dave says in a flat toned voice. "If you need anything, just hit zero on any of the phones you find on the floor. Oh, and so you know, there is a vehicle that you're welcome to use for local business. But, if you do decide to go out, I would strongly recommend that you get back before dark. Unfortunately, Veracruz has become unsafe now for Americans. You know, since we bombed their country over what happened in DC several months ago and all. But please, please understand," he pauses, "the vast majority of Mexicans are happy that our governments are working together. We need to end this plague that has hurt both countries for far too long. Okay then," he says, backing out of the door, "call if you need anything."

"Thank you Dave," I reply.

Clare decides to leave the floor with Pedro to look for the other children in the building. Fina pegs a couch for her afternoon siesta after she noses under the cushions for any lost food. Our temporary accommodations consist of two large rooms. One for sleeping - the other for everything else. It feels like a hospital with its dull white walls and the smell of bleach wafting in the background. Hoping to get some fresh air, I quickly discover the barred windows don't open and the thick smoked glass is bullet proof. My inspection is cut short by my cell ringing.

"Mom, I've been so worried about you - you okay?" I say.

"Fine Joseph, just fine. Stella and I got back to our condos after 11:00 last night. To be honest I haven't been able to sleep since I got home. I still can't believe it that the plane we were supposed to be on was shot down and crashed into the sea. Those poor innocent people, dead, because someone might have wanted us dead. It's tough to talk about. Now you tell me: what happened at the mission. Are Clare and Pedro alright? Diego?"

"Everyone's fine, Mom. I'm sure you heard from Carlone that both the Mission and I were targets for a MIG. But thanks to Pedro and Diego, I'm talking to you from the American Consulate office in Veracruz. We're here tonight and leaving for Brownsville, Texas in the morning. Pedro has a new family wanting to adopt him in the US. There's an orphanage in

Brownsville, a Saint Jerome's Children's Home, run by John and Sharon Hammond. Clare knows them well - trusts them."

"Wow Joseph, what you just said makes me both happy and sad. I'm thrilled that Pedro will have a family to love and raise him. But I'm sad since I thought maybe you and Clare might want to adopt him."

"Clare and I did speak about it, you're right, but felt it was best for Pedro to have a family that was a little more settled. The good news is the couple wanting to adopt Pedro may be related to him through a distant cousin or something."

"Well honey, whatever you and Clare decide is best for Pedro is good with me. Anyway, I'm too young to be a grandmother," Mom says with a laugh.

"Yes - you'll have to wait to be a grandmother because I'm too young to have a kid. Oh, the other thing I wanted you to know is that Diego's restaurants have been burned to the ground – most likely arson. No one was hurt, but of course he's devastated. He left last night to meet up his business partner, Darnell."

"Oh my God Joseph, poor Diego. I will try to contact him after we hang up. I'll ask my library staff to poke around and see what they can find."

"I gotta tell ya mom, I'm worried that we miscalculated the strength of the cartels – and how quickly they could regroup. Once we're in Brownsville, I hoping to convince Clare into staying put until we get a better handle on the situation. And mom, as the United States Library of Congress Director, I think it's time to put on your NSA hat and use your high level clearance to meet with the President."

"I've got a meeting with the President to discuss what's happening," my mother says. "From reports I've seen so far; it looks like the cartels are up to something – something big. We had an informant in Columbia who said an event, his word – "event," is being put together by the drug kingpins. Never used the word revenge, said it's been planned for a long time. Sadly, the informant's head was mailed to the California governor's office – even made it past security. Heard the governor's assistant fainted when she opened the box, saw the head - eyes and mouth sewed shut. The coroner's report stated that the man was very much alive during the stitching."

"Oh, that's horrible. Let me know if you find out anything that you can share with me. And before I forget, do you remember the package that was dropped off at the mission several weeks ago?"

"Your birthday package. Of course I remember that Joseph."

"Well, I finally opened it yesterday. Do you remember that stone – had the face carved into it, from my sixteenth birthday? That's what I found in the box. And, get this, it had words, inscribed at the bottom - written in Spanish. Clare translated it - reads 'snares of the devil.' I'm not sure what that means. Any idea?"

"Hang on Joseph, are you saying it's the same one you got on your sixteenth birthday, and now it's got writing on it?"

"Yea Mom, that's it. Oh, and to make things even stranger we had a group of visitors yesterday who were after the rock. The one who seemed to be in charge said he knew you. Had thick glasses and a mangled right hand. He said that this rock they were looking for was a gift from a pope and that it was stolen – said it belonged in some temple on Machu Picchu. We know it didn't come with any inscription fourteen years ago, but this time it did." Hearing only silence on the other end, thinking their connection must have been lost, "Mom, are you there? Mom, can you hear me?"

I hear Mom's best friend's voice come over the phone.

"Hey Joey, it's me Stella. I'm not sure what's wrong with your mother, but she dropped the phone, believe it or not – and her head's between her knees. You okay honey? Hang on a sec; she wants to speak to you. Love you."

"Joseph, please, listen to me. We need to talk about this, but not now. Listen to me: you may be in great danger! Make sure the consulate is secure. Please Joseph, hang up and check now," she cries hysterically. "Talk to the person in charge! I'll contact the NSA!"

Our conversation ends abruptly, followed by lights blinking throughout the room before going off. Running through the door out into the hallway, guided by emergency lighting, I hear a deafening explosion and feel the floor below me lift, sharply tossing me against a Coke machine.

Before I know it, the ceiling starts to break up and large chunks of cement are falling onto the floor. I quickly jump on the overturned Coke machine as the floor starts cracking below my feet. What I remember last is the floor giving way and my ride down on top of the Coke machine. Hoping the "real thing" is a real life saver.

CHAPTER 14

I find myself lying between a cement wall and the soda machine. Alarms are going off throughout the consulate. Crawling on my belly, I squeeze through a small opening into a stairwell, and venture down the stairs through a smoky haze. Regaining my bearings, I head for the consulate offices located near the front of the building. Walking down the heavily damaged main corridor, I hear people yelling in Spanish. Using weak translation skills, I'm able to make out the word surrender, "renuncier." I hide behind an overturned industrial type copy machine. The verbal warnings stop, followed by shots ringing out. A minute passes and the shooting ceases. After that, the only sound I hear is my rapid breathing and doors slamming.

I'm desperate to track down Clare. I stumble into the office area break room and find three dead men, lying on their stomachs. What causes me to stop and take a second look is that the man lying in the middle has a tattoo of a white tiger with black feet and stripes on the back of his neck. I've seen this marking too many times. It causes my stomach to churn, knowing it symbolizes nothing but torture and death. I start running down the halls, shouting for Clare and Pedro. Even with the majority of the building intact, I find no signs of life. Something just doesn't seem to add up. Looking at my watch, I realize that almost two hours have passed since the initial explosion when I was on the phone with Mom. I must have been unconscious for a while after I fell though the floor. Either no one came looking, or they couldn't find me behind the Coke machine debris.

After searching all three floors and finding no one, I run out into a barbed-wire fenced courtyard that has several picnic tables, a few trees and a thick carpet of green grass. Off to the left side of the enclosed area is a children's playground. Just outside the fence is an empty helipad. A ball cap lying on the ground near the opening in the fence catches my eye. The Boston Red Sox cap - it belongs to Clare. As I start to assemble the pieces of what might have happened, I hear my name being shouted from above. Quickly scanning the area, I see someone waving their arms on the roof. I shade my eyes from the harsh sun and am able to make out that the person signaling is Diego. Thank God for small miracles.

We finally run into each other in the consulate's cafeteria.

"Joe, what happened here? Where's everybody? You okay?"

"I'm fine, but a few hours ago several explosions went off throughout the building. I was on the third floor when it happened and woke up on the first floor two hours later. All I remember is that prior, just, just before the alarms started blaring, Clare and Pedro left, went to another part of the building to find a family, who were staying here – like us - had young children," I say out of breath.

"Your mother called me and told me you were here. I've not found anybody in this entire complex, except three dead guys on the main floor," Diego says. "I figured I'd check the roof and that's when I saw you."

"Where are the police – the authorities?"

"Joe, my first thought is that this attack was planned by powerful people who told everyone, including the Federales, to stay away for a time. I think we need to get the hell out of here – now! People are coming – good, bad – who cares! I have a vehicle parked in the neighborhood we need to get to quickly!"

"Diego, I can't go! I have to find Clare and Pedro! Not leaving – not yet!"

"Listen to me, nobody's here! We both looked – there's nobody! Most likely they were evacuated after the bombing."

"Or maybe kidnapped?"

"No, evacuated, probably by the military," Diego says.

"Military, who's military?" I shoot back.

"I can't answer that – don't know - sorry. Anyway, let's go. We'll figure it out once we get to the car – get away from here."

A decision is made to meet in twenty minutes on a side street behind the consulate. I run through the floors checking every room, shouting for Clare and Pedro. Stopping at our room, I grab my surf bag from under the bed. Doing a quick check, I find nothing missing and remove the fully loaded Colt 1911 and tuck it into the small of my back. Navigating around

36

the damaged room, it finally hits me. All of Clare's and Pedro's belongings are gone. Strange, but a positive sign. If they were kidnapped, they probably wouldn't have been allowed to take stuff with them – certainly not everything. I check again for calls or messages on my iPhone, but find it empty. Seeing I have three minutes left to search the building, I throw my bag over my shoulder and sprint for the stairway.

CHAPTER 15

My beeping watch tells me its 6:00 PM. I slip out through a side door of the consulate and see a great deal of damage. There's a deep hole approximately twenty feet from the main building, indicating a possible car bomb. The charred fender I trip over on my way to the street confirms it. There are numerous people walking by the consulate's mangled front gate, and I spot the steel encased cement foundation where the guardhouse once stood. The rest of it – gone. Few look at me as they go on with their daily routines - probably immune to this type of violence. When I get to the public walkway, I hear police sirens getting louder. At this point, I'm not sure what's worse, getting caught by the cartels or spending time in a Mexican jail. My fight or flight instinct kicks in and I almost knock over an elderly woman as I get out of there.

Once away from the consulate, I slow my pace to a brisk walk. It might be highly noticeable if I'm the only person running through the streets. Going up and down the side roads, I fail to find Diego – I don't think he ever told me what he was driving. I assumed he had Clare's Jeep. Deciding to give up and have Diego find me, I notice a small outside tavern with covered seating. I take the only open table at the far end and order a diet Pepsi from a girl who looks to be about twelve. She promptly returns with the can of soda and a tall colorful glass filled to the top with ice. Knowing firsthand the problems of the Mexican water system, I forgo the glass of ice and clean off the can's top with my shirt. I pop it open and take a large gulp that goes down smoothly. I realize how thirsty I am, and order two more cans, no ice, as a strange looking car goes slowly by. As I watch it disappear around a corner, it finally hits me where I've seen it before. My smartphone vibrates with a text from Carlone. "Clare Pedro Safe. Evacuated from consulate to Carrier off Veracruz. Where are you? Call me ASAP!" I type in a code and we connect after a few minutes.

"You scared the daylights out me Joe! What happened? You okay?" Jim says rapidly. "Nobody could find you in the building!"

"I'm much, much better now that I know Clare and Pedro are alright. Thanks."

"We were caught completely off guard. Got a call from someone at the CIA – tells me the consulate office in Veracruz is under attack. I sent you there for safety – an hour later the place is under attack. Sorry! We tried to make contact with you or anybody in the consulate – no good. Ended up getting a small team together to chopper in from the Carrier Group off shore. They got everyone out - except for you. Searched longer than they should have, but still couldn't find you - Clare wouldn't leave. Just glad you're alright – had me worried. Everything I've heard so far tells us the attack was executed by professionals. The NSA was able to tap into the consulate's camera system and counted about a dozen people - all wearing masks. There was no sign of you on the recordings. Where were you when all this happened?"

"Up on level three, when I felt the explosions. Ended up falling through two floors on top a soda machine. I was out for almost two hours - woke up wedged behind it - out of view. And, right now, believe it or not I'm sitting at an outside bar in Veracruz waiting for Diego."

"Diego? He knew you were at the consulate?"

"Yeah, Mom told him we were there. He found me wandering around the grounds of the consulate after the attack – long story. Tell me, how do I get a hold of Clare? I don't think her cell phone's working."

"Relax. I'll contact the ship and get a message to her right away – let her know you're okay."

"Thanks, find out about her phone. May need to get her a replacement."

"Don't worry; I'll take care of it. But, we have another issue to discuss. It has to do with your mother. She's very upset over something - you need to talk to her."

"Thanks – I think I know what it's about. I'll call her once I find Diego."

"Still going to Brownsville?"

"Yeah, think so - just need to talk to Clare. Need me for anything?"

39

"Not yet – just be careful. Since we're not exactly sure who we're at war with, stay in touch and be ready to jump in or get out of the country. Hey, I'm also going to alert our people in Mexico to stay close to you whenever possible. Contact me when you know where you're going. We can chopper you to the Carrier Group off shore at any time. Be safe, Joe."

"Will do."

"I'll get a hold of whoever's in charge of the Carrier to have Clare call you ASAP. Find out the status of her cell. Oh, I'll also ask, or beg who's ever in charge to support your requests as long as they're reasonable."

"Come on Jim, have I ever been unreasonable?"

"Too many times to count. And Joe, call your mother."

"Yes sir – Thanks!"

I see that strange car again moving slowly down the street. It does a U-turn and parks less than ten feet from where I'm sitting. I transfer the Colt 1911 into my jacket pocket and wrap my hand around it. Standing to leave, I see the driver's side gull wing door open on the stainless steel DeLorean. I expect to see Marty McFly or Doc Brown from Back to the Future; instead there's Diego frantically waving at me. I drop a twenty on the table and move quickly to the car. The passenger side door opens with Diego telling me to get in. Even before I have a chance to pull the door closed, we're merging into traffic.

"Tell me Diego, where'd you get this car – a museum? I'm sure it won't attract any attention. There must be 50 left in the world."

"Lay off," Diego says. "Darnell collects rare and odd cars. This was the only car that survived the fires at the restaurants. We've basically lost everything, but again, we're thankful no one was hurt," he says, shaking his head. "Any word on Clare and Pedro?"

"They're fine – I just got off the line with Carlone. They're on the aircraft carrier off shore. I'm so sorry about the fires Diego. Please let me know what I can do to help."

"Well, since you offered, maybe you can be the one to tell Clare that her Jeep was stolen last night – right off the street."

"I'm sure she'll be happy that you're alright. That's all Clare really cares about –people she loves. You and me, we're lucky, because she loves us both."

I pull my cell and a map out of my bag. Still no call from Clare. Left a message on my mom's voicemail. As I start putting a plan together, I begin humming the "Power of Love" sung by Huey Lewis and the News. Think it was the theme song for the Back to the Future movie. Not sure - Mom would know. That was her era, and she used to make us watch all those 80s movies together.

"Hey Diego, I think we should drive up the coast to Tampico. Looks about two hundred miles from here. I'm thinking we should be able to hook up with Clare and Pedro along the way. I know that even after all that's happened, she's gonna want to go with us to Brownsville. But for now, it's gotta be dangerous to drive these roads at night, so we'll have to stop someplace. What'd you think?"

"You're right - not safe. Why not leave Clare and Pedro with the Navy? You know they're safer where they are."

"Yeah right, but once Clare knows where we are, she'll insist on joining us. Anyway, let's just see what happens – Okay?"

"Alright, we'll find a place to stay tonight and put together a plan for all of us to get to Brownsville in one piece. Let me make a few calls – see what I can find. I do know of a hotel on the coast, about twenty-five miles from here. Caters to surfers, and I know the owners quite well. They moved here several years ago from the states after their kids graduated from college. Their dream was to live on the coast and own a surf shop. They found a shop for sale on Craigslist in Nautla - right on the water with a million-dollar view. Said when they got there, they found out the price included the shop, a small hotel, several boats and a beautiful home – adobe style. Apparently the owner had some trouble with the government and was very motivated. Wait till you meet them, they're good people."

"Sounds like a great set up." I say. "Can they be trusted?"

"I would trust them with my life, Joseph."

"Good enough for me then," I reply, thinking about my recent conversation with Clare about the Hammonds at Saint Jerome's Children's Home. Only a few people I'd trust with my life. Hope I don't need to find out who they are.

As darkness blackens out the surrounding landscape, the road gets bumpy. Diego slows the DeLorean down to forty miles per hour to keep

41

the car from getting a flat or breaking an axle. We talk very little and my thoughts go to Clare. I tried her cell several times and keep getting her voicemail. Same with my mom. Thinking about the package opened back at the Mission that contained the stone and Swiss Army Knife, I figure now's the time for a test. Reaching into the back seat, I grab a glass bottle of water, the type that needs a bottle opener to remove the cap.

"Hey Diego, do you have something to open this bottle with?"

"Don't know - look in the glove compartment."

Rummaging through it, I find stacks of folded newspaper from Mexico City held together by elastic bands. Strange.

"Can't find anything," I say. "What about your Swiss Army Knife? That has a can opener doesn't it?"

"Yes it does, but I can't find it. Looked for it this morning - might have lost it back at Holy Spirit. Maybe there's a toolkit in the trunk – a screwdriver might work."

As I'm about to respond, there's a loud bang and the car begins to swerve out of control. Diego manages to straighten the vehicle and brings us to a stop. "Sounds like we have a flat tire Diego. Wait, didn't the DeLorean fly in Back to the Future?" Just my luck, we must have the no frills model.

Standing on the side of the road with no flashlight or spare, Diego calls the owner of the hotel. We're five miles away and Diego says he's coming to get us in a flatbed truck that we can load the DeLorean on. My phone finally rings, and I see its Clare.

"Oh my God Joe, what happened? We couldn't find you," cries Clare. "We thought you were buried in the rubble or kidnapped."

I tell her the story of how I had rode the Coke machine to safety.

"I'm so sorry Joe – we all looked for you. Even the wonder dog – I guess she's no great blood hound. Ten minutes after the bombing a naval helicopter landed and wanted us to evacuate. They had a team that went in to look – still no you. I'm so sorry. Forgive me, please."

"It's okay Clare, I'm fine. Diego showed up and now we're on our way up the coast. Are Pedro and Fina alright?"

"Pedro is great, but Fina had to be restrained and carried into helicopter. She must have known you were still in the building somewhere and didn't want to leave," Clare says.

"We're all safe – that's what's important. Now we have to determine if we're still going to Brownsville. In speaking with Carlone, he informed me that things are heating up again throughout Mexico. He won't admit it yet, but I will. It's payback time."

"I think you're right. The rumor going around this ship is that the Carrier Group will be staying off the coast of Mexico indefinitely. Somebody said that over twenty consulate offices have been bombed in Central America and Mexico - embassies too."

"Wow, I haven't heard any of this - guess I'm not the only target. When the consulate was bombed, I thought I was being singled out. With what you told me, that doesn't seem to be the case."

"Joe, I need to tell you something. Meant to tell you before, but the subject never came up."

"What is it?" I ask.

"I hate boats. Large, small – doesn't matter. For some reason, I get severe bouts of vertigo – it usually means a trip to the ER. I need to get back on land."

"Oh, sorry to hear that. Can you stay on the ship tonight? Cause I need to figure out where the Navy can safely bring you to shore, and update our plan together that will get us to Texas. I hope to have you back on solid ground by tomorrow morning if all goes well. Will that work?"

"Yeah, I'll take something to help me sleep after I put Pedro to bed. Don't forget Joe, whatever plan you're working on needs to include all of us."

"I remember. I think Diego will be joining us for the ride to the US border. He has no place to go and besides, we're his family. Hey Clare, gotta go. I do believe this is our ride to a hotel. I'll call Carlone and arrange transportation, so we can meet up as soon as possible. I love you."

"I love you too, and thanks for helping me get off this boat. See you in the morning."

"Bye Clare, sweet dreams."

As the headlights draw closer, I see Diego move away from the DeLorean to greet the oncoming vehicle. To our surprise, a series of headlights go on, revealing three other vehicles coming up behind a flatbed truck. Hearing the sirens and seeing the flashing lights tells me that I'm about to have my first encounter with the Mexican Police.

CHAPTER 16

Diego gives me a nervous look as the vehicles come to a stop. He walks over to the flatbed truck and shakes hands with the blond-haired driver. Two Federales walk past Diego, nod, and head in my direction. In an attempt to prevent an ugly situation, I raise my hands over my head just prior to being tackled from behind. Within seconds, I'm handcuffed by a huge guy, pushing his knee into my back, and yelling Spanish profanities. Diego hits the ground as two men attempt to pull his hands behind his back. The melee goes on for a few seconds when two shotgun blasts go off by the truck. With my head pushed into the dirt, I see the blond, tall stranger standing on the back of the flatbed holding a double-barrel shotgun discharging the shells. He removes two new shells out of his shirt pocket. Looking directly at the fat guy kneeling on my back, he chambers the shells and leaps off the truck.

Walking in my direction, he helps Diego off the ground as his captors move away. The weight of the fat man quickly lessens as he begins to stand up and scramble backwards. The blond man starts yelling at the Federales in Spanish causing them to look away, cowering. I'm able to make out a threat that assures these guys that their boss will find out about this. He demands the handcuff keys from the fat man, who drops them on the ground and joins his buddies heading for their vehicles. Diego runs over, helps me up and brushes the cakes of dirt off the front of my North Hampton School Jaguars jacket. I feel someone behind me gently unlocking the handcuffs. As I turn, Diego jumps in with introductions.

"Joe, I would like you to meet Mark Temple. He and his wife Cheryl own and operate the Surfer Moon Hotel and Catch a Wave Surf Company. He's our ride," Diego says, breaking out into a smile.

"Nice to meet you Mark, and thank you," I say shaking his hand. "I think these guys meant to hurt us for some reason. Are they local cops?"

"No. They buy police cars at auctions, dress like them, and then shake down people stopped along the road. They must have heard me call my wife on the two-way to let her know I was picking up a broken down vehicle. Guess they thought they'd be able to strip the car before I got here. Us arriving at the same time most likely turned their plan upside down. Though, I am surprised they attacked the two of you, especially with me being here to witness it. Ya see, I surf with their 'boss' every Wednesday morning and I know he would never tolerate any of this nonsense. Must have been desperate or something. Look, let's load the DeLorean and get outta here."

The car is chained to the flatbed in ten minutes and the three of us squeeze into the front of the truck. The floor is littered with tools and the dashboard heavily coated with resin dust. The pungent odor of epoxy adhesive fills the cab, reminding me of a small surf shop in Key West where I attempted to build my own board. After taunts and jokes from my surf buddies during its sea trials, I decided that building surfboards should be left to the experts.

Driving for twenty minutes, we turn off the main road onto a gravel driveway past a rusty iron gate that's falling over. After a half mile we go through a thick line of trees and the view opens up. I see the moon casting its light on the breakers as they roll towards the shore along the Surfer Moon Hotel. My moment of Zen is broken when I see a Naval Sikorsky helicopter parked in front of the Catch A Wave Surf Company. I recognize the figure of the woman standing under the green neon ninguna vacannte – no vacancy sign. She's wearing faded jeans, a Library of Congress t-shirt and a small grey Bolivian cowboy hat she got many years ago. I'm completely caught off guard by her presence, but what surprises me the most is the military issued holster attached to her belt sporting a M11 Sig Sauer pistol, usually found on Navy Seals.

I look over at Diego and notice a guilty grin on his face. He must have called her, told her where we'd be spending the night. He looks at me, stops smiling, hunches his shoulders and looks away. The flatbed stops and I jump out to meet the woman walking briskly towards me. It's after midnight and I get the feeling I'm about to play I got a secret, or secrets.

CHAPTER 17

Wednesday / 12:34 AM
Surfer Moon Hotel
Nautla, Veracruz, Mexico

"Mom, what are you doing here?" I say as we hug. "I just spoke to you in Washington less than ten hours ago!"

"I know Joseph, calm down. Let me explain."

"I'm sorry – go ahead."

"When we spoke yesterday afternoon and you told me about the stone, the visit from the guy with the deformed hand - I had to talk to you. Not on the phone, but in person. So I called in a big favor and hitched a ride on a Navy jet. We made a stop in Key West for fuel and flew directly to the carrier group off Veracruz. Look honey, I apologize for not telling you I was coming. But I knew if I did, you'd try to talk me out of it. And Joseph, I was coming no matter what."

"What's going on, Mom? The last time I saw you wearing a holstered gun was when you came to visit me in Pakistan, five years ago."

Momentary silence takes over. I notice Diego off to the side, waiting to get his chance to say hello to my mother. While waiting for a response, I feel something grab my legs.

"Hi Joe!" Pedro says loudly. "We on a big boat and fly here. Clare sick on boat. We come here to find you. We find you!"

"Well I'm so glad you did Pedro," I say as I lift him and give him a big hug. "I missed you!"

"Me missed too Joe," Pedro says, followed by a big yawn, as his body collapses against mine.

When I set him down, Diego starts talking to him about going to bed. My attention quickly goes to the person walking towards me. She's wearing

47

white jeans and a grey zippered sweatshirt opened enough to reveal a simple silver cross. I walk quickly towards the stunning woman wearing a New York Yankees cap – my hat. Even though we saw each other less than twelve hours ago, she runs over to me and jumps into my arms.

"Oh my God Joe! I thought I'd lost you!"

"Thought you were coming later this morning," I say, as I bury my head into her neck.

"We were. Pedro and Fina were sound asleep and I went up on deck to get some fresh air because I felt awful. Anyway, somebody came to find me and I got ushered up to what's called "the island" and a jet landed on the carrier. Even though it was dark, I can see the pilots climb down onto the flight deck. One of the pilots starts to stagger and sits down. Within seconds a stretcher is brought out and the person disappears into the carrier," Clare says as she takes a deep breath. "Since I can't sleep, I go down to the kitchen – the "mess," for a cup a coffee and there she is, your mother sitting with the Captain. I couldn't believe it! She looked a little queasy, but happy to see me. She wasn't surprised I was on the ship. What's she's doing here?"

"To be perfectly honest, I'm not sure. I think it might have something to do with that rock in my surf bag."

"Well you two need to talk!" Clare says. "We only had a few minutes together. When she went off to shower and change, I was told to get our stuff together - get ready for a ride over to the mainland. Twenty minutes later, we're on a helicopter for a quick flight here. We just got here ten minutes before you did," she pauses. "It's getting crazy Joe."

Clare and I sit down on a bench made from an old surfboard, and listen to the waves crash onshore. I can see Diego carry Pedro into one of the rooms of the hotel, followed by Mom and Fina. I feel my iPhone vibrate and take it out of my pocket and read a new text from Carlone. Clare starts smiling as I read the message aloud from Carlone. "Your mother on way. Not sure why. Just found out. President authorized use of Navy jet. Heads up. Contact you when I know more. Be safe." When done reading the text, Clare smiles and says, "If he only knew."

My watch beeps at 2:00 AM, waking us both up from our short nap on the bench. We decide to go and check on Pedro. Walking with Clare, arm in

48

arm, on the warm Mexican sand reminds me again of how lucky I am. We come to an opening in the building that gives you a good view of the sand dunes bathed in the moonlight. Two people walking up the dunes holding hands grabs my attention. One male. One female. The female's wearing a Bolivian cowboy hat.

CHAPTER 18

I'm startled awake at 7:22 in the morning by the sound of a helicopter taking off. Clare and I slept on the floor last night since Pedro and Fina were sound asleep on the bed when we got in. I see I'm alone now and that the door is wide open. Clare must have gone out with Pedro and the dog. I can smell salt air mixed with the aroma of coffee. I throw on some jeans and a t-shirt, brush my teeth and wash my face, wondering about why my mother is here? Why is she wearing a gun? Holding hands with Diego last night - really? It's time for a family meeting.

I walk out onto the sand, following unseen familiar voices. Smoke is rising over the dunes, the smell of bacon wafting in the air - I'm hungry. Climbing to the top of the dune, I see a small group of people sitting around picnic tables eating breakfast. I recognize Mark Temple working the grill, with Fina sitting by his side waiting for anything to hit the ground. The wonder dog doesn't care about the five second rule. At one of the tables, I see Mom, Clare, Diego, Pedro, and the guy from the bombed out consulate in Veracruz. I think his name is Dave. Clare sees me walking towards the table and jumps up to meet me about twenty feet away from the table. She wraps her arms around my neck and whispers in my ear.

"Don't say anything Joe. Please don't say anything."

"Good morning to you too Clare," I say. "What am I not supposed to say?"

"Come on, you know."

"Know what?"

"Okay, maybe it's nothing," she says nonchalantly.

"Oh it's something alright," I shoot back. "Tell me why was my mother holding hands with Diego? They were holding hands - right? You saw it too!"

Clare pulls me in tight, tells me to calm down and that she loves me. I see my mother turn, look in my direction then go back to speaking with the guy from the consulate. Dave Shea – that's it, that's his name.

"Don't worry Clare; I'll not say a word. At least not now."

"Thank you. Anyway, give her time. She'll tell us when she's ready."

"You know something Clare; you had less power over me when I thought you were a nun a few months ago."

"Keep it up and I will join a convent," she whispers while biting on my ear.

As Clare and I start walking, my mom stands up to meet us and gives me a big hug. She still has the gun around her waist and is wearing the same clothes she had on last night. Was she out all night? Who am I to speak - I'm wearing the same clothes as well. She grabs my hand and leads me away from the table. Clare sits next to Diego, looks at me and mouths the words, "Be nice."

"Good morning Joseph," she says after kissing my cheek. "You look tired."

"I am. But I'm ready for you to tell me what's going on. Why'd you need to get here so fast? What's with the gun? Have you heard from my father? And were you holding hands with Diego?" Oops, sorry Clare.

"I thought it was urgent for me to get here so I finally took the President up on a long overdue favor. And the gun was given to me many years ago, when I flunked out of Navy Seal training. I think they felt sorry for me. We can discuss that at another time. And yes," Mom says with a long pause, "I have spoken to Tomas, even asked for his help. We'll discuss that later, after breakfast. And finally, I was holding hands with Diego. I wanted to tell you about us weeks ago at Holy Spirit Mission, but I never found the right moment. Let me just say right now that it's complicated."

She releases my hand and walks back to the table, leaving me alone to ponder the word "complicated." It's strange how "complicated" things became at the beginning of the year starting with the terrorist attack in Washington DC. The war with the drug cartels. Almost losing my best friend in that battle. Adding people to my family tree. Falling in love with Clare and almost killing her in the process. I still blame myself for all the bad stuff that's happened to her since we met. Anyway, it's "complicated."

51

I walk by the table on my way to the coffee pot sitting on the grill. I say good morning to Pedro and Diego, who barely respond since they're both engrossed in a game of fish, Pedro's favorite card game. Mark sees me coming and hands me a mug with K.B. Bagels painted on the side. I thank him for everything, and pour myself some coffee. Our conversation is brief due to Fina's high pitched howling as I spot two Sikorsky Seahawk helicopters flying low off the water, heading in our direction. They circle the buildings and find a landing spot down the beach about a hundred yards away. Pedro jumps up in excitement, allowing the cards on the table to blow away. Diego grabs him just in time before he's about to run off to the choppers. It must be a drop off since the GE engines aren't being shut down.

I get a little nervous when I see several people jump out of both helicopters wearing wetsuits. Did Mom call in her Navy Seal buddies? No. Seeing several surfboards being handed down to the folks in wetsuits can only mean well deserved downtime for some in the fleet. Mark taps me on the shoulder and says, "Surfs up!" and leaves to meet the group of sailors.

The person I'm most interested in is the last one to get off the Seahawks. I use a pair of compact binoculars lying near the grill to verify. He's wearing a Hawaiian shirt, checkered Bermuda shorts and flip flops. How can someone who tries so hard to fit in, seem so out of place. Even without the binoculars, Clare knows who it is. She stands up to wave as I put my mug on a rock above the grill. We look at each other and smile. As the helicopters lift off, I break into a run heading for the man in the colorful Hawaiian shirt. I promise myself this time, if we're assigned a job from our boss, Carlone, we'll not split up.

Things all of a sudden got less complicated.

CHAPTER 19

Wednesday / 8:49 AM
Surfer Moon Hotel
Nautla, Veracruz, Mexico

"Well, hello secret agent man Mike Lenoce! Didn't I just see you a few weeks ago at Holy Spirit Mission? I even think you were dressed in the same clothes," I say, giving him a big hug.

"Listen pal, when I heard about all the trouble you been causing down here, I asked Carlone to reassign me here. Ya know, someone who never gets tired of saving your worthless life. Actually," he grins, "I had to beg him. After being kidnapped by drug mercenaries and thrown in a Mexican jail, he didn't want me out of his sight. Heck, he made me his driver for a week to keep me close by. But then he said I was a lousy driver anyway, and ended up approving my trip down here with stipulations," Mike smirks. "Me a lousy driver? He even called Joanne to discuss my trip here. Ya know – checking to see if I was still having those nightmares. I know he loves me, but come on. Must have gotten all thumbs up cause I'm here."

"I really need you here," I said.

"I figured. Anyway, we have a job to finish," he says.

"You know something Mike; you're the second big surprise in less than eight hours. I got in with Diego early this morning, and guess who was waiting for me."

"Your mom."

"Yes my mother! How did you know?"

"Once Carlone heard the rumor your mother was on her way, he approved my reassignment – at 2:15 this morning. An hour later, I'm on a Navy Super Hornet flying at almost Mach two to get here. During the ride to the base, I swallowed four motion sickness pills. I was feeling queasy just being in the car. When I get to the jet, the pilot gives me patches to wear behind my ears, and a band to wear around my wrist. Plus, a dozen barf bags that I stuffed in my flight suit. Oh Joe, that suit – it's hot! So I'm sick, you know, sweating bullets before we ever leave the ground. I throw up twice within the first twenty minutes; pass out till an Air National Guard KC-135 fills our tanks off the coast of Florida. After that, I'm fine till we were about to land on the carrier," Mike says taking a deep breath. "I don't know how these pilots do it. Trust me, it's gotta be like threading a needle in the dark. Between us -man to man - I was scared out of my mind. If you hear a story of me kissing the flight deck after landing and throwing up on the guy helping me stand. Don't believe it. Even if you see a picture of it. I'll deny it!"

"Don't worry buddy. If those pictures come my way, I'll say it's someone who looks like you. Don't worry," I say, while feeling my iPhone vibrate in my pocket. Probably just some new jpegs being delivered.

"Thanks Joe. But the guys on the aircraft carrier told me all about your mother getting off the jet, mostly steady on her feet, asking for something to eat and a place to shower. They also said your mother left on the helicopter wearing a Navy Seal issued Sig Sauer M11. Because I'm your friend and love your mother, I won't tell you what else they said. And that I, me, Mike Lenoce let the words stunning, sexy, hard body and beautiful fly right over my head once I discovered they weren't talking about me," he says, busting out in laughter.

"Believe me Mike; none of those words come close to describing you. By the way, where's your stuff?"

"Oh, the first stipulation from Carlone is that I must live on the boat until we figure out what's going on. But hey, don't worry; I'm working on an escape plan. Anyway, I can't save your butt from fifteen miles off shore. You know me, I get bored easily."

CHAPTER 20

Back at the picnic table, Mike gets a hero's welcome. There's a group of surfers now out on the water paddling behind Mark, in search of the perfect wave. As I gaze out over the sea, I think about the events of the last few days. I struggle to find a connection between the stone; snares of the devil; the destruction of Holy Spirit mission; the bombing of the consulate; the man with the mangled arm, Diego and Mom holding hands.

My scattered thoughts dissipate when I see a white van kicking up dust as it approaches the hotel. It stops by the main entrance and a man climbs out, reaches in for something, pulls out a familiar cowboy hat and places it on his head. He takes off his sunglasses and replaces them with thick-framed black glasses. He waves me over, and I go off to meet him. Fina the wonder dog appears out of nowhere at full speed, barking, running towards the stranger. I stop, turn and ask everyone to stay here. "I'll see what he wants." Remembering I left my Colt 1911 under the seat of the DeLorean, I scour the area for some type of weapon if needed. Nothing. I hope we can be civil.

"Señor Dustan, how nice it is to see you again," the stranger says. I stop five feet from him. "The last time we met, I apologize for not having the opportunity to introduce myself. My name is Alvaro Morales and I'm here for the sacred rock - again. Do you have it Señor Dustan? I'm not looking for trouble. But, if I don't find the rock, others who have no conscience will come looking. Who knows, they may kill me first. So please – where is the rock?"

"Listen, Mr. Morales…."

"Please call me Alvaro."

"Alvaro, the last time we spoke, I felt you weren't being completely honest," I say lowering my voice. "I will tell you that I know of a rock with a face carved into it. When it came to our home on my sixteenth birthday, it was sent back to Peru."

"Mr. Dustan, I'm not stupid. Do I look stupid to you?" he says glancing over to the table by the dunes. "You told me some lie about your mother sending it back many years ago. For that is not true – ask her. I met your mother in February 1999 when she tried to return the stone to the Peruvian authorities. Unfortunately, the so-called authorities were very bad men. They set a very elaborate trap for your mother, which almost got us both killed."

"Hello Señor Morales!"

We both turn to see my mother walking towards us with her holstered weapon. Alvaro takes off his hat, places it over his chest and nods.

"Buenos dias Señorita Dustan. The years have been very kind to you," he says, smiling. "Please excuse my rudeness, but I've come for the stone. I've been searching for it over the last many years. The trail ends with you and your son," he says calmly, while putting his hat on.

"Señor Morales, why do you think we have the stone?" Mom asks.

"Señorita, please call me Alvaro."

"What? Okay, Alvaro. We were on the helicopter together in 1999. If I remember correctly, you were in shock from being struck by lightning. I passed out from almost drowning."

"Mom, what are you talking about?" I say a little too loudly, causing Clare to look in my direction. "You almost drowned? You never told me this!"

"Joseph, please relax," Mom says calmly. "It was a long time ago, and I came here to tell you about it. Unfortunately, Señor Morales beat me to it."

"Señorita, please Alvaro."

"Alvaro and I met in Bolivia in 1999. That rock you received on your sixteenth birthday caused quite a stir within the Peruvian government. Or at least I thought it did. I spoke to several Peruvian government officials and they insisted I bring the stone in person. It wasn't until I got there that I discovered it was a ruse. I ran into some trouble. Alvaro saved my life that day. Sorry Joseph for not telling you."

Staring over at Clare, I notice Diego moving in our direction.

"Look, I suggest we find a place to sit down and discuss this. All of us," I say loudly.

"Right Joseph, you're right," Mom says.

"Yeah, we, we talk," Alvaro says nervously. "Give me an hour to make some calls. But I must warn you, I'm not leaving without the stone - I must have it! Powerful people want the stone and will do anything to get it."

CHAPTER 21

I find Cheryl Temple, the co-owner of the hotel, sitting under a large shady tree, typing away on a laptop. She's updating their website and sending thank you emails to a group of visitors who stayed here last week. She tells me she manages what I'd call the tedious work of running the business, while her husband is property caretaker as well as the ambassador of fun. It seems to suit them both well. Every time she speaks of Mark and their two children, Trisha and Zach, her face lights up. She says she misses her children at this time of the year because they're both teachers at universities. Trish in California. Zach in Massachusetts. "They'll be here in May," she says, beaming. Cheryl points out the two wind mills about fifty feet from the low tide line. "Zach and Mark put those up last year. The solar panels on the roofs and two large diesel generators make us less dependent on the grid," she says. "We had power problems when we first got here because the electricity around here is unreliable. Anyway, Mark loves engineering projects, especially when someone says it can't be done."

Cheryl tells me how much they love being here after living hectic lives in Massachusetts. "What's funny is that we have more friends here than we ever had in the states." She does some work at the local school. From what I can tell, she's on the school board, maybe the Principal, all while teaching several subjects. It's easy to see why Cheryl and Clare hit it off so well. They both love children and will do anything for them.

I become distracted by the sound of the Seahawk starting up on the beach. It must be back to work on the carrier for the early morning surfers.

Cheryl allows us the use of the hotel roof patio for our meeting. It has beautiful red and yellow tile running along the floor in a circular pattern. It reminds me of the yellow brick road from The Wizard of Oz, except this path leads to a large outside bar of which I was given the key. There are ten square tables scattered throughout the rooftop, all with big orange umbrellas covering them. Looking out at water, I see Mark's surrounded by others on surfboards, including someone who looks familiar. Not having any binoculars, I give up trying to determine if I know the person closest to him.

Voices drift up from ground level. I walk over to the parking lot side of the hotel and see Clare, Diego and Mom huddled around an ice machine. I call out to them and point to the way up. Walking back over to the ocean side, I see Pedro coloring at a table a few feet away from Cheryl. She volunteered to watch him while we meet. As the group comes up the steps, I realize I haven't seen Alvaro in over an hour. Last time I saw him; he was doing something under the hood of the van. Checking the oil? Don't know.

"Alvaro's gone, Joseph," Mom says as she comes through the stairwell door. "His van's gone. Did he say anything to you?"

"No," I say as I walk to the edge of the roof to look in the parking lot. "You're right, no van!"

"What's going on?" Diego says. "Somebody clue me in. Please!"

Clare looks over at me and says nothing. I've already given her the Cliff Notes version of what I think is going on. But more needs to be discussed. I'm surprised to see Mom still wearing the gun. What bothers me the most is that it looks all too natural on her.

"Okay Diego, hang on a minute. Let's grab something from the bar and sit down."

Its 10:30 in the morning. We all decide on bottled water before taking a table that allows us to see Pedro building something in the sand. Fina is sleeping at Cheryl's feet.

"Anybody see Mike?" I ask.

"Yeah - twenty minutes ago heading into the surf shop. I reminded him about our rooftop meeting," Clare says with a smile.

Why is it every time Clare looks at me or says something, I lose my train of thought. Right now, at this very moment I want to take her hand and walk away. Far away.

"I'm here, I'm here!" Mike shouts sprinting through the door. Mike's wearing long board shorts. A Billabong t-shirt. Oakley sunglasses. Black and white checkered slip on rubber shoes. White goo on his nose. Hope he doesn't say "tasty waves."

Once Mike gets to the table, that's it. We can't hold it in. We all bust out laughing.

"Tell me Mike, why are you dressed like Spicoli from *Fast Times at Ridgemont High*," I say, laughing with Mom.

"Who's Spicoli?" Diego says. "What times where?"

I can see by the look on Clare's face that the only people to get the joke are Mom and I. We love old movies.

"It's a classic funny movie from the early eighties," I say. "Ah, forget it."

"Hey," Mike explains. "Cheryl was nice enough to give me a room so I could shower after my surfing lesson," he says. "When I got out, I found some puke on my clothes from the flight from hell I had last night, so I threw them all in the garbage and walked over to the surf shop – ok, in a towel. Cheryl saw me wandering around and gave me the key to the shop and told me to take what I needed. So I did."

We start to settle down after Mom takes the tags off his new clothes. He asks me if I thought Carlone would pick up the tab. "Sure," I say. "Why not."

Just as we're about to start the meeting, I hear someone yelling from the parking lot. I get up, walk to edge and see Mark waving.

"Whose white van is that in the parking lot?" he yells.

To my surprise, Alvaro's van has returned and is parked near an outbuilding. Mark has an arm full of wetsuits heading in the opposite direction. I yell down "It's Alvaro's. I'll take care of it." Leaving the roof, down the stairs, walking through the lot, I don't see him in or outside the van. Maybe he's in back. Mike yells my name from the roof. I stop and turn towards him.

"Something's wrong Joe, I don't like this!" he yells. "Get away from the van! I'm coming down. Get Back!"

Not moving, I hear a cell phone ringing. It's coming from inside the van. After one ring it stops. I move to the right to get a clearer picture of the back. I swear I see movement inside. The cell phone rings again. After two rings it stops. I reach down, pick up a large rock and crash it through the side window. The phone rings - stops after three. Sticking my hand through the broken window, I open the locked door. Muffled noises are

60

coming from the back. I climb over boxes and find Alvaro tied up - tape over his mouth. As I rip it from his mouth, the phone starts to ring. "Oh boy." On the second ring I pull open the slider door. On the third ring, I throw a dazed Alvaro over my shoulder and run towards a sand dune. Mike knows the game. I hear him yell for everybody to get down. I barely hear the fourth ring as we fall over the dune. A few seconds of silence pass before an explosion rips open the van, littering pieces over the lot and dunes. Peeking over the sand, I see thick black smoke is pouring out from the burning van.

"Thank you Señor Dustan, thank you," cries Alvaro.

"No problem, I'm Joe by the way. You all right?"

"Yes, si, thank you Joe, gracias. Please, in my pocket I have a knife. To cut the rope."

Reaching in his coat pocket, I pull out a knife. Not just any knife. A Swiss Army Knife. Am I the only person in Mexico without one? I cut the ropes, help Alvaro to his feet. He gives me a very strong one arm hug. We climb over the dunes, see Mark rolling up to the burning van in a tanker truck that says "WATER" on the side. Running over to meet him, I see one side of the outbuilding next to the smoldering van was blown away, exposing a large white propane tank. Mark walks slowly towards the van with a fire hose in his hand.

"Hey Joe," he says. "Do me a favor and turn the water on. It's a large stainless steel wheel on the back. You know, like the one for a garden hose, only bigger."

"Mark is there any propane in that tank?" I say pointing at the now burning building.

"We had them emptied when we bought the place. They weren't safe. The new ones are buried. Don't worry. We're fine," he says, calmly.

Walking to the back of the truck, I turn the wheel and hear the water start flowing. I see Clare holding Pedro's hand, standing near the main entrance. She has that worried look on her face. Diego and Mike rush over with fire extinguishers to help Mark put out the fire. Mom goes to sit on the ground next to Alvaro. He seems to be crying.

"Joe, you alright?" Mike says breathing heavy. "I knew, just knew something was wrong."

"I'm good Mike, thanks."

"How'd you know he was in the van?"

"I didn't, until I got close and saw it moving. I heard a cell phone ringing inside, stopped after the first ring. I just had a bad feeling about it."

"Don't tell me. You heard it again, but this time it rang twice," says Mike. "I can't believe someone is still using that old technology to detonate a bomb."

"Especially with the intermittent cell coverage in this area," Diego chimes in.

My eyes go to a loud noise coming from inside the garage adjacent to the surf shop. Rolling through the door at low speed is a large green John Deere tractor. One end has been modified to act as a tow truck. Driving this beast is Cheryl, wearing shorts, a grey Bose t-shirt and a New England Patriots ball cap. These two are some of the most amazing people I've met in all my journeys. Nothing rattles them. As the tractor makes a wide circle, I see Fina sitting on its green fender. Cheryl pulls up next to the water truck and shuts down the engine. Mark meets her, helps her down and they go off to look at the smoldering van. I owe them an explanation. Once I come up with one.

CHAPTER 22

Wednesday / 12:33 PM
Rooftop - Surfer Moon Hotel

Mark cleans up what's left of Alvaro's van. He refused our help, and said we should have our meeting. I bet they both want us out of here. Can't blame them. The bombing made me realize how isolated they are. No one came to help. Police. Fire. Nobody. I now understand their need for self-sufficiency. I tried getting hold of Carlone several times this morning, but kept getting voicemail. After navigating through the DEA's phone system, finally a live person tells me he's in "Very important meetings." I get the feeling that Washington's political parties are taking sides and Carlone's caught in the middle.

Thanks to Jim's assistant, I was able to get some navy personnel here to provide some low-level security. I heard the first thing they did when they got here was check out Mark's garaged Black 1969 GTO 400 Convertible. Diego said "It's no DeLorean, but it's still nice."

Clare decides to skip the meeting and takes Pedro into town with Cheryl to see the school she works at. She asked Clare to help her teach an English class this afternoon. Of course she said yes, and this is the happiest I've seen her in quite a while. Why do I get the feeling I'm ruining her life? As added security, Clare agreed to take along a person I met in Key West several months ago - Navy Ensign Kelly Rogers. I thought I recognized someone in Mark's surfing group this morning. Her showing up out of the blue makes me wonder, that she's more than an Ensign in the Navy. But I trust her.

Mom, Diego, Alvaro, and Mike start the meeting. I tell everyone that I just received an email from Carlone - no news. Except that somebody high up in the government authorized the carrier group to move north and anchor off the coast of Tampico. A couple hundred miles from here. Mike

63

jumps in to confirm that he and Ensign Rogers will be picked up here by chopper at 5:00 PM. He says that Carlone would like us to go with them, but because of Clare's aversion to boats, that's out of the question. Besides, they know we're taking Pedro to Saint Jerome's in Brownsville. Mom and Diego say nothing about their plans, but I can tell Mom is thinking of something. Alvaro? We'll see.

"Alvaro, what happened?" I ask.

"Joe. Mike. Diego. Señorita Caroline," he says slowly, pausing to take a drink from his water bottle. His hand is shaking so much; most of the water soaks the front of his shirt. He looks at Mom, takes a deep breath, and continues.

"Lo siento," he says. "Very sorry. Understand, the last time I was this afraid is when my beautiful wife, Leandra, died of cancer in 2000, March 21. Again, I feel so lost." His eyes tear up as he lowers his head, begins crying softly.

Mom slides over next to Alvaro. Places a hand over his and starts to talk.

"Please Alvaro, you have friends here. We'll help you," she says soothingly. "Let me start by saying what I know. On Joseph's sixteenth birthday, he received a box – left on our porch, I think. That was November 1998. It contained a stone with a face carved into it. Not sure whose face, but a face – maybe Jesus. The Smithsonian verified the rock was part of a collection from one of the temples in Machu Picchu, Peru." Mom removes her hand from Alvaro and looks at Diego, "So it looked like somebody stole the rock, and sent it to my son on his birthday. Why, I don't know, but Joseph got presents from someone on every birthday till he turned sixteen. We just assumed they came from someone I knew many years ago when I lived in Mexico with my parents. A man I hadn't seen since before Joseph was born. Anyway, no note, a rock wrapped in newspaper from Mexico City. No clues and," mom says as her eyes glaze over. It's my turn to take over.

"So, Alvaro, we never knew who sent us the rock. It was sent back," I say with a long pause. "At least I thought it was sent back." Mom jumps back in.

"As you know Alvaro, I came to Peru in February of '99," Mom says. "My contacts with the Peruvian government insisted that I bring the stone in person. Which I did. Something about an international antiquity theft ring. You see, they said this was an opportunity to solve a twenty-year-old mystery, but I was double crossed and almost killed. You - Alvaro, saved my life. During our escape your boat hit some rocks and broke up. A helicopter plucked us out of the water. The box containing the stone was taken from me after the helicopter crashed. That's the last time I saw it, three days later I find myself in Machu Picchu waiting for a bus to take me to Lima. I still don't know what happed during that time," her voice trailing off, her eyes getting watery.

"Where's the rock now?" Mike blurts out. "I'm confused. Whose face? Note or no note? And does this have anything to do with bombings and cartels?"

"Jesus, it's the face of Jesus. On the stone I mean," Alvaro says in a flat voice. "Hold on, hold on," says Diego as he raises his arms for attention. "Joe, when you got the stone, ten, no fourteen years ago was there an inscription?

"No."

"Alvaro, I'm under the impression that you think the stone always had this, writing, inscription. Snares of, devil, snares of the devil. Yes?" Diego says staring at me.

"Si – Trampas del Diablo," Alvaro says slowly.

Alvaro stands up and begins pacing around our table. He starts mumbling to himself and walks to the edge of the roof to look out over the water. I decide to get up and ask a few more questions.

"Excuse me Alvaro." He turns to me with tears running down his face. "You never saw the stone, did you? Look, I believe someone hired you to find it because you had a connection. On the helicopter in 99 – with my mother. What happened to you after the helicopter crashed? Where'd you end up?"

Standing five feet from him, waiting for answers, Alvaro soaks up tears with his shirtsleeve. Looking at me, he starts to open his mouth. His words are muted by a single gunshot that hits him in the back. The force is so strong; he falls into me, knocking me onto the yellow brick, tiled floor. I

65

hear Mom scream; a powerboat starts up and Mike asking me if I'm okay. My cheek feels stuck to the floor with blood flowing from my nose. Face sideways, looking down the yellow brick road, like the cowardly lion, I ask the wizard for courage before passing out.

Chapter 23

Wednesday 3:10 PM
USS Harry S. Truman – Supercarrier
Off Shore – Veracruz, Mexico

I wake up with my head pounding and hear the low hum of engines below. Looking across from me, I see several empty beds, perfectly made in white and blue sheets. I'm alone. Sliding my feet onto the floor, I feel dizzy, which causes me to lean against the bed. Wearing only boxers, I reach over to the adjacent bed where my clothes are folded in a neat pile. I dress slowly, happy to be standing and begin walking towards the exit. The noise of an aircraft taking off above me confirms that I'm on an aircraft carrier, probably the USS Truman - Mike's new home. I've been on several carriers in the past, but never the Harry Truman. I see a sailor outside sick bay and ask him to take me out on the flight deck to get some air. Before we go, he makes a call, talks politely to someone and we're on our way. Battling a fuzzy head, I think we go up two levels before I step out onto to the flight deck. Pulling the sunglasses from my pocket, I lean against a metal rail for support and notice we're moving.

"Joe, what are you doing out here?" It's Mike. "The doc thinks you might have a mild concussion."

"Mike, why are we moving?" I ask.

"Don't you remember? The carrier group is moving north," he says.

"Yea, right, I remember. But wait a minute. Where's Clare? Pedro?"

"You know that Clare wouldn't leave your bedside, but Diego convinced her to tour the ship with him and Pedro. Anyway, we're all on board except Alvaro."

"He's dead?"

"No," Mike says. "He disappeared after the shooting. Remember the shooting?"

"Yeah, maybe, what happened?"

"Alvaro was facing us, standing by the edge of the hotel rooftop. You were standing a few feet away. A gun shot. Next thing I know Alvaro's glasses pop off his head and he falls right into you - hard. You hit your head on the tile floor, knocked yourself out. Blood was spurting out of your nose. We thought it was broken. Don't worry, it's not."

"What happened to Alvaro?" I say, gently touching my nose.

"He got hit in the back - shot from a Cigarette style boat off shore. The Navy's looking for it. The sniper must've wanted to finish the job he tried earlier with the van."

"He's not dead?"

"No. After he almost got killed in the van, he was a nervous wreck. Told me they we're trying to kill him. I asked him who they were – he wouldn't tell me. So after the van explosion, I gave him my bullet proof vest – he wore it to the meeting. Damn thing saved his life," Mike says. "We were loading you onto the chopper so you could get seen by a doctor, and next thing I know Alvaro's gone. Mark and I looked everywhere – no luck. Maybe they got him - don't know."

"Mom okay?"

"She's worried, Joe. About you and everything else that's going on. She thinks it's all tied together. The Jesus stone. Holy Spirit destroyed. The bombing at the consulate. Alvaro showing up, almost getting killed - twice. You know your Mom. Her brain is trying to thread it all together. She's leaving for Washington tonight via the Super Hornet express. Jeez, better her than me. Told Carlone she needs her team. I'll find her. You alright?"

"Yea, fine Mike, thanks."

As soon as he's gone awhile, I hear my mom behind me.

"Joseph, I'm trying to be strong," she says. "I really am."

I turn to see her standing there, looking exhausted. Eyes with dark circles, shoulders slouched and whispers barely heard above the hum of the ship. We find a place to sit down, both silent until she speaks.

"I'm leaving tonight. Need to get back to the Library"

"I know, Mike told me."

"Something is going on here. I'll be damned if I can figure it out," she whispers.

"Mom, after the terrorist attack in DC several months ago, somebody was sending us clues. Granted at first we thought they had nothing to do with the attacks. But, looking back now, I think they had everything to do with the attacks. Come on Mom, you're the one who figured it out."

"Please, I had a lot of help. Don't forget you and Clare almost got killed following those clues. I'm still haunted by the whole thing. And you know what," she whispers, "it's happening again. I'm sure of it. That's why I'm going back to Washington. I need to take the stone with me – I already contacted the Smithsonian."

"Mom. I'm worried about you – I've never seen you look so tired."

"Don't worry about me; my assistant back at the Smithsonian will not let the stone out of her sight. Mr. Carlone has set up 24/7 security for anyone even remotely involved. Since he became DEA boss, he's been my closest ally. Even the President likes him."

"He's found a good friend in you," I say. "You'll need someone to pick you up at Edwards when you land?"

"Stella's picking me up. Thank God for her."

"Yeah mom, thank God for Stella."

"Joseph, I have to admit, I'm deeply worried. I feel something bad is going to happen. Something big. And I know the stone has something to do with what's going wrong down here. That's why I contacted Tomas."

"My father?"

"Huh, who," she says hesitantly. "I'm convinced he or someone he knows sent the box containing the stone to Holy Spirit Mission a few months ago. We both know the inscription on the stone is relatively new. That's why I think it's a warning. Snares of the devil certainly has religious connotations, but I feel it's something else. I ran across it somewhere - can't remember though. Some Intel we picked up in 2001 or 2002, think it was intercepted via our embassy in Columbia. Anyway, I haven't heard anything from Tomas, so I sent up another flare through Diego, but still nothing."

"Speaking of Diego," I say quickly.

"Sorry Joseph, gotta go," she says, getting up quickly. "It's after 5:00 and my jet leaves tonight at 6:00. I need to have a snack and suit up. Can't fly at Mach one and a half on an empty stomach."

"Come on Mom, we need to talk about it. You promised."

"Yes, we do - just not now," she says standing up. "Walk me down to the mess hall since I have more important things to tell you. Where's Clare?"

"Mike says she's taking a tour of the ship with Pedro and Diego. Anyway, my head is clear and we need to get back to the hotel to pick up our stuff, including the wonder dog. From there it's off to Brownsville."

"Come on Joseph, let's get something to eat," she says, finally smiling.

The Navy is right on schedule. Mom took off in the F/A18 Super Hornet at exactly 6:00 PM. Jetting faster than the speed of sound should put her back in Washington before 10:00. She did almost faint when I showed her the stone with the added inscription. Seeing it again reminded her of the trip Peru to in 99, an excursion that went horribly wrong. Not being able to remember what happened during the three days between passing out in the helicopter, meeting Frank Sinatra and the bus ride to Lima scared the hell out of her. But I'm still not quite sure why she dropped everything to come down here after I told her about the stone. I know she loves me and wanted to warn me personally. About what, I'm still not sure. At least I was able to trade the stone for her M11 Sig Sauer.

I find myself, alone, sitting in the mess hall at 7:40 PM. Clare, Pedro and Diego are back at the hotel because Clare could not stay on the ship any longer. Thankfully Mark and Cheryl allowed us back for another night as long as we "behave ourselves." Truthfully, I think deep down, they like the excitement. Me, I'm tired of it. Now I'm waiting for the doctor to clear me back to land. I so desperately need to spend time with Clare that I'll swim to shore if need be.

Chapter 24

Wednesday / 9:36 PM
Surfer Moon Hotel

Walking hand in hand with Clare along the shore helps temporarily erase the events of the last few days. After receiving a clean bill of health from the ship's doc, Ensign Rogers and I hitched a ride on a helicopter back to the hotel. Rogers has joined our group as a security expert. She's now sleeping in the adjoining room next to Pedro's. The last time I checked, Rogers was battling for space on the bed with Fina. Little does she know that it's only a matter of time before Pedro joins them.

Before leaving the Truman, Mike told me he had to remain on board until Carlone gave him shore leave. Or until he goes AWOL. The good news is tomorrow morning; an RV will be delivered for our use. Our "family" will pose as tourists heading back to Texas. This should be interesting.

"Joe, what about right here?" Clare asks. "We have the ocean, soft sand, and dunes to protect us from the wind. I like it. What'd you think?"

"Perfect, just perfect," I say while laying out the blankets. It could've been a bed of nails for all I care. The smell of strawberries is making me crazy. "Clare, I want to say again how sorry I am for everything that's happened over these last three months. You should've driven by me at the airport in Mexico City. Left me, right there, on the bench outside baggage claim. But no, you had to stop," I tease.

"Please Joe; don't you remember why I had to stop? Don't you? Think hard."

"Clare, you stopped because you saw this dangerously handsome man sitting alone outside the airport."

"Dangerous yes! Handsome, who am I to say?" She smiles. "But let me refresh your memory. I drew the short straw to pick you up, and the bus

71

I was driving broke down outside the terminal. You just happened to wander over along and helped me get it started. You were just another face in the crowd."

"Handsome face," I interject.

"Dangerous face," she throws back.

"Alright, you win! Dangerous Joe Dustan asks sexy Sister Clare Atwater for a ride on a multicolored bus with Holy Spirit Mission painted on the side. Dangerous Joe tempts the beautiful Sister to join him in a little danger. She gives in – eventually," I add.

"Sister Clare? No! Sexy and beautiful Clare? Yes! Giving in to danger? No! More like Dangerous Joe from naval intelligence brings trouble for those around him - whether they want it or not. Now please dangerous Joe, stop talking and get under the blanket before I find a convent to take me in."

I'm woken up by a mumbling Alvaro at 3:08 AM. I'm in my birthday suit, next to Clare wrapped tightly in all the blankets; maybe I should change my name from Dangerous to Precarious Joe. Sounds right. Note to self: look up precarious. Hearing voices on the other side of the dunes tells me he's not alone. Did he bring his group of merry men?

CHAPTER 25

"Las fresas, huelo fresas," Alvaro says.

"What?"

"Fresas, I smell strawberries," he replies.

"Listen, never mind strawberries," I say pulling on my pants. "Where've you been?"

"Getting help Joseph, getting help." He says, barely able to keep his eyes open.

"Alvaro, how many drinks did you have last night?"

His eyes go wide, and he begins to smile. "Please Joseph, excuse me, but someone tried to kill me – dos veces – two times. This is a new experience for me. Your Clare is beautiful," he says staring at her. "She looks like an angel."

While getting the rest of my clothes on, three other men show up, two drunker then Alvaro. They give me a quick glance then move their attention to Clare. I get the feeling that Alvaro doesn't know these guys, and probably just met them at a bar. I sense the situation about to get out of control when Alvaro jumps in.

"Thanks, for the ride," he says to the men slurring his words. "Muchas gracias!"

I can tell the men are deciding what to do at this point. Looking down at the sand for my gun, I notice it's missing from the holster. The men turn to leave. Stop. Turn back around. This time the skinny, shirtless one in the middle has a pistol in his hand.

"Please my friends, we don't need guns." Alvaro says clearly. "Let me pay you for the ride – please."

One of the men, a heavyset guy wearing one shoe, starts moving towards Clare. I step in his way.

"Listen, we don't want any trouble. Find a spot along the beach and sleep it off." I say, staring into his eyes. Where have I seen this guy before?

He stops a few feet from me, close enough for me to smell a mixture of alcohol, urine and vomit. Now that we're face to face, I see blood dripping from his right ear and one eye partially closed. Tears flowing from the other. Has he been in a fight? Anyway, doesn't look like he's ready for another. Before I have a chance to say anything, I hear ruffled movement behind me followed by a loud, clear voice.

"Move back sir! I said get back! Now!" Clare says moving around me holding my mother's gun in her right hand. Wrapped in a camo blanket, she's pointing the Sig at the disheveled man standing in front of me. For a moment, I forget all about the strangers until I see them running away down the beach. The third man with the bloody face falls to his knees, begins to cry and begins mumbling something in Spanish that I can't translate. Alvaro backs away and sits awkwardly on a large piece of driftwood before falling onto the sand. Clare hands me the gun, puts her hair in a ponytail and slides into her jeans. She finds my New York Yankee t-shirt and puts it on - can't take my eyes off of her.

"Clare, can you please grab the other flashlight out of my bag?"

"Sure."

"Sis, Sister Clare!" the stranger cries out. "Is that you really you Sister Clare?"

"Who are you? And where do you know me from?" she says softly.

I lower the gun as Clare moves close to the stranger. Seeing the man and hearing his voice takes me back to when I first got to Mexico - after the attacks in Washington. Clare picked me up at the airport in a multicolored school bus that looked like it belonged to the *Partridge Family*. It was something like a three, four hour ride from the airport to Holy Spirit Mission. Let's see, we made a few stops along the way. Picked up supplies. Stopped at a church. Played baseball with orphaned children. Ate pizza and ice cream with them. Wait. Pizza, ice cream, baseball. Oh my God, it can't be. No, can't be. Clare yelps as we both figure out who it is at the same time. She falls to the ground, cradles his head and begins crying and sobbing like I haven't seen for quite some time. Her words come out as she grabs his large hand and places it against her chest.

"Yes, it's me, Clare! Please, what happened?" She pleads. "Never mind, don't matter; we'll take care of you. Don't worry, never mind, you found us," Clare says, calming down. Then it hits her. "Oh my God TG, where's your wife?" As he's about to speak, I see his leg start to spasm. He looks over at Clare, touches his arm and starts grabbing his chest. Clare's background as a nurse causes her to yell out orders, as TG goes into full cardiac arrest. "Alvaro! Hotel lobby! Defib paddles! Now! Joe, call the Truman! We need to medevac TG to the ship! Please help me," she cries. I quickly reach into my bag; hit a button on the emergency locator beacon. We'll have help in less than ten minutes. I pull out a flare gun, point it towards the water and pull the trigger. Can't hurt. It lights up the area, exposing Clare conducting CPR on TG. She takes a break and I jump in. Staying alive, staying alive. Thank you Bee Gees.

Within minutes, Mark shows up and takes over for me. Clare's on the phone with Mike, telling him what we need on the chopper. "Don't forget the doctor!" she yells. Ensign Rogers arrives with Cheryl, holding Pedro in her arms. It's 3:43 in the morning. Eight minutes since heart attack. Fina breaks out into a howling tirade letting us know the helicopter is close, reminding me of the character Radar on the 70's TV show *MASH*. We carefully move TG on to a surf board and strap him down. It looks like Clare managed to get him stable even without the paddles. Alvaro seems to have disappeared – again.

Mark and I carry TG over the dune toward the beach where I see Diego waving flashlights, guiding in the chopper. Upon landing, Mike jumps down and rushes over to help. Is he wearing New York Yankee pajamas under his life vest? The Naval doc who signed me out last night is on board, hanging out the open door. Mark and I hand the stretcher to several people inside the chopper and move away. Clare gives me a hug and climbs inside. "Call you when we land – when I know something – love you," she yells over the engine noise. Mike pulls me to the side. "Joe, we need to talk very soon. All hell is breaking loose inside the halls of DC. Talk later," he yells as he jumps inside the cabin just before the door closes. We move away, watching the helicopter take off and fly low over the water lit by the moon. Cheryl lightens the somber mood when she says, "coffee anyone?" I take Pedro from Ensign Rogers, hold him against my shoulder and we begin walking to the Surfer Moon Hotel.

CHAPTER 26

It's 4:18 in the morning and we're sitting in the lobby of the Hotel sipping our coffee in silence. Pedro's wrapped in a blanket sound asleep on one of the red velvet couches. Fina followed Cheryl into the kitchen 20 minutes ago to watch the art of baking muffins and is surely keeping the floor clean. I decide to break the silence when Mark comes in to join us.

"TG's someone Clare knows from Puebla. He's like a father figure to her. I met him for a few hours several months ago. He and his wife Sandy own a restaurant named Amalfi Pizza. But more importantly, they're like foster parents to hundreds of street kids," I say.

"TG, Sandy and Clare worked together, placing these kids in good homes throughout Mexico," Diego jumps in. "My business partner Darnell and I helped in screening families while traveling on business. Clare would house many of these children at Holy Spirit Mission - sometimes up to fifty at a time. I saw him a few days ago in Puebla – he asked about Clare. He heard about our restaurants being torched. I told him where we were heading. He seemed distressed, not himself. Said Sandy was in the States."

"How sad – about the children, I mean," Cheryl says, walking into the room carrying a tray of freshly baked muffins. "We have homeless kids at the school - it's terrible! No place to go at the end of the school day – so they just wander the streets - many younger than ten. We teachers have worked out a schedule to take the children home with us. Last year, Mark and I had eight children living with us all summer."

"What'd you think happened to TG?" Rogers asks. "He looked like he'd been in a fight or maybe a car accident."

"I'm not sure," I reply slowly. "When he first showed up, I thought the same: a fight, an accident, maybe mugged. But, when we loaded him into the helicopter, the lights exposed possible signs of torture. Maybe, not sure, anyway let the doc check him out."

"He had a gun, but it was really a lighter," says Mark. "Picked it out of the sand."

"TG liked Cuban cigars. I saw him use that very same gun to light a cigar after a baseball game with the kids. He asked me if I wanted one - cigar. I can't smoke – it makes me dizzy. Allergic too."

"I've smoked a few Cubans with TG," says Diego smiling. "Delicious aroma, excellent quality."

Seeing the sun break through the lobby windows, I decide to go out and look for Alvaro. Ensign Rogers comes along. Diego takes charge of Pedro as Mark and Cheryl head for the kitchen. "Breakfast at 7:00," Cheryl says cheerily. Still no call from Clare. We need to move on so the Temples can get their lives back, and not be dragged into my troubles. Cheryl said the hotel will be fully booked in a few days due to Spring Break.

"Captain Dustan, can you please stop calling me Ensign Rogers? You can call me Kelly or Rogers, I don't care. Ensign's too formal," she says politely, while stepping around a large rock pile.

"Sure Ensign Rogers. From now on I'll call you Kelly or Rogers – sounds good." "Great – thank you – appreciate that."

"But you gotta stop calling me Captain. It kind of freaks me out. When Mike and I got in trouble in the military, he'd say, "How will you, our captain, get us out of this one? He's a captain too - much better one than me. Anyhow, call me Joe. And please not Joey. Only use Joey when you're trying to tell me something. Like life and death type stuff – you know, get my attention."

You got it Captain, I mean Joe, not Joey unless in danger. Sort of code word – I like it."

Kelly and I split up to cover a wooded area that runs adjacent to the hotel. She takes a trail going east and I go north. Within ten minutes, I hear her yelling, "Joey, Joey you need to see this."

Backtracking down the trail, following Kelly's voice, I come to a small clearing. I find her looking at a hole in the ground, surrounded by several large sand piles. Moving in closer, I see the top of a red, opened umbrella, pointing towards the sky. Kelly gives me a nervous look as I peer into the hole. She's found Alvaro. He's holding the umbrella in his good, non-deformed – left hand. His thick black glasses are hanging off one ear,

78

exposing a dime sized bullet hole between his eyes - ants are crawling into his nose. I reach down into the hole, shoo away the pests and close his eyes. Kelly goes back to the hotel to find a blanket while I contact Mike on the Truman, letting him know we need a forensics team right away.

While on the line he tells me TG's in surgery and Clare's with him in the operating room. He adds that Carlone gave him permission to leave the ship and join us on dry land – "quarantine over." Needless to say, I really need him.

Kelly returns with a blanket and a hot cup of coffee. I cover Alvaro's face with the blanket to keep the bugs away while trying not to disturb the crime scene. After about ten minutes of standing guard over his body, I hear the wonder dog break into nonstop howling. Minutes later, I hear a chopper landing nearby. Soon after, a team of eight find their way to us following Diego. They begin securing the area with stakes and yellow tape. We get asked a series of questions read off a clipboard. Once complete, we're granted permission to leave. Looking over at Alvaro one more time, holding the umbrella, I say a quick prayer. Even though he was a little strange, I liked him, and he did save my mom's life back in 1999.

Walking in silence down the path with Kelly, I get a bad feeling.

"Why would someone shoot Alvaro and put an umbrella in his hand?" I say aloud.

"Maybe, maybe it was in his hand when he got shot. You know, killed instantly, hand muscles lock up – maybe?" Kelly says.

"It's possible I guess."

"Maybe the killer shot him and once he or she knew the victim was dead, they used the umbrella to make the body easier to find," she says. "But you're right, it doesn't make sense."

"Unless maybe it's some sort of clue," I reply. "Maybe the killer didn't open the umbrella. Someone else opened it? I guess we'll see what the Navy finds."

Just before joining the others for breakfast, I get a call from Clare aboard the Truman.

"He's gonna make it Joe," cries Clare. "TG's gonna live, thank God!"

"I'm so happy to hear that – great news!"

"He'll have to stay on the ship for several weeks to recuperate. But I know they'll take good care of him," she says.

"Clare, do we know any more about what happened to him?"

The phone goes silent. "Clare, can you hear me? Clare?"

"Sorry, Joe, I'm here. Give me a minute. Please."

"We'll talk later. Clare? Call me back."

"I'm back. Sorry. One of the doctors is telling me that TG was tortured. He has burns on his legs, chest and groin area. They're certain he has a fractured jaw, but he's too unstable right now for x-rays. The Navy doctor put him in a deep coma so his system can start to repair itself. Oh and they found nothing wrong with his heart - minor blockage in an artery – I guess it's quite normal for someone his size and age. The doctor thinks that the cardiac arrest was probably caused by all the trauma he's been through. Everything just shut down. Mike tells me Alvaro's dead – murdered?"

I hear Clare's voice begin to break up and the phone connection becomes muffled. "Yes, Alvaro is dead," I say loudly, so she can hear me. "Rogers found him. Anyway, I'll call you back."

"Wait, sorry about that. I'm okay. Anyway, Mike and I are flying back to the hotel at ten this morning," she says pausing. "That's in about an hour and a half. Hey, how's Pedro?"

"He's fine. Between, Cheryl, Kelly and Diego, I think I've only held him once. Anyway, he keeps asking about you."

"I miss him, Joe. Can't imagine how it's gonna feel when he goes off with his new adopted parents in Brownsville."

"I know, but listen, the RV will be delivered here this morning and that will be our ride to Texas. We'll make the most of our time spent with him along the way. I figure we can leave after lunch. Alright?"

"Sure, but we'll need to stop in Puebla on the way. Since TG's in a coma, we need to try and find Sandy. We'll go to their restaurant, home - ask around the neighborhood. I know she may still be visiting her elderly mother in North Carolina, but I'd like her to hear what happened from us, if possible. Anyway, that needs to be our first stop."

"No problem, good idea. Diego said he saw TG a few days ago in Puebla and that Sandy was in the States. Either way, I'll have it all mapped out before you get here. Love you."

"See you around ten," she says. "Love you too."

Not wanting to hang up, I wait till the line goes dead. I grab a seat at one of the picnic tables facing the woods and sadly get a front row view as they carry Alvaro, sans umbrella, to the waiting helicopter. A member of the forensic team joins me at the table.

"Captain Dustan, I'm Chief Petty Officer Gerry Rigby."

"Please, please sit down. You want a cup of coffee? Some in the kitchen," I say.

"No thank you Captain – chopper's waiting for me. I wanted to give you my opinion on what we found. The man as you know was found dead, with the umbrella. It was placed in his hand after being killed. At first, we thought he'd shot himself. But, the location, angle of the bullet hole made it physically impossible," he says as he gets up to leave. "Thought you should know."

"Officer Rigby, hold on a sec," I say. "Anything else?"

He looks around and sits back down, pulling a Ziploc plastic bag from his pocket.

"Captain Dustan, the man in the hole was not shot by the same person who put the umbrella in his hand. In my opinion, the victim was shot, thrown in the hole. I think someone came by later and placed the umbrella handle into the dead man's hand. My assumptions, I repeat, my assumptions are based on time of death and rigor mortis. Also found two pairs of footprints at the scene – under the body. Bare feet - no shoes."

"Interesting. Ensign Rogers and I never went down into the hole," I say. "We knew he'd been dead a while. I did lean in, checked his pulse anyway and closed his eyes."

"We found this in his mouth, under his tongue."

Officer Rigby hands me the plastic bag with a small piece of white paper inside. Flipping it over, writing, in pencil, printed neatly – "Trampas del Diablo." Below it, the print is smudged, but I think it says Saturday. Two days from now?

Chapter 27

Thursday / 12:00 Noon
Surfer Moon Hotel

Our travel plans are set. Clare, Pedro, Diego and Ensign Rogers will head towards Brownsville this afternoon in the RV. Mike and I will drive to Puebla to look for TG's wife Sandy. It's about a two hour ride and Mark's volunteered to drive us in his Tahoe Hybrid. Carlone promised a pick-up in Puebla so we can rendezvous with the RV in Tampico later tonight. Pick up by whom? Mode of transportation – unknown.

Sitting alone in a beach chair waiting for the RV to show up, I watch Pedro and Fina playing in the sand when my iPhone rings. It's Mom.

"Hi Mom," I say trying to sound cheery.

"Good Afternoon, Joseph," she replies in a professional tone. "I'm calling from my office in the Library of Congress. You're on conference with five members of my team. Can you talk with us?"

Mom and I have a code worked out when she calls me from the office. You see, she has two offices. One above ground where she spends most of her time collecting and digitizing old works. At least that's what I think she does. Her other office is below ground. This is where she works on various government research projects, usually assigned by high-ranking officials. Sometimes even the President. Mom is recognized as one of the best research librarians in the world. Her team has a knack for pulling data together, analyzing it and recommending solutions. Ninety-eight percent of the time, they're correct in their assumptions. So anyway, when she calls from her office in the Library of Congress, I know she's below ground, working on covert type stuff. A call from just the office with no mention of the Library is above ground.

"Joseph, can you hear me?" Mom says.

"Yes, I'm here."

"Joseph, we just received the initial report on the death of Mr. Alvaro Morales. Also, information concerning the other two attempts on his life prior," her voice cracking. "The forensics report says Mr. Morales was shot, close range, in the forehead. Suicide ruled out. The report goes on to say that he was killed someplace else. One to two hours later dumped in the pit. After which, an umbrella was placed into his right hand with fingers wrapped around the handle. What do you think, Joseph?"

"That's what I was told by the Navy Forensics team as they were leaving this morning. Based on that report and being at the scene, I guess I agree with those findings."

"Joseph, can you confirm that the umbrella was open when you found him."

"Yes – pointing towards the sky."

"Confirm the color of the umbrella was red?"

"Yes."

"Did the umbrella look new – old?"

"Old, faded, had several rips in the fabric. Couldn't have been good for keeping out the rain," I say.

The line falls silent except for some shuffling of paper in the background for a little while.

"Hello Joe, I'm Joan. Sorry about that. I'm part of Caroline's, I mean your mother's, team. The report states that a white piece of paper with writing was found under Mr. Morales's tongue. Can you confirm this?"

"Yes. I was shown the paper by the officer in charge - before he left for the Truman," I say. "I did not see the paper extracted from under the tongue. It was shown to me from inside a sealed plastic bag after the body was moved."

"Thanks Joe," Joan says. We have not yet seen the slip of paper. Were you able to read what it said?"

"Yes,"

"Can you tell me, us, what the note said?"

"Yeah. Trampas del Diablo – translation - Snares of the Devil with a day written below it -smudged. I mean the print was smudged. But, I think it read Saturday. This, if correct, is two days from now."

"Joseph, hang on, wait a minute," Mom says, barely audible.

I hear voices, movement followed by a door being closed and locked. The receiver is picked up and the annoying echo during the conference call is gone.

"Joseph, it's me. I've adjourned the meeting, asked everyone to get working on the latest findings."

"What's going on Mom?"

"Joseph, when I went to Peru in 99 to return the stone, I ran into some trouble. I didn't want to worry you with the details. Especially since I made it back to Washington in one piece. Over the last ten years or so, I was obsessed with what happened back then, but finally put it behind me as a random event. Now, with everything that's happened, I think there's a connection," Mom says, with a deep breath. "That's why I rushed down to see you. Thinking my experience in '99 is somehow related to what's happening now."

"You said you wanted to warn me – in person."

"Yeah, kind of. But also tell you about what happened years ago in Peru. You and I, we, I think we know just about everything about each other. The thing that happened in South America, returning the stone, I never told you. I'm sorry," she says softly.

"That's okay; it had no effect on our lives." I say.

"Till now," mom replies.

"Okay - till now."

"I have a meeting with Jim Carlone and the head of the NSA in ten minutes," she says. "I'm going to tell them about my trip to Peru, the stone and why I think it's connected to the events happening now. Joseph," Mom says softly. "It's the how and why we need to work on. Somebody is trying to tell us something - warning us. Whoever sent you that statue, and…"

"What makes you think that?" I ask.

"The umbrella, open and in Alvaro's hand was meant as a warning. To me, I believe."

"How's that mom?"

"In '99, on my way to Peru, I had a layover at Miami International. The weather was dreadful, heavy rain. Anyway, I forgot my umbrella at home," she pauses. "Our flight was delayed a few times, until it got canceled. I rebooked for the next morning. You see Joseph, outside

84

baggage claim, it was pouring rain as I was waiting for a taxi to take me to a local hotel. I ended up sharing a taxi with a woman with an English accent, no luggage, briefcase, nothing. Except, a large red umbrella."

"Come on Mom, please don't tell me you think there's a connection to that umbrella and the one we found with Alvaro's body," I say jumping in.

"Of course not Joseph," she says slowly. "Until I read the forensics report stating Alvaro was killed, placed in a hole with Umbrella after death – and opened. Anyway, when I got to the hotel, the taxi driver grabbed my luggage. The woman walked me through the parking lot - under that umbrella."

"I don't get it Mom."

"When we got inside the lobby, she offered to give me the umbrella. The red one," she says. "I refused, saying I'd just buy one in the morning if needed. "Don't need the bloody thing if the sun's shining," she'd said. She tells me something about it being bad luck to open an umbrella on a sunny day. I joked back, saying she should tell that to all the golfers and sunbathers. She didn't laugh - just stared at me. The last thing she said was to keep an eye out for open umbrellas on sunny days. "Might mean danger – just some friendly advice," she said.

"Okay Mom, a strange lady at the airport becomes even stranger at the hotel. She talks to you about open umbrellas, sunny days, and danger. I'm sorry; I don't get the connection to Alvaro."

"Joseph, listen, a day later I'm in Peru, walking up to my hotel, going to check in. I hear someone calling my name. I look behind me and see a man telling me to wait. He too has an English accent – like the woman at the airport. Remembering our conversation, I can't help but notice his umbrella's open. Joseph, there's not a cloud in the sky - it's a beautiful day," Mom says, as if reliving that moment. "After he calls my name, I hear police sirens from cars that eventually end up in front of the Peruvian hotel. Several of the men go in, while some others start walking through the crowds - like they're looking for someone. I glance back at the opened red umbrella, panic and run"

"Did you ever find out if they were looking for you?"

"Yes, yes I did – the hard way. They saw me running towards the shore of Lake Titicaca, gave chase and started shooting at me. In my attempt to get away, I meet up with that guy – the Englishman. This time he's in a rowboat, offshore telling me to go with him. That's when Alvaro shows up in his power boat and saves my life. Now he's dead," mom finishes sadly. "Now he's dead."

"I don't know Mom - sounds like a stretch," I say softly.

"Hang on Joseph – there's more. After Alvaro picked me up, a strong storm moved in. He was hit by lightning - it struck his crippled arm. The boat hit an outcropping of rocks – smashed to pieces. We're thrown into the water, plucked out by a helicopter," she says. "Just before passing out, a man takes the box from me. You know the one that contains the stone. In the helicopter is the English guy - with the umbrella. Sorry Joseph gotta go - finish the story later."

"Okay Mom, but one quick thing before you go. Let me say that I understand the possible connection. Do we have any idea who the Englishman is?"

"No. But my team is working on all leads – including this one. I'm off to my next meeting. Love you Joseph. And please, be careful. As soon as we figure anything out, I'll contact you. Give Clare and Pedro a big hug for me. Have a safe trip to Brownsville," she says.

"Thanks Mom, I love you too! Should I hug Diego for you as well?" I say sarcastically.

"Yes, please do! Bye Joseph – call you later," she says and the line goes dead.

My head's spinning after our conversation. I agree with her premise that someone is warning us and sending clues. The question is who, and why. I lose my train of thought as a large, white RV pulls into the parking lot. The writing on the side says, "Flame Keepers ZX Racing" with two lightning bolts forming the "X." As it drives by, I notice "Brownsville Texas" written in smaller letters on the back. Completing the ruse is the "Lone Star State" license plate – "BLKnBLU." It stops in front of the lobby door. As I walk towards it, a door under "ZX" opens and a tall, pale man steps down to the ground. Either I'm seeing things, or the man is dressed in a three-piece suit. What really catches my attention is the item in his right hand. As I get closer, he turns to me; holding some sort of cane, begins shouting.

"Excuse me! Excuse me my good man. Can you tell me where I can find a chap by the name of Dustan, Joseph Dustan?"

Pulling the Colt 1911 out of the small of my back, pointing it to the ground, I stop.

"I need you to put your hands over your head," I shout. "Drop the cane!"

He pauses for a few seconds, sees Mike moving off to the side, gun in hand. Dropping the cane, he slowly raises his hands over his head, saying nothing. Mike stops, gun drawn, I move closer. At about ten feet, I clearly see the item he was holding, now on the ground, is not a cane, but rather, an umbrella. What's going on here? The eerie silence is interrupted by a ringing cell phone. It's mine.

CHAPTER 28
Thursday 1:35 PM
Surfer Moon Hotel Parking Lot

Colt 1911, right hand, pointing at a stranger wearing a three-piece suit with arms in the air. Cell phone, left hand - call from Carlone. Snap a picture. Hit send.

"Hey Mike, you got this?" I yell across the lot. "It's Carlone – I need to take it."

"No problem buddy."

"Hello Mr. Carlone," I say.

"Hi Joe, did I catch you at a bad time?"

"You tell me. Download a photo I just sent you."

I notice the guy's arms drooping - getting tired, I tell him to lower them and sit on the ground. Mike moves in closer, gun still drawn. Carlone's back on the line.

"No way Joe, I can't believe it," he says. "I'm speechless!"

"How do you think I feel? Now you see my dilemma. Hey buddy, I need your help on this! This needs your attention right away."

"Okay, now I get it! All your whining and complaining. I thought you were just joking. He actually wears those shorts in public?" Carlone says.

"Darn right he does!" I yell knowing Mike can hear me. "He never dressed like that when the three of us were wandering the Pamir Mountains in Afghanistan."

"Alright, alright, I'll talk to him," Carlone says. "I know Joanne would never let him leave the house in those shorts."

"Thanks Jim. Maybe check his bags the next time you send him out – please."

"No problem Joe. Hey, by the way, the guy next to Mike is Victor Kingman - British Special ops guy. He's to drop off the RV and disappear,"

Jim says. "Well not really disappear, but rather fade into the background. Anyhow, we have so much going on in the world, we're shorthanded. So our friends in the British government are helping us out."

"I guess this happens when you act as the world's policeman," I say.

"Look Joe, I don't like it either, but I'm thankful for the help."

"Do me a favor and share the picture of Victor with my mother ASAP. Oh and be ready, ready to catch her if she faints."

"What are you talking about? Why would she faint?" he says.

"Listen Jim, it's a long story and I gotta get going. Mike and I are off to Puebla to check on something - right after he changes out of those shorts. Just show the photo to her. She won't believe those shorts either."

"Okay Joe, I'll do it right away."

"Thanks Jim. Oh and by the way, can you have someone email Victor Kingman's file to me? I need to find out where he was in 1999, early February I think. Also, an umbrella has been flown out this afternoon via a naval transport. We found it open in Alvaro's hand after he was dead for several hours. Maybe check for prints. I'd bet they're a match to our English spy, Victor Kingman. Think he has a collection that goes back to the late 90's."

"What makes you say that?" Jim says.

"Look at the picture again – see that cane looking thing on the ground – it's Victor's umbrella." I say. "Till I hear back from you, Vic's on my most wanted list."

"Understand. I'll get with your mom on this right away. You all be careful."

"Yes sir, boss – we'll be careful. Bye," I say moving towards the man sitting on the ground. I nod at Mike, tuck the 1911 into the front of my pants and start my interrogation.

"What's your name?" I ask the stranger.

"Kingman, Victor Kingman," he stammers. "But my friends call me Vic."

"Okay Mr. Kingman. I understand your job was to drop off the RV. It's here. Thank you. Tell me, where did you get it?"

"You're Joseph Dustan, right? Son of Caroline Dustan?"

"Yes. How do you know my mother?"

"I'd rather you ask her," he says. "The RV came from Mexico City, large warehouse operation called Doc Fuller's Specialty Auto. If you don't know, it's run by the US government."

"If you say so Mr. Kingman. Did you pick it up yourself?" I say watching Mike walk up behind Victor.

"No. The chap who owns the place drove it about ten miles from here," he says pulling out a business card from his vest. "Name is Bill Fuller, 'Automotive Doctor.'"

"Mr. Kingman, if you don't mind - where were you last night?"

"I do mind Mr. Dustan. My employer doesn't allow me to divulge such information - to anyone."

"I'm sure the British government won't mind if you tell me."

"Mr. Dustan, the keys are in the ignition. Gas tank is full. I must be going."

He reaches to the ground, grabs his umbrella and starts to walk down the driveway. On his way out, he passes Diego walking in my direction. I can't help but notice that Diego gives him a strange look as they pass. Fifty feet away, the Englishman stops, turns towards me, opening the red umbrella.

"Mr. Dustan," he yells. "Tell me; is the sun always this strong in Mexico? I hear the next several days will be virtually cloudless. Saturday is to be sunny and hot up near the border. I find it all bloody dangerous, skin cancer and all – can't be too careful. It's why I have my umbrella handy. Things get hot, I open it. See you soon Mr. Dustan. Tell your mom I said hello!"

"Thanks for the report," I shout. "Sounds like weather one might find in Peru this time of year. Stay safe Mr. Kingman – from the sun I mean."

The three of us watch him disappear into the heat ripples rising off the hot tar.

"Who wears a three-piece suit in this weather?" Mike says.

"You're one to talk in those shorts," I reply.

"I'm not allowed to wear them back home," Mike says.

"Oh really, what a surprise," Diego says jumping in.

"Mike, you need to change before we go," I say.

"Okay," he says sounding dejected. "I was going to anyway."

90

"Joe, who was that guy with the umbrella?" Diego asks.

"Some English guy named Victor Kingman," I reply.

"I know him from somewhere - can't place him though. It'll come to me."

By now, I'm use to Diego's deep thought process. He tunes everything out. Squints his eyes, causing his nose to wrinkle – a little like mom.

"Oh, Diego," I say. "I have something from my mother."

I turn and give him a big hug. Followed by a kiss on the cheek.

"The hug is from mom, kiss is from me," I say laughing.

Mike closes in from the other side and kisses Diego on the opposite cheek.

"I thank you all, especially Caroline," he says backing away. "But, I don't want any man kissing me, especially wearing those shorts!"

The three of us break out in laughter, soon quieted by Fina's excessive howling. We see her sprint out between two buildings and disappear over the sand dunes. A minute later, we hear the engines of a Navy Seahawk. Clare's back.

Chapter 29

It's 4:08 in the afternoon as I watch the Flame Keepers Racing RV pull away from the hotel. They got a late start due to Mike and me checking every nook and cranny for suspicious items like explosives and GPS tracking devices. Anything left behind by Victor Kingman. At this point, I don't like him or trust him, even though he might have been involved in saving Mom's life in '99. We'll see. Anyway, the RV's clean. The Flame Keepers Racing team consists of Diego, Pedro, Kelly and Clare. And the wonder dog. The plan is to meet them in Tampico around midnight after Mike and I swing through Puebla to check on Sandy to update her on TG's condition. That's if we can find her.

The latest update from Clare is that TG's still in a drug induced coma. She said the doctor was sure he was tortured, probably left for dead. Thank God he found us – somehow. Not sure how. I must be leaving a trail of breadcrumbs.

The toughest part is splitting from Clare - again. We promised each other that after Brownsville, we're going on vacation. Where – who knows? As long as we're together. I know Clare's upset about Pedro's adoption, but she knows it's for the best. Especially since they may be Pedro's extended family. We'll find out more on Saturday when we get to Saint Jerome's in Brownsville. I feel better knowing that Rogers is traveling in the RV. I get the strong feeling that she's a Navy Seal ordered to keep an eye on us - me. Lucky for us, Carlone convinced the Admiral of the Navy to have the USS Harry Truman Carrier Group track us up the Mexican coast to Texas. While waiting for our ride, two Super Hornets fly a few hundred feet over the Surfer Moon Hotel. Go Navy!

Mike joins me at the picnic table wearing jeans, sneakers and a Central Connecticut State University t-shirt. Normal clothes – thank God.

"Hey buddy," I say as he sits down, laying his Colt 1911 on the table. "You know one day you're gonna find out the truth about that gun."

"What'd you mean?"

"Come on, you know. We've talked about it many times."

"Please refresh my memory," he says sarcastically.

"Okay! It's that nonsense about that gun – right there!" I say pointing. "You believing that General Omar Bradley fired that exact same gun during WWII…"

"For your information smartass, I have the paperwork certifying its authenticity," he says.

"Mike, the serial numbers are missing! Filed off!"

"Don't matter," he says. "His initials are etched into the ivory handle – Look!"

"I've seen them at least hundred times," I reply.

"Then let me read them one more time – ONB - Omar Nelson Bradley. He was one of our finest Generals throughout WWII. Patton had nothing on this guy – except fame and glory," he snickers.

"Mike, listen, this is like an old Seinfeld episode from the nineties. Remember when George thought he bought a car that belonged Jon Voight, the actor."

"I don't think so," he says scratching his chin and looking at the sky.

"You remember! George's excited about the car because he thought Jon Voight owned it. Jerry ends up looking in the glove box and finds the old registration or something with the previous owner's name on it. John Voight. John spelled J-O-H-N. Not J-O-N – like the actor." I say laughing. "It's the same as your gun. The initials ONB probably stand for Owner Never Bradley. Not Omar Nelson Bradley."

"Think so?" he says.

"Yes I do! Anyway, the "B" looks more like an "R.""

"No way," he says starting to laugh. "It's a "B" as in Bradley."

"What are you guys laughing about?" Mark says, joining us at the table.

"Mark, please take a look at the initials on Mike's gun handle," I say. "What do they say?"

Mike removes the bullets and hands it to Mark. He takes it, moves it around to get the proper lighting before giving his answer. "O-N-R, yeah that's it, O-N-R," he says.

"Wrong answer!" Mike says quickly. "They're O-N-B. The gun once belonged to General Omar Bradley," he says proudly.

Just as I'm about to salute, Mark says "Okay, if you say so."

"Thank you," Mike says.

"If you want to make sure, I've a high powered scope in the shop," Mark says. "We can see if that's a *B* or an *R*."

"Not necessary, but thank you anyway," Mike says.

Mike and I bust out laughing when Mark lays the gun on the table and asks if we ever saw that Seinfeld episode. "The one where George buys the car, Volvo I think, from the actor. What's his name?"

"Voight, Jon Voight," Mike says.

"That's Jon without the "H"." I add grinning at Mike.

Chapter 30

It's 6:15 PM. We're approximately thirty miles east of Puebla. Mark's Tahoe is pulling an enclosed trailer. Inside are small turbine prototype blades designed by his son Zack, built by Mark in the surf shop. Many of these blades can be found in wind towers throughout Mexico, powering anything from individual homes to small communities. What the father/son team are most proud of is a smaller version of their blades that are installed in high tech pumps that bring clean water to those in need. Mark's plan is to drop us off and deliver the blades to a business associate who works for a local relief agency.

Mike and Mark are sitting up front chatting away. Me, I'm downloading information on Victor Kingman, an interesting character to say the least. He's officially been working for the British government since 1996. The last fifteen years he's been stationed throughout Central and South America. Mr. Kingman has a bachelor's in political science and two master degrees. One in Anthropology. The other in Archeology. In 2001, he was severely reprimanded, dropped a few pay grades for shooting his boss, "by accident," in La Paz Bolivia.

Much of the information is blacked out, but from what I decipher, justified. It looks like Victor's old boss was playing both sides with the drug cartels – double agent? Kingman discovered this when staking out a dinner held by the local drug boss. He was working undercover as a waiter. According to his statements, he recognized a voice during the toast. "I left the kitchen to find it and wouldn't you know – there he was - sitting bloody right next to one of the biggest criminals in South America. They were like, buddy buddy - chaps!" Reading through the transcript, Victor says he took a photograph, "Because no one would believe him." After that, "I pulled a gun from my boot, aimed for his head, bloody missed. Caught him in the shoulder. Ran!" It looked like the British tried to cover it up, but the story got out.

The Prime Minister was forced to do something. He was quoted as saying "British intelligent officers should not be shooting at each other. No matter what the circumstances." In the final paragraph, it states that Victor's boss disappeared after the shooting. Said he's on a capture type hit list – most wanted. "Last seen – Mexico City, November 2012." I've been in this business long enough to know that if the real story ever got out, Victor would've been a hero. When the politicians see blood in the water, the cowardly ones stay on shore – which means most. I think I'm starting to like this Victor Kingman. I click an icon to download Victor's photo on to my iPhone. Noting the weak signal, it's gonna take a while.

Listening to Mike tell Mark about his wife Joanne puts a smile on my face. Mike explains how he met her in college. "It was love at first sight," he says. "Fell in love with her right away."

"Getting her to love you back was truly a miracle," I chime in. "Matter of fact, I wrote it up and sent it to the Pope – begged the man – we need a miracle please! Ya know Mark, after seeing Joanne fall in love with my buddy here; I figured that walking on water stuff must be true."

"Joe, hand me one of those water bottles besides you. I need to make a little wine!" Mike says. "Anyway, the truth is, I'm a very lucky man. It is a miracle that she fell in love with me. Even while I'm away, I feel her near me, whispering to me, saying to me, go ahead, wear those shorts - piss off Joe!" Mike laughs.

"Hey buddy, the real miracle is that Joanne still loves you. Sorry, loved you yesterday," I say seriously.

"Listen, I haven't spoke to her yet today, but I know she still loves me. Today, tomorrow – always and forever!"

"You might want to check," I say.

"Check, why? What'd you do?"

"Nothing, now that I know it was her idea for you to wear those shorts today." "Come on Joe, what'd you do?"

"I emailed her a picture of you. Looking courageous. Handsome. Confident. Your standard kick butt looks, take no names attitude."

"Why thank you Joe," he says.

"He wasn't wearing those shorts?" Mark jumps in.

"Oops. He was." I say. "Cancel all that handsome, kick butt confidence nonsense!"

"Canceled!" Mark says.

"Next time – head shot only," Mike suggests.

The three of us continue our laughing fest until we cross into the city of Puebla. Seeing the road ahead blocked by cars with flashing lights, I swear I can hear a pin drop.

Mark stops the Tahoe behind one of the police cars, off to the side. He tells us "not to worry" and gets out. Three uniformed men come walking in his direction – all smiling. One stops to talk with Mark, the others approach us in the car. Mike and I decide to get out and stand next to the trailer. Flashlights hit our faces followed by Spanish and broken English. Both men look to be quite young, early twenties maybe, clean shaven with spotless uniforms. One with a minor limp starts talking as the other walks behind the trailer.

"Hola Señores!"

"Hola," Mike and I say back.

"Tell me, explain what you do, here in Puebla," he says. "Please, yes, explain."

"Dropping off wind blades," Mike replies. "You know wind power," he says waving his arms.

"Si, I understand Señor. Gracias. Do you have any firearms, weapons?"

"Yes," I say. "We have permission to carry in your country."

"From whom."

"Your president," Mike says, watching the other cop climb over the trailer hitch.

I sense the two inexperienced policia are getting nervous. They're whispering back and forth, smiles gone. I'm starting to feel like Doc Holliday at the O.K. Corral. They must have found who they were looking for. Cars once blocking the road are making u-turns, back to the city. Our silence is broken by a beep followed by, "File's done" coming from my pocket. Victor's photo finally finished downloading. Before I have a chance to say anything, Mark walks up to us, says something to the officers in Spanish, and they head for their car.

"I told you not to worry," Mark says. "Told you I'd take care of it. And I did."

"Thank you," Mike says.

"Yeah, thanks," I say. "What'd they want?"

"You two," he says calmly. "They know me – it's fine. It seems you both are in a little trouble."

"What kind of trouble?" Mike asks.

"Not sure. All I can tell you is that it's not enough to bring you in – now. But they'll be watching you. Speaking to the man in charge, he said he got an anonymous tip from someone, initials D.H."

"Who is D.H.?" Mike asks.

"Don't know," Mark says. "But the officer was told, by this D.H. person, that if either of you was wearing an ugly pair of shorts, haul him in!"

"Who is this D.H. person?" Mike asks, confused. "What do shorts have to do with this?"

"Diego, Diego Hugo," I say smiling. "My uncle sure knows people – doesn't he?"

"What comes around goes around," says Mike. "Mr. Hugo better be careful," he smiles. "Last time I ever give that guy a kiss."

Mark opens the Tahoe door, jumps into the driver seat. Mike quickly joins him on the other side. Standing on the side of the road, I click on my iPhone, view Victor's photo. I count seven men sitting behind a table, eating and drinking. Even though the picture's quite blurry, there is a face I recognize. Or should I say half a face. The right side of his face is heavily bandaged. Almost like a mask. Is that my Dad? Hand written note at the bottom of the photo says, "La Paz Bolivia 2001." Whoa – wait a minute. Is that what I think it is? On the table – in front of a bandaged Tomas Amos – dad. I forward the picture to Mom.

Feeling a little dazed, I walk slowly over to the Tahoe. As I'm about to get in I hear a horn beeping. It's from a car moving in our direction with only one headlight. As it passes, I see Victor Kingman sitting in back of the open Chevy El Camino – waving. No umbrella in sight. I wave back. I climb into the backseat and we begin moving. I look at the photo again – more closely. Looking for details. Something, someone.... I send a text to

Carlone. "Resend Victor Kingman's dinner photo. Higher resolution please. Copy Mom. Joe."

Chapter 31
Thursday, / 8:10 PM
Puebla, PU, Mexico

The GPS is telling us that we are only 2.2 miles from TG's restaurant. The streets are relatively quiet except for a few cars and people scattered around the outside cafes. The Eagles "Hotel California" is drifting out into the streets through the open doors of the El Cardenal. Mike and I finish the song with our best air guitar – ever! Even though it's been a few months since I've been here, I remember it like it was yesterday. Clare picking me up at the airport and making a stop here, in Puebla at TG's restaurant, Amalfi Pizza, playing baseball with children. Finishing our game with Pizza and ice cream. Clare crying when we left. That's when I fell in love with her, even though at that time I only knew her as Sister Clare.

I hear the GPS tell us we've arrived. Looking out the window, I realize we must have the wrong address. I jump on the internet, recheck the address. It's right.

"Mark, can you do me a favor and plug this location into your GPS?" I say handing him my iPhone. "Something must be wrong with my equipment."

Mark loads the data. Seconds later we hear a sexy Australian woman's voice tell us "you've arrived at your location on left."

"Must be something wrong with the satellites," Mike says.

"Must be," Mark says. "If this is the right address."

I get out of the car to get my bearings, seeing what might have been the field where we played baseball back in January –it can't be. If correct, then the spot where TG's restaurant stood is now a vacant, empty lot.

"Mike, grab a flashlight, will ya?" I say before he exits the SUV.

"What're ya thinking, Joe?" Mike says joining me.

100

"I think we're standing where Amalfi Pizza once stood," I say, slowly, trying to work it out in my memory. "It was a two-story wooden structure. Large glass windows on the front. TG and Sandy lived in an apartment above the restaurant."

"Are you sure it was here?" Mike asks.

"Not at first. But I think so now," I say shining my light over the ground ten feet away. Running over to something reflecting the light, I bend over, pick it up. It's a large piece of broken glass half buried under the dirt. Painted on it is a large letter "A" followed by a broken "M," looks more like "N."

"Joe," Mike yells from thirty feet away. "Found a piece of glass with two "Z's".

Amalfi Pizza was here – I wonder what happened.

"Joe, Mike, it was firebombed," Mark says, joining us. "Called a friend of mine who lives in the area. Knows the area well – and is actually friends with TG and Sandy. Said it happened a few nights ago."

"By whom," I ask. "Why?"

"He didn't know," Mark says. "Did say that it must have been somebody who was connected – you know, had pull. Because the day after it was bombed, a group of men with heavy equipment came and cleared the area. All in the same day. He said that never happens. Buildings usually just rot away before they're torn down and the land cleared. He said we should be careful."

We get back in the Tahoe, traveling northwest of Puebla. Mark's dropping the wind blades at a private delivery company adjacent to the airport. It's a ten mile ride to Hermanos Serdan International airport. Mike and I are getting picked up for our ride to Tampico. In what – I don't know. Whatever it is, pick up is 10:30 PM. Since we're early, we decide to help unload the blades.

Mark pulls the Chevy into a small parking lot at 10:06, stops at the loading dock.

"I've got a key," he says stepping out of the vehicle. "I'll turn on the light so we can see what we're doing."

It's strange to be across the street from an international airport that's almost completely dark. From where we are, I'm able to see blue taxiway lights as well as the white and green beacon flashing near the control tower. I leave Mike in the SUV talking to Joanne and walk out towards the road, where headlights are moving in my direction. Ducking out of the way, back into the lot, two eighteen-wheel fuel trucks pass me - slowing down. I see nothing written on the sides of the truck. It's the logo on the back that catches my eye. No way. Can't be.

Smelling burning rubber, I see the two trucks take a right about 100 yards from me.

"Joe, you gonna help?" Mark yells.

"On my way!" I shout back.

Mark's trailer is unloaded in less than ten minutes. He turns out the lights, locks up the building.

"Thanks for your help, guys," Mark says.

"It's the least we can do since you gave us a ride," Mike says. "Joe, it's 10:23 and our pick up is at 10:30. You know where, Joe?"

"Sorry, don't know, let's walk over to the airport and wait." I tap the location beacon app on my phone and should get a return text when our ride is close.

"I'll stay with you guys 'til your ride gets here," Mark says.

"Appreciate that, but I'm sure you need to get home," I say.

"A few minutes won't make any difference. Anyway I'm curious to see who and what's picking you up."

"That makes three of us," Mike says as two cars pass us in the lot heading away from the airport.

"Mark, are you familiar with the gas tanker company a few doors down?" I ask.

"Not really, just driven by. I figure they haul fuel for the airport. Why'd you ask?"

"Not quite sure. Except that I need to take a picture of one of the trailers."

"What's up, Joe?" Mike asks.

"I think I recognized a marking, logo or something. Back of the trailer, when it went by a few minutes ago."

"Okay, let's go," Mark says starting the engine and driving us out into the road.

102

"Pull over," I say as we pass a chain link fence enclosing the two trailers.

"Wow, this place is empty!" Mark says. "Anytime I've been here - driven by, I've seen at least two dozen tanker trailers. They must be out on a fuel run or something."

"Let's hope," I say climbing out the door and walking down the outside of the fence.

"I asked Mark to stay in the car," I hear Mike tell me from behind.

"I think if we follow the fence to where it borders the next parking lot, we should be able to get a good shot."

Mike and I see several security dogs inside the fence, prowling for uninvited guests. We stay quiet enough not to be noticed. Hanging a left into the open, adjacent parking lot, we run up to the back of the trailer. Mike sees it before me.

"Holy cow," he says softly. "You gotta be kidding. I don't believe it."

Too stunned to talk, I turn on the flashlight, hand it to Mike, and snap several photos. While checking the quality, I notice a large hole in the fence. This time they see us before we see them. Two very large dogs come bolting through the break in the fence, baring teeth. I feel Mike pull me out of the way and see him turn quickly to the attacking dogs. As they are about to pounce, I see flashing lights followed by yelping. Immediately they drop to the ground and start to spasm. Mike turns to me, helps me off the ground and gives me some advice.

"You gotta get one of these things Joe," he says showing me the Taser he used to immobilize the dogs.

"I'll make a note out of that. Let's get outta here before the rest of them find that hole in the fence!"

Sprinting back to the Tahoe, I notice an object floating in the dark, moonlit sky. Its 10:33, my iPhone starts to vibrate telling me I got a message. Outside the vehicle, I read the text – "FLASH LIGHT 5 TIMES. SKY." Mike gets the same message, points the flashlight towards the sky – on and off five times. After a few minutes we hear the sound of an engine coming towards us. Thinking someone's driving without their lights on, we move quickly behind the trailer, out of the road. The noise gets louder, but we can't see anything coming down the road. Making sure we're seen by whomever, Mark turns on the Tahoe's parking lights and I see the wheels of an airplane fly about five feet over our head.

"It's crashing," Mark says.

"No, it's flying," Mike says.

"Both wrong," I say. "It's landing. Here to pick us up."

"We're right across the street from the airport. Why is it landing in the road?" Mark says.

"Airport's closed?" Mike shoots back.

We grab our stuff out of the Tahoe, thank Mark with a big hug and start running for the airplane. This time, several dogs are chasing us. No time to Taser. Especially since we're outnumbered. Sprinting towards the dark plane idling in the shadows, we run directly into a family of nocturnal skunks looking for food. Mike and I leap over the soon to be noxious group just before their tails go up. Looking over my shoulder, I see the dogs slow and begin chasing the skunks. Not a good idea. We get to the airplane, or should I say bi-plane. Standing under the wing, is a man, maybe mid-fifties, wearing a beat up brown leather jacket, white scarf around his neck. On his head, a baseball cap that says "I'd Rather Be Sailing."

"Hey buds," he says in a deep, loud voice. "You are about to take flight in a 1932 Brunner-Winkle Bird CK. My one and only Waltzing Matilda," he says while pointing at the words painted in white above the landing gear.

"Did you say 1932?" Mike asks.

"Yes sir Bud," he says clearing his throat. "Don't worry, maintain the bird myself. Also, the motor on my sailboat," he adds. "My name is Bob Roe and I'm your pilot to Tampico. Little over a two-hour flight."

"Hi Bob, I'm Joe and that's Mike."

"Welcome aboard! Let's get going before somebody wakes up in the Control Tower across the street. Oh, and don't step on the wing, you might put your foot through it."

"Put my foot through it?" Mike asks.

"Yeah Bud, that's what I said. Let's go – climb in. Don't want the Mexican Air Force chasing us – do ya?"

We climb into the bench seat up front, stow our two bags on the floor, and start looking for the seatbelts.

"Find your belt?" I say looking at Mike.

"No. You?"

"No."

"Maybe they didn't have seat belts in 1932," Mike says. "He did say 1932 – right?"

"What're you boys looking for," Roe says climbing in behind us.

"Seatbelts!" Mike shouts. "Seatbelts! Ya know – restraining apparatus. In case of a crash."

"What crash? We aint gonna crash!" he yells. "In my thirty-five years of flying, I only had to ditch seven times. No, excuse me, nine times. Yeah, right – nine times. That's without counting the times I was forced down," he says winking at me.

"I feel much better now," Mike says. "You hear that Joe, only nine times."

"Better than ten," I reply.

"Listen buds, you'll be happy to know that I just re-bolted the seat you're sitting on. Serious rust problem ya know. Now we can fly upside down and the seat will not move an inch. Oh, and I used Loctite on all the bolts – the red stuff. Been to one of their adhesive seminars – very informative – now I'm kind of the expert around town."

"Excuse me Mr. Roe," Mike says nervously. "Thank you, the work on the seat and all. But, you understand that, if we fly upside down, which we shouldn't, you know inverted like; the seat will stay - bolted. Hey, I believe you when you say it won't move. Even a little bit. The problem is with Joe and me. We have no darn seat belts to hold us in. That is, if we fly upside down."

"Please bud, don't worry, I'm not planning to fly upside down. Who does?" he says laughing. "Well maybe once – lost in a darn cloud bank."

"Quiet!" I shout. "Quiet."

Listening to the engine purring at idle, I hear it again. Mike does too. Our pilot perks up when he hears it.

"Well buds," he shouts. "I guess they do have a few Mexican Air Force jets at the airport. Gotta go amigos! Fasten your seat belts!"

As Mike and I turn to give him a dirty look, all the lights at the airport go on, giving us a perfect view of two military style jets taking off. The engine of the bi-plane goes up to full power and we start rolling down the center of the road.

"Hey buds! Buds!" Roe yells from behind. "Smell that? Think we ran into a few skunks. Say some prayers will ya?"

We lift off the ground, threading our way through the night sky in an open cockpit airplane. I see the taillights of Mark's trailer moving down the deserted highway – heading home. My plan of seeing Clare by one is questionable with the sight of two military aircraft flanking both sides of our slow moving bi-plane.

CHAPTER 32

We're thirty minutes into our flight and still being followed by the two Mexican military jets. As soon as we left the ground, Mike sent out an SOS to USS Harry Truman. He also sent an email to Carlone to let him know we're flying in an open cockpit airplane named Waltzing Malinda, made in 1932 with no seatbelts. I emailed Mom and Carlone the pictures I took of the logo on the back of the tanker trucks. Told them "We need to talk" early in the morning. Turning around, looking at our pilot, I see him talking to himself, no he's singing. At first we thought he was yelling to us. He wasn't. Just singing the same song about a pair of bowling shoes, empty closet, dinner for one, blue pickup and a dog that barks all night. Must be country. He's certainly not bothered by our escorts. Mike gets a text back from the Truman – "CATAPULT DOWN-NO JETS –NO ESCORT."

It's after midnight when the two Mexican jets disappear into the night. Mike's sound asleep wrapped in a sweatshirt to stay warm. I start to drift off, listening to our pilot singing. He actually has a good voice that's getting noticeably louder. I hear every word. Now wide awake, I realize why he sounds louder, the engine stopped. I turn around to see him give me a thumbs up sign as he tries to restart the engine. After the sixth time, we're both looking over the side for a place to land. The good news - lights of Tampico look about ten miles away. The bad news – at our altitude, we'll never make it. I turn and see our pilot rapidly tapping his fingers on an iPad or something. He sees me, again gives me thumbs up and shouts, "don't worry!" and "hang on!" I figure now's not the time to wake up Mike. Barely able to see what's in front of me, we slip to the left, dumping altitude, level off. In the distance, I see a pair of headlights flash off and on. Pilot Bob slips the airplane to the right and heads for the flashing lights. After a few minutes, I can clearly see the ground below. It's paved. The headlights come on again – stay on. The bi-plane floats over the vehicle and touches the ground so softly, I can barely feel it. As we roll along the ground, I see the RV tucked into the woods, Diego standing off to the side waving a flashlight. It's 12:48 AM.

Mike wakes up as Bob and I climb out of the aircraft.

"Well Bob, that was some flying," I say patting him on the back. "I gotta tell ya, that running out of gas thing made me a little nervous."

"Heck, I'm sorry about that," he says. "My fuel calculations must have been off a little. Or, I have a hole in a gas line or something."

"Hey guys, you made it," Diego says, happy to see us. "Bob, that engine of yours is so quiet; I didn't hear you come in."

"That's because we ran out of gas several miles back," Bob says smiling.

"We ran out of gas!" Mike says joining us. "First no seat belts! Now no gas! Hi Diego, where'd you come from?"

"From there," he says pointing to the RV in the woods. "Bob was homing in on our position via a radio signal. Ensign Rogers set the whole thing up before we dropped her in Tampico. I drove here based on her GPS coordinates. Told me I should be expecting contact from Bob around 12:30. Sure enough, I get a text telling me to flash the headlights. And here you are."

"Safe and sound," Bob jumps in.

"Hey Diego," Mike says. "Thanks for that little episode with the local police in Puebla. I owe you one. I'd watch my step Diego Hugo. Or should I call you Mr. DH."

"Maybe this will teach you not to kiss me. Especially when wearing those shorts," he laughs.

"Maybe, but I doubt it," I say.

We siphon about 10 gallons of gas from the RV and transfer it into the airplane after making sure there are no leaks. Pilot Bob says that's more than enough fuel to get him home, but decides to leave in the morning. Mike and I help him push the Waltzing Matilda off the road, under several large trees for cover.

"Ya know Charles Lindbergh gave his wife Anne flying lessons in a Bird CK," Bob says proudly. "They don't make 'em like this anymore."

"Thank God," Mike says. "I prefer airplanes that have seat belts in case we get in an accident, or run out of gas or something. I bet Mrs. Lindbergh used a seat belt."

"I have seat belts! Just forgot to put them back in after I fixed the seat. I told ya I fixed the seat – right?"

"Yes and thank you," I jump in. "The new seat was so comfortable, Mike slept most of the trip. Even through the running out of gas part."

Bob pulls a sleeping bag out of the plane's cargo hatch, unrolls it under the wing and climbs in. Mike disappears inside the dark RV. Too wired to sleep, I sit in a lounge chair and check email - forward more pictures to Mom and Carlone. I realize that once they see them, the United States will go on alert. No confusing color coded system, no public panic, mainly awareness. Behind the scenes, nations around the world will be on the lookout for any suspicious activity. Based on my gut, I'm afraid we moved past the suspicious part. Saturday's date, Snares of the Devil written on a piece of paper found under the tongue of a dead man. A red open umbrella held by a dead man. All pieces of a puzzle we'd need to put together – before time runs out.

After hearing the 2:00 AM beep from my watch, I begin to doze off. Not sure how long I was out, I'm awakened by a blanket being placed over me. I feel someone climbing under, settling against my chest and holding my hand. The relaxing scent of strawberries mingles in the cool air. The last thing I hear before I fall asleep is, "Love you Joe."

I slip into a strange dream where I find myself in a dark cave. I'm wet. Freezing. I try to walk – can't. Someone is next to me starting a fire. Paper falling out of file cabinets. Fuel source. I crawl over to the fire. See Mike throwing paper onto the fire. Body starts to warm. It's three of us, Mike, Carlone, me. Skimming files, burning em. I feel something in my hand. An umbrella?

I'm startled awake to find Clare gone and see it's only 5:38 in the morning – too early. Thirty minutes later I wake to find Fina the wonder dog staring at me. So close, her breath reminds me I need to get up to brush my teeth.

CHAPTER 33

Friday / 6:30 AM
Outside Tampico, Tamaulipas, Mexico

Camping. That's it, it smells like camping. I lost my love for this activity after being in the military. Not much call for it now since I'm in the Naval Reserve, which usually puts me at a desk somewhere. My eyes follow the rising smoke and I see Diego and Pedro side by side, toasting marshmallows. It's something Clare taught Pedro back at Holy Spirit Mission. We had this ritual several nights a week. Local children would come over to play baseball, have dinner, and toast marshmallows. Of course Clare would extend an open invitation to parents, relatives - just about anybody. Most nights we had close to fifty people laughing, singing – having fun. Boy, how I miss that. We'd get up in the morning and find wooden boxes of fresh fruits, vegetables, and bread, left by our friends from the night before. I fell in love with the Mexican people over the last several months. They took me into their hearts, treated me like family. For that, I'm grateful. I hope one day I can return that love.

Diego informs me that Clare is in the RV's shower. Ensign Rogers is on her way from Tampico with an additional vehicle found at a US Military salvage yard. Mike and I felt it was needed in case we had to ditch the RV. Walking over to the Bird Bi-Plane, I see the back of Mike's head, wearing earbuds, sticking out of the passenger cockpit.

"Hey Mike," I yell. "What are ya doing? Does pilot Bob know you're messing around in his airplane?"

"I certainly do!" says Bob walking up behind me. "I have him installing the seatbelts he was crying about. Found 'em under my seat. He's a good kid, that Mike. I like him. He thought my Bird was named Waltzing Malinda not Waltzing Matilda. Smart kid, but can't read worth a lick."

"That really was some great flying last night, Bob. I thought we might clip some trees and have a hard landing – didn't happen."

"Listen bud," he says, "what's nerve wracking is landing an A6 Intruder on something that from the air looks the size of a postage stamp bobbing up and down on the water. Did it for twenty-five years in the Navy. Loved every minute of it – miss it dearly. But now I run a small charter company in Tampico with my buddy Jute. He handles the water charters. I manage the flying part. Our wives pitch in when they're not too busy saving the world."

"What about last night?" I say. 'How'd that job come about?"

"Listen Joe, I know who you are – what you do," he whispers. "Jute and I run several trips a year for the US and Mexican governments. Transportation is our game, not covert opps. We don't touch anything that smells the least bit illegal – no sir. Anyway, got an urgent call last night from a guy I know in the government. Said he needed my services - pick up - drop off job."

"What government?" I ask.

"Does it matter?" he says.

"Maybe."

"Okay, English."

"As in US English?" I ask.

"No, British," he says.

"Does this contact wear a three-piece suit – carry an umbrella?"

"Can't say – never met 'em. Sworn to secrecy type thing," he replies. "But what I can tell ya is after I spoke to him, a Warrant Officer from the USS Truman contacted me. Gave me the coordinates, logistics. Worked on the timing with Diego – done."

"Well thanks again," I say shaking his hand. "Where are you off to now?"

"Back to Tampico," he says smiling. "Jute and I are taking some Volkswagen executives sailing this afternoon. They have an auto plant in Puebla – been there since mid-sixties, I think. Anyway, we do a lot of business with 'em. Nice people. Get discounts on their cars."

"Maybe we'll see you again," I say.

"Most likely," he replies.

111

"Why'd you say that?

"I guess it's alright to tell you," he says slowly. "I'm on call – for the next six days. Being paid to fly if needed. Possible pick-up/drop-off type stuff."

"By whom?" I say.

"Can't say. But it's all legal. No guns or drug money garbage," he says.

"Done!" Mike yells looking at us from the passenger cockpit.

"Did you use the red *Loctite*?" Bob yells back.

"Almost done!" Mike shouts back head disappearing inside the plane.

I hear an old fashion school bell being rung at the RV – time for breakfast.

After breakfast, we line up and wave to Pilot Bob as he takes off into the wild blue yonder. The ten gallons of gas we gave him will be plenty to get him home if his calculations are correct. I get the feeling that Pilot Bob is just a happy-go-lucky sort of guy. Wants every day to be fun with a mix of excitement. He seems to live a life most only dream of – including myself.

It's 7:45 AM when I get a call from my mother.

"Hey Mom!"

"Joseph, can you talk?"

"Yeah sure," I reply.

"Is there anybody else nearby?" she asks.

"Well, yes," I reply.

"Joseph, I need to talk to you alone," her tone is serious.

"Okay Mom," I say moving away from the RV. "I'm good, go ahead."

"First off, Jim and I looked at the pictures you sent last night – of the tankers. The picture of the white tiger with black paws almost caused me to hit the floor. We know this is not good. I still have nightmares of headless bodies with that very same picture – that tattoo. The same logo on the flag in front of Missing Acres Farm run by the cartels. Underground tunnels with torture chambers. I'm afraid this is turning me into a nervous wreck.... Your friend, you know from the hotel, Mark Temple, he was right about there being more tankers like that earlier. Our satellites took some pictures over that area two weeks ago."

"Don't tell me," I say jumping in. "Parking lot full of white tanker trailers."

"Yes Joseph, twenty-eight of them to be exact. Now there's two – only two. The NSA has people working on this to try to locate the other twenty-six."

"What about who owns them?" I ask.

"It's being worked on. All we know is that the majority of transactions go through the Caymans, to South Africa, to someplace in the Middle East. That's all we know right now."

"How about the other picture? Cartel dinner at a restaurant," I add.

"Joseph, that's the main reason for calling. We think it's Tomas Amos, his face bandaged at the table. Did you recognize the item on the table, in front of Tomas?"

"I think so. Even though it's blurry," I say. "It's the stone – isn't it?"

"Yes - no doubt about it. The experts from the Smithsonian confirm its authenticity. They tell me it's probably worth at least two hundred million to an unscrupulous collector."

"Does that explain why so many people are trying to steal it?"

"Maybe, but it's safe here in Washington. Joseph, there's someone else in the picture who looks familiar. At least I think so. He's standing in the back, off on the right side. We digitally enhanced the photo, I'm still not sure – but it could be."

"Who is it, Mom? Tell me."

"I think it's Diego. I'm not a hundred percent sure mind you, but quite possible."

"Mom, send me the enhanced picture right away – please."

"Joseph, you can't say anything yet – I need to be sure. Our best photographic experts are reviewing the photo to see if additional improvements can be made. Should be done by the end of the day. Please honey, don't say a word."

"Alright mom, I'll stay quiet for now."

"He's a good man Joseph. I know that much in my heart - trust me."

As I'm about to reply, the line goes dead, followed by a series of beeps. I hear a voice.

"Captain Joe Dustan. This is Warrant Officer Dave Shea calling from the USS Truman. Confirm line is secure."

"Confirmed," I reply.

"I'm informing you that Ensign Kelly Rogers went missing this morning at 5:05 AM in Tampico. Vehicle found burning on a dead end street in an Industrial Park. No body found. Naval Intelligence has been mobilized. Out."

The line goes dead. Information only – no questions allowed.

CHAPTER 34

I break the news about Ensign Rogers to the group. We all agree that we won't leave Tampico without her. Diego immediately gets on his cell calling contacts for any information of her whereabouts. Mike contacts Naval Intelligence for updates. Due to the recent events with Rogers and TG's home and restaurant, Clare and I finally realize that having Pedro with us is too dangerous for him. As we discuss options, my cell rings – no ID.

"Yes," I say.

"Captain Dustan, it's me – Kelly. Sorry, I mean Ensign Rogers."

"Where are you? Are you hurt?" I shout.

"I'm fine. Took a wrong turn, got ambushed by some type of street gang. They wanted the vehicle, and me dead. Got neither."

"Where are you?" I say, relieved starting to calm down.

"At a coffee place across the street from the Airport – sign says Aeropuerto De Tampico painted in large white letters. Named after a General I think – Francisco something."

"Send Mike your position and we'll pick you up," I say loud to get his attention.

"Done," she replies. "Captain, I've got a message from the guys who saved me. They must have been following me. The message is for you."

"Please Ensign Rogers, call me Joe."

"Okay, the man in the mask wanted me to tell you to be careful. He was kind of strange, but nice. He said something's going down tomorrow. Not sure what or where."

"The mask covered the right side of his face?" I ask.

"Yes, definitely," she replies. "Do you know him?"

"Yes, I believe I do."

"The last part of the message came from the other guy, an Englishman, and I quote. "Watch your arses near the border." He's quite charming. He also said to have your mother check old Mossad files that reference something called snares of the devil."

"Don't tell me," I say jumping in. "He wears a three-piece suit - carries an umbrella."

"Yeah that's him," she replies. "Wait a minute. Is he the Kingman guy you were talking about?"

"That's him," I say quickly as Mike nods, letting me know he got her signal. "Sit tight Ensign, I mean Rogers, we're on our way. Mike's telling me twenty minutes. Stay safe. Make sure to call your boss."

"I will. See you soon."

The RV's already running when I climb in with Diego at the wheel.

"Your brother's in Tampico," I say whispering in his ear. "He and Kingman helped Kelly during an ambush from thugs trying to steal her car. Speaking of that, we'll need one. Can you get us car?"

"Tomas is here?" Diego asks. "With the English guy?"

"That's what Kelly just told me. Two odd looking men. One wearing a mask. The other in a three-piece suit carrying an umbrella."

"Strange," Mike says, joining our conversation. So much for whispering.

"Mike, take over the driving," Diego says as he pulls off the road. "I'll make some calls to get a car - try my brother again."

"Diego, I get the feeling that Victor and Tomas must be following us," I say. "Why, I don't know. Oh and by the way, have you ever met Victor before yesterday, do you remember? I don't know, airport, hotel, maybe a restaurant."

"I don't think so – why?" he says looking off to the distance. "I feel like there's something you're not telling me. What is it?"

"We'll talk later," I say. "Please find us a car first. Thanks."

During our trip to pick up Kelly, I text Mom about checking Mossad files for any mention of snares of the devil. I also inform her that Tomas is close, maybe too close. "Think he's following us." The biggest problem I have presently is Diego. I'm not sure what's going on, but him being in that picture with his brother and drug runners is a problem. Before I have a chance to talk to Diego, my cell phone rings – it's Carlone.

"Good Morning Jim," I say.

"Joe, the President's coming to the border. Some type of NAFTA celebration, free trade, democracy type of rally."

"Does this mean apple pie for everyone?" I ask.

"Only those waving the flag," he says.

"Let me guess, he's coming on Saturday."

"You guessed it."

"Where?"

"Only a few will know the details until Saturday morning. He'll be meeting with the Mexican President. Kind of a joint, informal news conference. Supposed to last an hour."

"Jim, I'm worried. I don't care how secret the planning has been. We both know this was planned months ago," I say. "People know about it – logistics and all. You gotta stop it, Jim. Have 'em pull the plug – it's just too dangerous. The President of Mexico can come to America. There have been too many warning signs telling us something is going to happen this Saturday. We're on our way to pick up Ensign Rogers after she went missing for a few hours. Spoke to her less than 30 minutes ago – told me Kingman and Tomas – yes Tomas, my supposed father – saved her life. Kingman told Rogers we need to stay away from the border – on Saturday. Jim you gotta stop it somehow!"

"I've tried Joe, but the President and his staff won't listen. This will be his first time on Air Force One since the terrorist attack on Inauguration Day. The media says he's hiding from his responsibilities as the leader of the free world. That he needs to act presidential. Joe, the bottom line is that his ratings have dropped significantly," he says. "The American people want the new President to get out of the White House, get caught up in rumors, scandals, fighting with the congress. I repeat my friend; this is what the public wants. Forget the facts. We need to sell newspapers. Enjoy our talk radio. Drown in the minutia of 24/7 news coverage."

"Jim, listen," I say. "Something's building down here. And all signs point to Saturday. I just don't know where or when which means nobody can guarantee his safety."

"Joe," he continues, "that border is almost 2000 miles long. If we can't stop the President from going, let's hope his location remains a secret for as long as possible."

"You need to talk to my mother. I believe she's on the verge of figuring this out."

"Call you later with an update. Hey, by the way, I will personally pass your concerns to the President when I see him later. I don't think it'll make a difference, but thanks."

After hanging up, I go up to the front of the RV and tell Mike about my conversation with Carlone. He says "I'm not surprised. Everyone knows the media's been brutal towards the President. Even with the deaths of his son and mother-in-law less than two months ago during the attack in DC."

"Hey Mike, new subject - let me ask you something," I say.

"Sure, go ahead, ask away."

"Do you remember the time we got caught in that snowstorm in the Afghan mountains several years ago?"

"Which one?"

"The time I got hypothermia. We found a cave loaded with filing cabinets. Burned the files for heat."

"Yeah, that one I remember."

"Most of the files were either written in a foreign language or some type of code. Remember?"

"Yeah, there were a few files in English, Spanish that we didn't burn for warmth."

"I've never been so cold," I reply.

"Me too," he shudders.

"The files – English and Spanish ones. Did you read any?"

"Maybe about five or six."

"I read some too," I say. "What I remember was a lot of religious ramblings mixed in with military stuff. Adam and Eve. Moses. The Ten Commandments. We thought maybe they were code names for terrorist military ops."

"Yes," Mike says. "Water to wine. Temptation of Christ. Last Supper. Crucifixion. Seemed right out of the bible, not the Koran. Odd, especially in that part of the world. But remember Joe, we know the files proved to be a link between Al-Qaeda and drug lords in Mexico, Central and South America."

118

"Yeah, Al-Qaeda had a money problem. Needed to raise some," I say. "Formed alliances with large drug cartels. Opened their terrorist training camps to them."

"Right," Mike says. "All well documented – read about it in Newsweek."

"What happened to those files? Do you remember?" I ask.

"The two guys who rescued us, they took them. You were probably too sick to remember. We had to carry you out."

"Right - I remember being carried out. Thank you."

"You're welcome," Mike says smiling.

"Thank you for that. I also remember a helicopter picking us up right outside the cave. Some Russian piece of junk," I say.

"Yeah, it was red – doors missing."

"Back to the two guys who rescued us, took the files."

"Yeah, I remember," he says.

"Who were they?"

"Israeli CIA – Mossad I think. Yeah, Mossad. Might have died if it wasn't for them. Said they saw smoke coming from the cave. Think they made up the story."

"Okay, thanks," I reply. "Just wanted to check my memory."

Pulling up along the curb across from the airport, Mike parks the RV under a billboard promoting cheap flights to Miami's South Beach. The flight may be cheap, but once you get there, be prepared to open your wallet. I see the outside café that Rogers was talking about, but no Rogers there. As a matter of fact, most chairs, tables are empty. I cross the street to find her while everyone else stays in the RV. I see Clare and Pedro waving from a back window. As I enter the café, I count less than ten people. No Rogers. Thinking she might be in the restroom, I knock on the door; call her name, no answer. I put my ear up to the door, and hear someone punching the numbers on a cell phone. Making a call, maybe. Thinking I need Diego's Spanish skills to ask questions, I walk back outside. To my surprise, Victor Kingman is sitting alone at one of the tables, hidden by the front of the building. I hadn't seen him on my way in. Umbrella up, sunglasses on, it looks like he's napping. I say "hello" and tap him gently on the shoulder. His head slumps forward, sunglasses fall onto the table. Eyes barely open, he looks at me, lips moving, manages to whisper.

"Mr. Dustan, get, go away, now. I beg you. You are in grave danger. Stay away, far away from the border. I cannot help you or your mother anymore. They took Kelly."

"Who took Rogers? Listen Kingman, get up, you're going with me," I say, urging him up. "Let's go."

"Can't, go, you must leave – now!" he says loudly. "Military – took Kelly."

Following his eyes to the ground, I see his ankles are bound and chained to the table. I also notice what looks like a wire protruding from inside his collar. The buttons on his vest look like they're about to pop. Too much bulk under his shirt. I realize he's wearing a suicide jacket under his shirt.

"Kingman, how much time you got?" I say in a normal voice.

"Don't know," he says. "It's controlled remotely - nearby I think."

"Okay," I say sitting in the chair next to him. "I take it I'm not the target since we're both still here."

"Again Dustan, I don't know."

I look over at the RV and notice Mike outside standing on a ladder, cleaning the windshield. I wave. Hit call on my iPhone; lay it on the table between Kingman and me. I hear it ring across the street.

"Yes."

"Don't talk," I say normally. "Listen. Our friend Kingman is chained to the table at his feet. Chain size, about an inch. Suicide vest under his shirt. Controlled remotely – close by." A phone rings from under Kingman's shirt, I pause. He looks at me and says "go now." It rings four times and stops. Remembering the situation with Alvaro, the van, bomb, and a ringing cell phone, I know I have less than four minutes. Four minutes until Kingman turns to dust. Looking over at the RV, I see Mike's gone.

"We have less than four minutes," I say aloud knowing Mike will hear me over the phone. "Have Clare move the RV down the street." When I finish speaking, the phone inside Kingman's shirt rings again – three times.

"Now we have three minutes." The RV starts to move away, leaving Mike and Diego standing out in the open. Tools in hand.

"Think I know, Mike –got it. Ready?" I say into the phone. "Now!"

As the words leave my lips, Kingman's cell rings twice, stops. I'm up, running at full speed, dodging tables. Mike and Diego are sprinting towards Kingman. I burst through the café's door with a quick look at the few occupants. Satisfied, I head for the restroom, again I hear a number being dialed – the last ring. I crash through the door and see a young woman standing inside a stall, punching numbers into a phone. She drops the phone into the toilet, pulls out a small handgun and begins shooting wildly. As I duck behind a metal trash can, the shooting stops. I hear the toilet seat being dropped in place, followed by a single gunshot. Peering over the can, I see the woman's head lying on top of a white roll of toilet paper, quickly turning red from the blood flowing out near her right ear. I walk over, check for a pulse – dead. Moving her off the seat, I reach into the disgusting toilet and grab the cell phone – still working, and decide it's best to cancel the call.

Washing my hands in the dirty sink, someone – the owner or manager, maybe - comes in, sees the dead woman, and starts yelling in Spanish. The only thing I understand is that I'm a "un muerto" – dead man. Realizing he's involved is this mess; I grab him by the throat, force him to his knees and ask one simple question. "Where the hell are the towels- la toalla?" No reply. The guy passes out. I dry my hands on his apron, under which I find a pistol and a large hunting knife. I take 'em, and walk out of the restroom.

Moving past the pickup counter, I notice two uniformed employees – kids really – standing by the register. The rest of the place is empty. I yell at the kids to get out. They move quickly. Outside, I wave to Mike, Diego and a shirtless Kingman standing across the street. The suicide vest is lying on a table; I walk over and pick it up. Amazed by its simple design, I carry it inside and place it under the stove where the gas line comes into the building. Leaving, I turn the sign from ABIETO to CERRADO – closed, and lock the door. I sprint across the street and jump into the RV. Clare pulls the Flame Keepers RV onto the main drive. I hit the redial key on the dead woman's cell phone, thinking of my recently murdered friend Alvaro. R.I.P..

CHAPTER 35
Friday / 10:30 AM

"What do you mean she's gone?" I say a little too loudly. "Rogers called us to pick her up at the outdoor café where we found you."

"I know Mr. Dustan, I know," says Kingman. "We dropped her off and helped her – during the ambush. Darn bloody road punks I think – carjackers."

"Listen Kingman," Mike jumps in. "We realize what you did, but why you're following her is another story. And it was Joe who saved your skin. Keep that in mind!"

"Everybody calm down," says Clare. "Pedro is sleeping in back and I don't want him woken up. Now Mr. Kingman, tell us what happened – but quietly, please."

"Yes, right, okay," Kingman stutters. "As some of you may have heard, I'm somewhat keen on following you to the border. You see," he whispers, "I believe there's a very serious terrorist plot being put into action, right now, somewhere in Mexico. I'm quite certain it will happen tomorrow – Saturday."

"What makes you so sure," I whisper back.

"Mr. Dustan, I have been chasing this thing for a long time. Not the event, but rather the changes going on in Mexico since the mid 1990's. So we have no secrets, I've been here since '94, working undercover. The bombings of drug manufacturing sites in Mexico and Latin America by your government a few months ago started a chain reaction."

"Look Kingman," says Mike. "Isn't your paycheck signed by the British government?"

"I cannot confirm that," he says. "Anyway, my employer is not important. What's critical is that an act of major terrorism will happen soon unless we stop it."

"We have very smart people working on the problem, but my immediate concern is that Kelly Rogers is MIA."

"I can't help you," he says loudly, getting a hard look from Clare. "Your Miss Rogers was grabbed by three guys, wearing masks, from the exact table you found me. The thugs threw her and Tomas inside a large brown military vehicle, strapped me with explosives and then chained me to the table. Next thing I know, some stoned out looking woman carrying a cellphone walks past me, gives me the finger and disappears into the café. You blokes show up five minutes later. Bloody good timing, I'd say."

"What happened to the guy in the mask?" Diego asks from the driver's seat. "You know, my brother – Tomas!"

"Injured I think," Kingman says slowly. "Got roughed up. You see, Miss Rogers got punched, hard, in the face – nose bleeding and all. Tomas jumped in and was hit several times with a wooden club. Last I saw, they threw him in the truck. I'm sorry Diego, but you know your brother, always the hero. Like the time he saved my life at that cartel dinner many years ago. Remember?"

Diego pulls the RV over to the side and stops. "Yeah, now I remember," he says while placing his head down on the steering wheel.

Hearing Diego confirm that he was at that cartel dinner with Tomas when Kingman tried to kill his boss helps fill in some of the blanks. I just need to find out the rest of the story.

Mike takes over the driving. Diego, sitting next to Clare on the couch, holding her hand, begins to tell stories about his brother when they were kids. Even though Tomas is supposedly my father, my emotions run cool. I never knew he existed until a few months ago and that was right around the time he saved my life after getting shot in the shoulder. Guess I thought we would get to know each other someday, but truth be told, he's been tied to some very bad people – who do horrendous things. I just don't know whose side he's on. Now, maybe I'll never know.

Our family RV is a flurry of activity at 12:30 in the afternoon. Mike's looking for a place to gas up and grab lunch. Clare is sitting at a table with

Pedro, who is deeply involved in coloring outside the lines of a *Charlie Brown* coloring book. Diego's asleep on the couch and Kingman is silent, staring out the window while rubbing the ears of the wonder dog. I leave a message for Carlone, letting him know what happened to Rogers and Tomas. Also, left a message for my mom to call me ASAP. Our plan is to be through Tampico by 5:00 and stop for the night in San Fernando by 10:00 PM. That leaves us a two-hour drive to the Matamoros – Brownsville area on Saturday morning. I'm not sure if we'll be able to cross into the US due to the President's undisclosed visit somewhere along the 2000-mile border. We have a meeting scheduled at Saint Jerome's in Brownsville at 2:00 PM. Clare has told Pedro about visiting the school and seeing relatives - he's quite excited. My thoughts are interrupted by my vibrating cell phone – it's Mom.

"Hi Mom," I say talking softly. "You got my message."

"Yes, Joseph. I also spoke to Mr. Carlone. He filled me in on Ensign Rogers and Tomas. How's Diego? Are you alright?"

"Diego's quite upset. You know he loves his brother and won't accept he's missing. And I won't either. We'll find them. Or like in the past, Tomas will find us."

"Listen Joseph, I just spoke to a high-ranking individual at the FBI who told me that all available personnel are searching for them. You know about the President's visit tomorrow, which unfortunately is consuming much of our manpower and resources."

"Did you have a chance to look for those Mossad files, the ones recommended by Victor Kingman?" I ask. "Who by the way is sitting right across from me."

"I'm quite positive he saved my life in Peru in 1999. The time I blacked out a few days and found myself on a bus heading for Lima. I always thought Mr. Kingman had something to do with that. Don't know why, just do."

"That's one of many questions I plan to ask him. First, he needs to come out of the shock of almost being blown to pieces," I say softly. "Even though he's a little strange, I like him."

"Are you sure you're okay Joseph? I mean about Tomas," Mom says. "I know you didn't know him long, but he did save our lives a few months back. We would've never gotten out of Mexico alive if it weren't for him."

"I'm okay. I'm more worried about Rogers and Diego."

"Me too Joseph."

"What about the Mossad files? Any updates?" I ask.

"Yes, I just briefed the President and the National Security Council. Mr. Carlone was there as well," she says. "Anyway, Mr. Kingman was right about documents being taken by Mossad several years ago from caves in Afghanistan that mention snares of the devil."

"I knew it! I saw the files that time Carlone, Mike and I almost died of exposure in the Afghan mountains. We were burning files to stay warm. I passed out, but Mike said we were rescued by Israeli agents. Who by the way took the remaining files - the ones in Spanish. What'd they say?"

"You almost died from exposure?"

"Did I say 'die?' I meant sick. Anyway, I'm here now. Please continue."

"Jeez Joseph, you certainly make it hard to continue!"

"Please?" I ask.

"Alright, where was I? Yes, snares of the devil. Okay, as you know Al-Qaeda had many years when they couldn't raise any money to fund their terrorist activities. During that same time, the drug lords in Mexico, Central and South America had too much money. Ran out of places to hide it. Enter Al-Qaeda, with weapons, training camps and secret Middle East bank accounts. It was a match made in heaven. No – hell."

"So a partnership was born," I say.

"Yes, we tracked their movements from the Americas to the Middle East. Took pictures of the training camps from space and intercepted their cell communications. Over the last decade, we bombed as many camps as possible. Not very effective though."

"How about snares of the devil - what does that mean?" I ask.

"From what we can tell so far, it has nothing to do with religion, per se. It's more related to a military maneuver, some type of attack, or trap."

"So, getting the stone delivered to me, back at Holy Spirit last month was a clue. The inscription *snares of the devil* was some type of warning.

125

Someone knew that we'd figure it out. What it really meant. I don't think Alvaro ever knew about the drug cartel/Al-Qaeda tie. He was simply there to find something that meant a lot to the Peruvian people – their culture. Alvaro wanted to bring the stone back to the temples at Machu Picchu. Maybe get a little reward money."

"Sadly, I agree Joseph," Mom says.

"But we don't know if he was killed by the cartels trying to keep that snares of the devil thing a secret. Or simply treasure hunters looking to make a lot of money."

"My bet is with the cartels," Mom says. "Somehow they found out about the stone and Alvaro somehow knew you had it. Maybe the cartels informed him – we don't know."

"Sounds about right," I say. "They were most likely using him because they knew about his love for the religious culture of Peru. Alvaro firmly believed that the face on the stone was Jesus. A gift from the pope. An actual stone used by the devil to tempt Jesus."

"I don't think he was involved in the drug trade or a treasure hunter. His involvement held much higher meaning," Mom said sadly. "Something we all need."

"Mom that explains it! That's why they're coming after me – us. Alvaro failed. They think I still have the stone," I say. "Think about it. Destruction of Holy Spirit Mission. Bombing at the consulate. Alvaro chained inside a bomb rigged van. Shot at on the roof of the Surfer Motel. Kingman wearing a vest filled with dynamite. Kelly and Tomas missing. All these things have two things in common if we're correct in our hypothesis."

"They're chasing the stone. Thinking someone will figure out the clue. Oh my God, Joseph!" she screams. "The other thing in common is you!"

"Calm down Mom, relax, hear me out. I agree those are the two things in common. Where's the stone?" I ask.

"In my basement office in the Library."

"Where are you?"

"Third floor office in the Library."

"Call your friend at CNN – Cindy More."

"You mean Cindy Morin," Mom replies.

126

"Yes, tell her you have a breaking story. Tell her to bring a camera crew. Get Carlone involved. Make up a story, doesn't matter. Please get that stone on TV. It might help call off the dogs."

"Great idea Joseph! I'll call Cindy right now. In the meantime, be careful. Call you later – bye – love you!"

Who knows, it might work. Can't hurt.

Looking out the window and thinking about our conversation, I notice Mike has decided to take us on the scenic route - through a very busy neighborhood. The small houses jammed together provide no privacy. Kingman is sound asleep, his shoulder leaning against the RV's tinted glass. Every time we hit a bump; his head bounces off the glass - still sleeping. After a few minutes, I get my timing right and place a small pillow between his head and the window. That's when I see it. I walk quickly up front and tell Mike to take a right at the next street. The turn comes up quickly and he decides to take it at the last minute. All tires on the right side hit the high curb, causing a thirty percent tilt in the vehicle. By the time he stops, everyone's up front wondering what's going on.

"Kingman, get a shirt on – now," I say barking out orders.

"Clare, get behind the wheel – please,"

"Pedro honey, sit here next to Clare," I say lifting him into a seat.

"Mike, get your Colt," I say softly, hoping Pedro can't hear me. Doesn't work. He starts saying "Bang – bang!" pointing his fingers in the air as Kingman joins us.

"Listen, Mr. Kingman, I think we just passed that brown military truck that took Kelly and Tomas. Parked in the neighborhood around the corner."

"You can't be serious," he says. "How do you know?"

"You told me what it looked like – remember? Anyway, I know for sure we just passed one. It's worth checking out."

"Let's go Joe!" Diego says loudly, scaring Pedro. "I'm ready!" he says softer opening the door.

"Diego, you can't go," I quickly reply. "You're staying here with Clare. I need you to find out where the nearest hospital is - directions and everything. The rest of us don't know anything about this area – or your connections. Mike, you stay here but, let Clare drive the RV in case I need

127

Kingman,

you – call Carlone. Kingman and I are going. Diego, please get on the phone, internet, whatever – find the hospital."

"Okay Joe, I'll stay – for now," Diego says.

"Thanks - ready Kingman?"

"Clare, drive the RV around the neighborhood. Try to stay off the same roads. This vehicle sticks out like a sore thumb. Love you," I say, kissing her a little too long on the lips.

"Time to go Mr. Dustan," Kingman says, tugging at my sleeve. "Bloody thugs await."

Clare mouths " I love you" as I step out of the RV. As soon as I hit the ground, the RV jerks forward, leaving us out in the open. Pulling my New York Yankees hat down on my head, we sprint for the house with the familiar truck parked in the driveway. If Kingman's nervous, he doesn't show it. His mind and movements are being controlled by one thing – revenge. Can't say I blame him. We're crossing the busy road and that's when I notice it. Speechless at first, I finally mange to get out some words.

"Kingman, did you really have to wear my Yankees World Champion t-shirt?"

"You told me to get a shirt on - found this one on the chair," he says while pulling on the neck. "It's a little tight."

"And short," I reply. "On you it looks like a belly shirt. Does wonders for showing that foot long scar over your naval."

"For all you know, I may be a huge Yankee fan. I think I even cheered for them during a Super Bowl!" He says proudly.

As I'm about to respond to his nonsense, I see the military vehicle backing down the driveway. No time for a plan.

CHAPTER 36
Friday / 1:13 PM
Tuxpan, Veracruz, Mexico

Kingman and I split up. He runs into an alley circling back towards the house. I stumble into the street, hoping the driver will stop or slow down when he sees me. The truck is getting close and accelerating. I see two heads in the cab as it comes barreling down the street towards me. I duck behind a parked car and hear the screech of brakes being locked up. I peek around the car to see the truck stopped fifty feet from me. The passenger side door opens and a tall man steps down, pistol in hand. Just as I'm thinking it's a fair fight, the flap on the back of the truck goes up and at least a half a dozen men, dressed like soldiers come pouring out. Knowing the odds are against me, I do what anybody would do – run for my life!

Sprinting through the neighborhood, over fences, around gardens and teeth baring dogs, I end up in a shopping mall parking lot. Not slowing down to check my shopping list, I run inside towards the Food Court. Still being followed by at least two, I pull out my iPhone and call Mike.

"Kingman's at the house and I'm at a mall!"

"Just picked him up – says the house's empty! What the hell are you doing at the mall?" replies Mike.

"Picking up lunch!" I shout into the phone.

"We're coming to get ya!" he says. "Diego knows the neighborhood – says he knows where the mall is. Hey, I'll take two beef tacos."

Bursting through two sets of doors, I'm back on the outside just in time to see the truck cruising slowly through the lot. Must be here to pick up the troops. I pull out my Colt and dash for the truck. There's one person at the wheel. I jump onto the driver's side running boards, and jam the gun into the side of his head. He starts talking rapidly in Spanish while pushing the accelerator to the floor. Hanging on to the mirror with my left hand, I point the gun down at the truck's floor and shoot him in the foot. Talking is replaced by screaming and the truck slows to a stop. I pull him out of the passenger seat; toss him to the ground, throw the truck into neutral. I run to the back, lift the flap and find two people bound by duct tape: Rogers and Tomas.

Giving Rogers the "I'll be back sign," I check on the driver squirming along the ground holding his right foot, trying to stop the blood flow. Under the seat, I find a large knife, two sawed-off shotguns and two black kittens. Grabbing the knife, I run to the back and begin cutting the sticky restraints off Kelly. There's no movement coming from Tomas, so I check his pulse; he is still with us. I remove the tape from Roger's lips, her speech is slow and disjointed. Probably drugged.

Since I have no time for translation, I throw her over my shoulder and carry her out the back and into the passenger seat. A group of people wearing camo outfits are running in my direction. I quickly buckle her in and run around to the other side. As I pass the guy on the ground, he grabs my leg, turns me around while pulling a pistol from his jacket. I look at him, wink and shoot him in the other foot. No time for small talk. I jump into the truck and fire it up. Using all my strength, I get the truck into first gear and we're up to forty miles per hour in no time. Bullets ricochet off the truck as I turn off onto a dirt road moving at close to sixty. Not knowing where I am, I get Mike on the phone, Rogers screaming in the background.

"Got Rogers and Tomas!" I yell into the phone. "Roger's been drugged and Tomas still has a pulse. I'm lost, driving alongside what looks like a river."

"I see you!" Mike yells. "We're on the other side. Diego says it's the Tuxpan River! We see you!"

"Alright, got you," I yell sighting the Flame Keepers Racing RV across the river moving at a strong clip. "How do I get to you?"

"Diego says there's a bridge in about a mile," Mike replies. "Hey Joe, do you know about the two green Kawasaki motorcycles right behind you. Both with double riders."

"That depends," I yell into the phone.

"On what?"

"Only if you've noticed the four police cars right behind you!"

"See you at the bridge Joe!" Mike yells back.

Rogers is now vomiting all over herself as she bounces against the seat belt. Remembering the shotguns under the seat, I slam on the brakes, causing the motorcycles to fly right by me. Reaching under the seat, I get scratched a few times by the kittens before I'm able to find one of the guns. Quickly checking the chamber, I find one shell. Not much help against four people on motorcycles. The green machines head back in my direction. I throw the truck in gear and get her moving again. The two passengers on the bikes stand up on the foot pegs and start shooting wildly in my direction. I grab Rogers by the hair and move her head away from the windshield. To my surprise the windshield is bullet proof and deflects the onslaught. They pass the truck on both sides, slam on the brakes and turn around. Within seconds, they're back alongside as I swerve, attempting to take them out – no luck. Looking ahead, I see the bridge with the RV parked on the other side, surrounded by several police officers.

Hoping the cops are on our side, I decide to cross the bridge. With motorcycles on each side, I yank the steering wheel to the right at the last second in an attempt to cross the bridge. The bike on the right crashes into the passenger side door and disappears from sight. I feel the tires on the left lift off the ground before slamming down on the wooden bridge. Closing in on land on the other side, I see an old man drop his fishing pole to chase his dog out of our path. Unfortunately, they're both now in the road. I slam on the brakes and swerve out of the way. The truck begins shuttering across the lane to the other side. It's at this time that I notice that the guard rail is made from flimsy wood and won't be able to stop our momentum. We plow through the rail and finally come to a stop with the wheels on my side over the edge. Clare comes running up to the truck as my side dangles over the edge. She pops her head into the passenger side window and immediately understands my predicament.

"Hi Clare!" I say loud and cheery. "Can you open the door and pull out Rogers?"

"Okay Joe," she cries. "You come too!"

"Can't, not yet" I reply calmly. "Tomas is in the back – unconscious. We need to get him out too. As you help Rogers out, I'm gonna move to her seat, hoping to keep it balanced. Alright Clare?"

"Okay Joe, got it," she says, looking terrified. "Makes sense."

As Clare starts to grab Rogers, Diego comes to help her.

"Diego," I say. "Tomas is in the back. Very carefully, see if you can get him out."

He disappears and I see the Truck's flap being thrown back and feel movement in the truck bed. Through the windshield, I see Clare with Rogers sitting on the side of the road. Clare's holding her hair away from her face as she continues to throw up. Seconds later, I see Diego in the mirror, standing behind the truck, holding his brother in his arms. Time for my escape. Moving slowly towards the open passenger side door, I feel movement around my feet. Scampering up my leg, the two kittens jump onto the dashboard and wedge themselves into a small space over the steering column. I can't leave them to die, so I slowly move back to the driver's side. I open my shirt and mange to grab one kitten, show Clare through the windshield and place him inside my shirt. Reaching for the remaining kitten, I hear a series of crunches under the truck. I grab the other kitten, stuff him into my shirt with the other. Realizing the truck is tilting upwards, I quickly climb up the seat to scramble out the door. Just before I'm out, the truck flips onto its side and begins a free fall into the river. Unsure if cats can swim, I quickly button my shirt just before we hit the water.

CHAPTER 37

I'm not sure what hurts the most, hitting my head on the dashboard, or the kittens scratching under my shirt. The truck lands softly on the muddy river bed about ten feet below the surface. Thankfully the current is weak, but the clarity is poor. I manage to get my bearings and pull myself out of the open passenger side window and swim towards the light. As I break the surface, I feel a splash a few feet away from me.

"Joe, Joe, are you alright?" Clare screams, paddling to me.

"Fine, I just need help with these two," I yell pulling the two, wet kittens out of my shirt, placing them on my chest as I start a slow back stroke.

"Where'd you get the kittens?" Clare says, bumping me in the water.

"They lived in the truck, I guess."

"So that's what you were showing me?" she asks. "When the truck was falling off the bridge. Come on, let's get to shore."

As I get closer to shore, Mike wades in and grabs the kittens from me. He gently wraps them in a white towel, says "I can't believe it" and heads for shore. I turn around to see Clare coming out of the water next to me. I'm pleasantly surprised to see her barely dressed in just her bra and underwear.

"Ya know Clare, in the time it took you to get undressed, I could have drowned," I say, looking at her with a straight face.

"I figured you needed someone to save your life. You know – mouth to mouth CPR stuff. And that you might respond better to someone almost naked," she smiles.

Clare stands dripping wet, sun behind her, blue eyes wide open. I pull her close and hug her as we're standing in about two feet of water. Just as we're about to kiss, a commotion breaks out behind us. We turn to see a large crowd of people lining the bridge and shoreline, breaking out into loud applause. Realizing it's for us; I bend Clare over and kiss her

133

passionately on the lips. When finished, Clare faces the cheering crowd and bows several times while laughing. I'm catapulted back in time two months ago when I first met Clare at the airport. She drew the short straw and had to pick up a stranger in Mexico City. She picked me up in a tired old bus that crapped out, right outside baggage claim. Clare managed to get the bus started, again to the applause of onlookers. When she took her bows back then, I felt I was about to meet one of the most fascinating women ever. Clearly I'm right about some things.

Holding hands, we walk up the embankment to the RV. Kingman hands Clare a nice fluffy towel. Mike gives me something he laid on when changing the oil in the RV. But he does hug me. Mentions he was right behind Clare, and would have jumped into the water if needed. Standing outside the RV, I notice most of the police are up on the bridge walking around with men in hard hats surveying the damage to the bridge. A pair of officers next to an ambulance helps load the two dead motorcyclists into the back. Clare goes off to shower in the RV and check on Rogers. Fina watches the kittens from a distance as the local kids quickly adopt them. Mike says Diego went to the hospital with his brother, and that it was just a few blocks from our location.

With all the danger associated with this trip, I make an executive decision - call Carlone to ask for a favor.

CHAPTER 38

Friday / 4:00 PM

Tuxpan, Veracruz, Mexico

The Sikorsky Seahawk lands inside a highly secured industrial complex where oil platforms are manufactured and assembled. It's mostly empty, which makes it a great place to land the chopper. It's been decided that Clare, Pedro and Ensign Rogers will fly up to Brownsville, Texas this afternoon. Mike, Kingman, and I will continue in the RV and meet up with them on Saturday. Clare doesn't like being separated from me, but realizes that exposing Pedro to all this violence is not good for him. Rogers is still sick from the drugs her kidnappers injected her with, causing her to mumble and hallucinate. The local doctors gave her the okay to travel, stating that it will take time for the drugs to pass through her system. Anyway, she'll receive additional medical treatment when they arrive in Texas. We're unable to reach Diego on his phone and decide to go to the hospital once the helicopter departs. Clare and Pedro are helped into the helicopter with Fina on their heels, leaping into the cabin. She'll follow Clare anywhere. Kingman and I load Rogers's stretcher into the Seahawk. Just as we lay her on the cabin floor, she grabs my arm, pulls me down to her face.

"Joe," she whispers. "Can you hear me? Somebody turn down the music!" she yells. "Forget it, leave it up! I love Elvis – in the ghetto," she sings. "Learns how to fight."

Kingman gives me a strange look as she continues to sing – loudly. I'm not sure if it's because no music is being played or because her voice sounds like a pack of hyenas. Either way, someone in the chopper, not wearing headphones, gives her an injection, which calms her down immediately. Her grip loosens, but her mumbling continues.

"Captain Joseph Dustan," she says. "Joe, can you hear me? I need to tell you something – now."

"Right here Kelly," I say holding her hand. "I'm here."

"Captain Joe, Captain Dustan, Joe, please listen."

"Go ahead Ensign Rogers," I say using a formal tone.

"Have you ever caught a rabbit?"

"You mean hunted with a gun?" I ask.

"No," she says softly starting to fall asleep. "With a tarp, no trap."

"No Ensign, I've never hunted or trapped a rabbit."

"I hear it's quite simple," she says slowly. "Using a snare, you know to trap someone, animal or something. Lure them in – make 'em feel comfortable, takes time."

Her mumbling changes to a soft, rhythmic snore as she releases my hand. I kiss Clare on the way out of the Seahawk, joining Kingman outside the RV. As the helicopter lifts off, I'm thinking about what Rogers just said. "Snare."

After the chopper departs, the local police allow us to leave after checking our paperwork and inspecting the RV. We drive over to the hospital to find Diego. Walking into the emergency room, leaving Mike and Kingman in our vehicle, I find out that the so-called hospital is really a large office with curtain dividers. The young American woman at the front desk calls it a clinic. Tells me she's been here all day and that no one named Diego or a man wearing a mask came in. Mostly "screaming children" she says, "along with a construction guy who cut off his thumb using a saw." She told me how she put his "disgusting thumb" in a Ziploc filled with ice. The vet cleaned up his wound, gave him a shot to prevent infection and lessen the pain. Said his wife kept calling him "estupido" and finally drove him to the big hospital in Tampico. I ask about the "vet" comment. She says Dr. Solana is filling in for the regular doctor due to an emergency, but the doctor/vet is very capable.

She allows me to check for my friends behind several of the dividers. I find Dr. Solana, children of all ages as well as three dogs chained to a pipe that disappears into the floor. I check inside an empty bathroom with no door, but in a quick search of the trash find Tomas's mask in the bottom of a trash can. After showing it to the woman up front, she nervously

136

confesses that two men did come in earlier. She apologizes for not telling me, but said the doctor had warned her to be quiet about this. One man was carrying a sick man wearing that mask. She said the doctor seemed to know one of the two, and drove them to the hospital in Tampico. "Bene hospital on Hidalgo," she says. That explains the vet doctor and the emergency. "Dangerous people may come looking," he'd said. I thank her and walk out the door across the street to the RV. I inform Mike and Kingman that we need to stop at the hospital in Tampico on the way to Brownsville. I say as I throw the mask on the table.

CHAPTER 39

Friday / 8:30 PM
Bene Hospital / Tampico, Tamaulipas, Mexico

Parked behind the Hospital in between two tractor trailers, we decide Mike and I will go in, and Kingman will stay with the RV. He still seems a little traumatized by the event early this morning, mumbling nonsense to himself. Mike and I decide to split up. He heads for the ER entrance. Me, the front door. Relieved by the lack of metal detectors, I walk over to an older woman sitting behind a large wooden desk wearing a blue hospital smock. As I get closer, she lifts her head, pushes her glasses up her nose and smiles. Two things stand out. She has no teeth that I can see. And, she's knitting – mittens. Nametag says Francine.

"Excuse me Señorita," I say slowly. "Do you speak English?"

"Why of course I do sonny," she yells back. "Oops, hang on a sec hon."

She disappears under the desk for a moment and returns holding a hearing aid, the type that goes inside the ear. It's hard not to notice the amount of ear wax attached to it. She looks at me, smiles, and I see not one pearly white, yellow, brown or anything. Blowing the dirt and wax out of the hearing aid crevices, she places the device back into her ear.

"Sorry, sonny, where were we?"

"Gracias," I say. "I'm trying to find two family members that came in today – both men, a few hours ago. Might have come in with a doctor from Tuxpan."

"We don't admit patients here," she says. "I mean we admit patients, just not here. All go through the Emergency Room – except the occasional visitor – like you hon. Follow that sign," she says pointing at the wall across from her desk.

"Is there any way to see if two men came by here, signed in as visitors?" I ask nicely.

"Here you go sonny, take a look yourself," she says, handing me the visitor's log.

As I scan through the book, she goes back to knitting. I quickly notice that all the dates are from last month.

"Excuse me Francine," I say. "Do you have the latest visitor book? This one has dates from last month."

"Let me see," she says grabbing the book from me. "You're right, wrong one." Moving all her knitting stuff out of the way, she finds the right one. "Here you go," she says handing me the book.

A quick scan provides no information. "Thank you Francine," I say giving her back the log. "I'll go over to the ER."

"Hey, excuse me, one more thing," she says. "Can you try on this mitten for me? I think you and my son-in-law have about the same size hands. He and my daughter live in Canada. Don't know how they do it. Too darn cold for me," she yells.

As I try on the mitten, I notice her hearing aid is dangling off the side of her ear.

"Fits perfect," I say loudly pointing at my ear. She gets the gesture and refits her hearing aid.

"Damn pain in the neck," she says. "Thanks hon."

"Bye. Good luck with the mittens," I say, walking away.

Turning the corner towards the ER, I see a message on my cell – from Diego. As I hit the play button, I feel the ground shake from an explosion somewhere outside. Running through the exit doors, I sprint out back to where the RV's parked only to see it engulfed in a ball of flames. Mike comes up behind me. There's nothing we can do so we move off to the side. I hear screaming behind us. Turning towards the noise, we find our luck is holding out.

"What bloody thing happened here?" yells Kingman. "I go out to stretch my legs and next thing I know our home on wheels is on fire."

Standing in the parking lot in bare feet, wrinkled suit pants and wearing my too-small Yankees t-shirt, Kingman finally realizes what just happened. As he starts to faint, Mike catches him just before he hits the ground. A black Toyota Sequoia comes barreling towards us. It squeals to a stop two feet from us with the passenger window down.

"Get in quick, we don't have time! They'll be here any minute!" shouts Diego. "Didn't any of you idiots get my message? What's wrong with Kingman?"

"Bad clams," Mike says laying him on the seat.

"Bad clams?" Diego says.

"More like he almost got blown up twice in less than then twelve hours," I say.

"I think I'd rather eat bad seafood," Diego replies.

"Me too Diego, me too," says Kingman, coming around.

We move slowly out into traffic, trying to avoid suspicion from everyone running to what's left of the smoldering RV. Next stop, the border – hopefully.

CHAPTER 40

Friday / 9:55 PM
In Route to Mexican – Texas Border

The drive to the border is close to 300 miles and will take at least six hours. Diego tells us how the doctor at the clinic in Tuxpan is a friend. How he was able to stabilize Tomas at the office and insisted on driving them to the hospital in Tampico.

"I had no car," says Diego. "And Tomas was going to die. I'm sorry I left without telling anybody, but he's my brother. Anyway, I knew one of you geniuses would figure it out."

"Where's he now – Tomas?" I say jumping in.

"Still at the hospital we just left – very private room," Diego says. "He's okay, but lost a little blood. The doc says the beating wasn't enough to kill him. But, leaving him to bleed out in the back of the truck was. Where's Ensign Rogers?"

"Probably in Brownsville by now with Clare and Pedro," Mike says. "After the truck-off-the-bridge incident, the US Navy sent in a helicopter to fly them out."

"Why didn't you guys go with them?" Diego yells.

"Because we weren't gonna leave you," I say looking at him in the driver's seat. "We didn't know where you were!"

"Wow, I'm touched," says Diego. "Thank you. But, you gotta know how dangerous it's getting. As Tomas came in and out of consciousness during the ride to the hospital, he said something about the border. Nothing specific, just stuff he heard."

"You're bloody well right Diego," says Kingman.

"That's from a song," Mike interrupts.

"Yes, bloody right," I say. "Supertramp, mid-seventies I think."

"Will you two shut up?" Kingman says.

"Sorry, must be the stress and lack of sleep," I say.

"Me too," says Mike. "Sorry."

"May I continue?" Kingman asks.

"Please do," Diego replies.

"Tomas and I have known each other for many years. Ever since I tried to kill my boss at that restaurant. Remember Diego?" Kingman says.

"Yeah, tried to forget," Diego says. "Some people still think I had something to do with it. Including your old boss, who I see from time to time."

"That bloody traitor," Kingman says. "If I ever see that scum again, this time I'll finish the job – promise! Now, where was I?"

"What you and Tomas heard," says Diego.

"Right, thank you," Kingman replies. "Something's going to happen at the border. Most likely tomorrow – timed around a visit from many foreign dignitaries. It's some celebration of a revamped NAFTA. I heard the new trade agreements will include countries in Central and South America – eliminate barriers – tariffs and such."

"How can the President's office be scheduling this?" Mike interjects. "Heck, we're at war with them – the cartels I mean. Don't the VIPS's know it might be dangerous at the border."

"Their war is with the cartels, not the people," I reply. "Listen Kingman, when Kelly was loaded into the helicopter, she talked about snaring and trapping – being lured. Granted she was out of it, but it must go back to this snare of the devil thing. You said it yourself."

"Correct Joe," says Kingman. "I believe snares of the devil refer to a terrorist act – military action. A snare is a trap of some sort. Miss Rogers must have heard this when she was kidnapped. But, I believe this plan – concept, whatever it is – snare devil thing started a long time ago. Many years ago when I first got to South America, I heard a story about the cartel bosses getting together to discuss a worldwide illegal drug strategy. That's when I first heard the phrase Trampas del Diablo – Snares of the Devil. They discussed methods for trapping – snaring people, into using the drugs they sold. I was told there were agreements on pricing, manufacturing and distribution."

"Interesting, Alvaro described snares of the devil from a biblical standpoint," I reply. "When Jesus was fasting in the desert for forty days, the devil would tempt him with stones. He'd say things like you're hungry, turn these stones into food. Alvaro was after a stone he believed to be from that event. Said someone stole it from Machu Picchu, sent it to me. Only this time it had an inscription on the bottom – three words – Trampas del Diablo."

"I have to say that Kingman's explanation makes a lot more sense," Mike adds.

"Agree," Diego jumps in.

The conversation ends when my Timex beeps, telling me it's midnight – Saturday. We pull into a gas station to fill up and get some needed supplies. I pick up a message from Clare telling me they're in Brownsville – they're all okay and staying at Saint Jerome's. Kelly was flown to a hospital in Houston and that Pedro was excited about seeing his relatives. Clare realizes she has to "let him go." She mentions going to Key West after this is over - a "vacation" she calls it. Clare probably won't call it a vacation once she sees how small my apartment is. She says she "loves me" and "can't wait to see me." While waiting for Kingman to buy a shirt and shoes, my cell begins vibrating in my pocket. I see it's Mom, and walk outside to a picnic table.

"Good morning, Mom," I say cheerily. "Shouldn't you be sleeping?"

"Hi Joseph," she replies. "You know I don't sleep well when my team and I are searching for answers with very few clues."

"What have you found out mom?"

"Not a hundred percent sure, but I'll tell you the same thing I told Jim Carlone. Let me start at the beginning," she says. "Back in 1999, when I tried to return that stone, Alvaro and I get rescued by helicopter. After racking my brain for the last 48 hours, I now know that Victor Kingman and Tomas Amos were on that chopper. I'll even go out on a limb and say Tomas might have been the one who took the box from me on the helicopter – the one with the stone. When we crashed, I lost the box in the jungle."

143

"Mom, I'm here with Kingman right now. As a matter of fact, I can see him trying on different shirts through a store window. I'll ask him about it when he's done. He owes me since I recently saved his life."

"That's alright Joseph, I'm sure he was there. I just don't know why," she says. "The thing that bothers me the most is Tomas was also on the chopper – I think."

"How'd you know it's Tomas?" I ask back. "Was he wearing a mask?"

"Don't know - I didn't see a mask. It's just after seeing him a few months ago, I just sense it – that's all. Can't explain it," she trails off.

"Mom, maybe it was his brother – Diego."

"Why would you say that?" she asks. "Why would Diego be there?"

"Something is going on between these brothers that I can't explain – yet. But I will."

"I have to go. I was going to surprise you, but I think it's too late for that. Anyway, I'm getting ready to board a plane to Brownsville. DEA Director Carlone asked me if I wanted to go down for the big NAFTA border celebrations taking place in less than twelve hours," she says. "You know me, normally I wouldn't, but since you and Clare are there, I figured, why not?"

"Mom, please don't come – stay in Washington. All signs point to something happening tomorrow."

"Honey, I agree that something is brewing on the terrorist front. But there always is," she says. "You know better than I that we can't lock ourselves in our homes. We have to continue to live our lives. My team is coming with me. Also a special friend."

"Can't you guys work out of Washington? And who's your friend"

"We have no confirmation that anything will happen today, tomorrow or any day for that matter. All I can say is that this has been planned for months and security is very tight. Anyway, my team and I will be helping to coordinate security logistics for all countries involved."

"Be careful, Mom, and call me when you get in."

"Hang on Joseph, somebody wants to say hello," she says in a muffled voice.

"Buenos Dias Joey! Can't wait to see you in Brownsville!"

"Buenos Dias to you too Stella!" I reply, her infectious personality always makes me smile. "You gotta tell me how Mom talked you in to going on this trip. I thought you're going on a book tour?"

"I am Joey, on my book tour," Stella laughs. "It starts Sunday at the Waldenbooks in Brownsville. My publisher moved a few things around and here I come, packing my autograph pens. Even on such short notice, I hope at least a few people will show up to get an autographed edition of Hell on Eight Wheels. Anyway your mother needs an ex-roller derby queen to keep an eye on her. Gotta go Joey, plane's about to take off – love you – see you soon!"

"Love you too Stella - bye," I reply as the line clicks dead.

Right after the terrorist attack in DC, Stella's daughter, Natalie was murdered. Found in a garbage bin, arms and legs broken, handcuffed to a man with no head. He had a tattoo of the white tiger with black feet and stripes on the back of his neck. The head was found in the carriage of a homeless person, mixed with empty bottles and cans. The police called it a drug related crime. Even though Natalie had a history of drug and alcohol abuse, I still think it was something else. Especially since the headless man pulled me out of a burning vehicle several days prior his death. Some things are beyond coincidences.

I've known Stella for almost ten years now. She's Mom's next door neighbor at the Watergate Condo Complex as well as her best friend. Stella spent thirty years as a professional roller skater wiping the hardwood with her opponents. Today as a widow, she writes books about her derby days, volunteers with different charities and most recently, she imagines herself as my mom's bodyguard. Thanks to Carlone, Mom and Stella have real security people whenever they travel. My thoughts are broken up as the Toyota Sequoia pulls up alongside me, stops with Diego climbing out of the driver side door.

"Your turn to drive," Diego says. "Kingman and Mike had a few beers inside and I'm getting tired. If you're tired, we can spend the night at the hotel across the street."

"No thanks Diego – I'll drive. That hotel looks a little shady. Mom and Stella are on their way to Brownsville."

"What?" Mike and Diego say at the same time.

"They're coming down for the NAFTA celebrations. Carlone is leading the delegation," I say.

"Come on Joe, excuse my tone - but this is crazy!" Mike yells. "Your mother knows how dangerous it is down here – especially now. And, it's such last minute! Carlone should not allow her to travel down here – wait till I see him!"

"Listen Mike, I was just on the phone with her - tried to talk her out of it. They were calling me while boarding the plane. Mom said she wanted to surprise me – us," I say looking at Diego. "It's too late now."

"It's at least five hours to the border – let's get going," Diego says softly.

I pull onto the main road. I can see Mike and Kingman in the rear view mirror eating something out of grease-stained brown bags. Diego seems to be in a trance, staring out the passenger side window. I can't help but wonder if he knew mom was coming to Brownsville. When I said they were on their way, he seemed the least surprised. Driving by the run-down hotel with a bar next door, I see at least thirty Harley Davidson motorcycles with Texas license plates lined up. The music of Pink Floyd flows out into the street through the open doors pushing me towards the Dark Side of the Moon.

CHAPTER 41

Saturday / 2:30 AM
San Fernando, Tamaulipas, Mexico

I'm driving on highway 101 through San Fernando early Saturday morning, two and a half hours from the border. The rest of the crew is sleeping, filling the Toyota's interior with snoring that's annoying my poor eardrums. In need of caffeine, I pop open a can of diet Pepsi. I wonder about why I'd been sent this stone twice in my life. I believe Alvaro's motives were true, wanting to return the stone to the lost city of the Incas - Machu Picchu. He somehow got mixed up with treasure hunters and or drug smugglers. Maybe when Alvaro realized this, it was too late. The nagging question is why the stone was sent to me – by whom? When it arrived at our house on my sixteenth birthday, it held no meaning – maybe a prank, but not a clue for something that might happen fourteen years later. Whoever sent it knew Mom would try to figure it out; its value – where it came from. I think the sender wanted attention. And they got it. Mom goes to Peru to return the stone, and almost winds up dead.

Then last month, the stone shows up at Holy Spirit Mission. The box was addressed to me, with the stone inside wrapped in newspaper from Mexico City. Only this time it had the inscription. Same words, on paper, found in the mouth of a dead Alvaro – Trampas del Diablo. I'm convinced its code for a trap. Whoever wrote those words is sending a message. Who and why – I don't know. What the trap is – no idea. When the trap will be sprung – probably today. Where – US Mexican border. My thought process is interrupted by a call on my iPhone. Who's up at three in the morning?

"Hello," I say softly.

"Hi Joe?"

"This is Joe."

"It's me, Mark – Mark Temple, from the Surfer Moon Hotel."

"Hey Mark, how are ya? And why are you up so early?"

"Since I don't have a regular job, I keep odd sleeping hours. I'm in my shop right now, laying down some glass on a new blade design," he says. "Anyhow, speaking of wind blades, I made another delivery yesterday to that warehouse by the airport. Remember?"

"Sure," I say. "Can't forget being chased by those dogs near the parked white trailers."

"Right – that's the place," he says. "Well I thought you'd want to know that it's shut down – trailers gone. Chain link fence, guardhouse - gone. Several signs on the property, EN VENTA – FOR SALE. Somebody cleaned up the lot, laid down new gravel. You'd never know the place once parked over two dozen semis."

"Anybody know what happened?" I ask.

"The owner of the place, you know where I ship my blades from, said it was done at night. Said he drove by on his way home, six-thirty at night – all quiet. Next morning, the place was empty and for sale."

"That's strange, Mark – thanks. Oh hey, was there a phone number on the for sale signs?" I say.

"No, just the name of a Realty company," he replies. "Hang on, I wrote it down – gimme a sec. Sorry Joe – here it is. I'll spell it. F-A-L-T-A-R, ACRES, followed by P-R-O-M-O-T-O-R, D-E, P-R-O-P-I-E-D-A-D-E-S. Need me to spell it again Joe?"

"No, that's okay – got it," I reply.

"I think it translates to absent or missing acre properties, maybe developer," he says.

"You're right Mark – that's it," I reply. "Unfortunately, I've heard the name Missing Acres. Wasn't what you'd call a good experience."

"Sorry to hear that," says Mark. "Gotta go, resin is about right. If you need me to do anything, let me know. Bye now."

"Thanks Mark! Tell Cheryl I said hi."

As the line goes dead, my mind rolls back a few months when I walked, mostly ran through the Missing Acres property near Holy Spirit Mission. A few of us, including Clare, almost died there. The Mexican farm was owned by a powerful drug cartel associated with the deadly terrorist

148

attack in Washington DC on Inauguration Day. Missing Acres was destroyed by a series of coordinated aerial attacks conducted by the US Military. Good to know Missing Acres has real estate added to their business portfolio of farming, drugs and terror. Gotta find out where all the trailer trucks went. My guess is they're either at the border or on their way. Think I'm starting to understand this snare of the devil thing. I just hope I'm not too late. I try to get Carlone or Mom on the phone – no luck. I type out a text to both – "URGENT – CALL ME – Joe."

CHAPTER 42
Saturday / 5:23 AM
Matamoros, Tamaulipas, Mexico

Our Toyota Sequoia is parked across from a Catholic Church on Morelos in Matamoros. Before Diego goes inside, he tells me its name – Catedral De Nuestra Señora del Refugio. With his help, I'm able to translate it to the Cathedral or Church of Our Lady of Refuge. Mike and Kingman go looking for coffee, based on directions from an elderly man opening up his street vegetable stand. I get out of the SUV to stretch my legs when a familiar white semi drives by - white tiger black stripes logo on the back. Being that Matamoros is a Mexican border town separated from Brownsville Texas by the Rio Grande, this is more than a coincidence. I jump in the Sequoia, fire it up and punch the accelerator in pursuit. The streets are virtually deserted at six in the morning, and I quickly catch up to the truck.

After about two miles, it pulls into a large parking lot designated for trucks crossing the border. Pulling in behind them, I spot a border patrol vehicle heading in my direction. Not yet ready to discuss my hunch, I make a quick u-turn and head back out into the street. Unfortunately, two other border control vehicles come barreling towards me in the opposite direction, causing me to slam on the brakes in the middle of the road. Several men in uniform unload from both vehicles, run in my direction with guns drawn. One yells for me to "Get out of the car, show your hands!" in perfect English. Leaving the Colt 1911 under the seat, I open the door, hands on head, and step out onto the ground. Several of the men throw open the doors on the Toyota and begin conducting a thorough search. They're all wearing the same police type uniform with a Mexican flag embroidered on their jackets. Feeling like something bad is about to happen, I reach into my pocket and hit the panic button on my iPhone. It's supposed to bring military help to this location within ten minutes. As I get ready to tell my ten minute story loaded with excuses, I feel a sharp pain in my back that forces me to the ground in a fetal position.

Before passing out, I hear my name, followed by someone pulling the iPhone from my pocket. Crawling along the ground - unable to stand, it hits me that there are three border crossings into Brownsville – only one allows commercial traffic. I think the trap – snare is being set. I'm lifted off the ground, hands and feet are zip tied and they throw me into the back of their vehicle. I feel a sharp pain in my right arm followed by the strong urge to sleep. The radio clicks on and Procol Harum's A Whiter Shade of Pale fills my ears pulling me down into the darkness. Unable to stay awake, I stumble down the rabbit hole – "the room was humming harder as the ceiling flew away."

CHAPTER 43

Saturday / 11:08 AM
Location Unknown

Waking up in the dark doesn't scare me. But, waking up inside a long tubular tanker truck, hands and feet bound near an object the size of a small couch with a blinking LED clock scares me to death. Something tells me it's not an alarm clock. Using the light from my Timex Idiglo watch, I'm able to see wires running out of the clock that go down into the sides of a large metal box. I'm thankful the tanker hasn't hauled fuel for quite some time since the smell of gas is barely noticeable. I see stray light coming through a closed hatch at the top of the tanker. Below the hatch is a metal ladder that ends a few feet from the bottom. As I think about an escape plan, the semi moves slowly for about a minute then stops. We're stuck in traffic. Sliding on my side along a metal platform that's welded to the tank floor, I'm able to see that the flashing LED clock is counting down the time. If the red blinking digits are correct, I have thirty-seven minutes to get my hands and feet free, disarm the bomb, climb out a hatch that's probably locked, and warn the public. Since I don't know much about bombs, I'll skip the whole disarming part.

I reach into my boot with three fingers and pull out the thing that has saved my life on too many occasions – a Swiss Army Knife. Thank God it's the one with the tiny gadgets. Holding the knife in my duct taped hands and using my teeth, I pull out the scissors. With the skill of a surgeon, I'm able to cut off a torn piece of fingernail that was causing me much pain. Pushing the scissors back into the knife body, I then pull out the largest blade. With shaking hands, I begin to cut through the heavy layers of tape around my feet and legs. I'm about to start slicing through tape around my hands when I hear a noise from somewhere behind me.

"Hello – who's there?" I say loudly. No reply.

I go back to shredding the tape around my hands when I hear the noise again. It sounds like muffled wheezing.

"Who are you – Hello?" I shout. No answer.

Peeling off the last of the tape and slicing through the zip ties, I glance at the bomb clock to see that I have thirty-one minutes left. About the time it takes to watch a sitcom. I hope it's a lousy show because those seem to go on forever. Hearing the noise behind me again, I struggle to my feet and carefully move towards the back of the tanker. Walking slowly along the flat metal floor using the light from my watch, I see what looks like the shape of a body under the platform where it ends.

"Hey you! Can you hear me? Can you move?" I yell.

As my eyes focus on the figure lying under the platform, I think I see movement. I hit the button on my watch to illuminate the light and drop the Swiss Army Knife on the body below. I reach down below the metal platform and touch the nose and the forehead of the person lying on their back. Feeling along the sides of the mouth, I know what I must do. Using my right hand, I rip off the duct tape; it's followed by a curdling scream.

"Sorry, I'm really sorry!" I scream. "Fast is better than slow – I thought you couldn't breathe!"

Using the light from my watch, I peer down at a face with a half moustache. Oops. This might be my fault. As I'm about to apologize, again, I hear several curse words, both in English and Spanish come from the man with the sore, half bare upper lip. As he begins to calm down and civility returns, I'm a little surprised by his first question.

"How'd you get my Swiss Army Knife?"

CHAPTER 44

Saturday / 11:43 AM
Inside Empty Fuel Truck

"Diego, why do think it's your knife?" I yell. "Seems like everyone in Mexico has one except me!"

"Look at the large blade!" he says while touching his upper lip. My initials are at the base – look!"

It's at this very moment that Diego figures out what has happened. He starts to stand and looks up at the LED clock counting down the time. He sits back down as I cut away the tape from his wrist. He doesn't say a word. He reaches down near his leg and picks up the piece of tape I ripped gently from his mouth. Okay, maybe not so gently. Anyway, he brings the tape close to his face, his eyes wide open, staring at all the hair stuck to it. He again touches the space between his upper lip and nose. Imagining I see smoke coming from his ears, I move away towards the bomb. I may be safer there.

"Joseph, what did you do? Look at me!" he shouts. "I've had this moustache since I was old enough to grow one. Now it's mostly gone," he says, in shock. "Gone."

"I'm really sorry. But look on the bright side, it's not all gone, you still have half," I say, trying to lighten the mood. "You can hardly notice. I think you actually look better, ya know – younger. Anyhow, we have much bigger problems. If you haven't noticed, we're locked inside an empty fuel truck with a bomb and a timer that seems to indicate it will be detonating in – let's see - less than seventeen minutes."

"Are you crazy Joseph?" he says while stuffing the hairy tape into his pants pocket. "I won't look better! Younger is total nonsense and you know it!"

I climb the ladder to check the hatch at the top of the tanker. No surprise, it won't open - much. It's not locked, but a thick chain on the outside allows me to open it only about four inches. I take off my right Timberland boot and jamb it under the hatch forcing it open enough to provide some light. In the belly of the tanker, I see Diego looking up at me. I can't help but break out into uncontrolled laughter as I see his poor moustache.

"Keep laughing Joseph – very funny," he says staring at the LED clock. "In less than thirteen minutes, the joke will be over."

"I apologize."

"Cut the crap!" Diego says sharply. "We'll talk about this later."

"Maybe there's something in here to help us escape? Look around!"

Unfortunately, Diego has quickly fallen into some type of funk. He's sitting in front of the large metal box, right hand over where some of his moustache used to be. His unblinking eyes, staring at the bright red numbers telling us we have ten minutes before liftoff. As I continue my search, I hear noise coming from outside the tanker.

"Hello, you hoo, did somebody call Triple A?" I recognize Mike's voice. Relief floods through me. "We got a message that some poor bastards got trapped inside a tanker trying to sneak their way into the USA via the Veterans Bridge. Just so you know, this is illegal and the Border Patrol can't wait to meet you."

"Mike!" I scream. "Are we on a bridge with traffic?

"Well yeah buddy, bumper to bumper!" Mike shoots back.

Running up the ladder to the top of the tanker, I see parts of Mike's face peering through the small opening. "Listen carefully," I say. "Inside this tanker is a bomb. Set to go off in less than nine minutes. You must clear this bridge – now. Do whatever you need to do, but clear the damn bridge."

I hear Mike yelling out orders to someone on the outside. I quickly climb down the ladder, grab Diego and force him to his feet. I shove him over to the ladder and tell him to start climbing. As he nears the top, I hear Mike yell, "watch out below" as a piece of the cut chain falls inside the tanker and catches Diego in the face.

"Don't you know you're supposed to say 'Watch out below!' before you cut the chain," Diego yells.

The hatch opens above and Diego climbs out. A quick glance at the clock tells me we have over six minutes to evacuate the area. On my best day, I can run seven minute miles. Climbing the ladder towards the sunlight, I hear Mike laughing. Must be the moustache thing.

CHAPTER 45

Saturday / 11:54 AM
Veterans International Bridge
Border Crossing – Matamoros, Mexico / Brownsville, Texas

The bright sun forces me to cover my eyes as I crawl along the top of the fuel tanker. I hear people screaming as my eyes begin to adjust to the light. Mike was right, the bridge is a parking lot littered with now deserted cars. Doors have been left wide open. Throngs of people are running, navigating the narrow alleyways formed by the parked autos. I see Mike running full speed back in my direction as my Timex beeps, letting me know the bomb will detonate in five minutes. As I climb down the truck's ladder and hit the pavement, three Navy Super Hornets screech over my head at Mach speed. Looking towards the truck's cab, I see a familiar sight. A red umbrella sticking out the driver's side window. I run and jump up on the cab's side boards, peer in to see Kingman lying behind the front seat, semi naked, wearing an "I'm With Stupid" t-shirt, gnawing off the tape holding his hands together. This is not a pretty sight.

"Where the bloody hell have you been!" he yells. "I could have been killed – again."

"Sorry I couldn't get here any sooner Kingman – really, sorry, but we have a bigger problem." I pull him from the cab onto the ground. Looking at the white mini van parked in front of the truck, I see yet another problem.

"Oh my God Kingman, why aren't you wearing any pants?" Mike says, hoarsely, his voice spent from yelling at people to get out.

"Mike," I point to the van, "forget the pants!" I scream pointing at the van. "Get those kids out of their baby seats and run for Texas! We got

157

about three minutes before the tanker blows – take Kingman with you. Where's Diego? Diego, where the heck are you?" I scream.

I jump back into the truck cab, fire up the ignition and look through the windshield. I see Mike and Kingman turn towards me with puzzled looks on their faces. I gotta tell ya, I'm also puzzled looking back at them. Mike in his bright red shorts standing next to a guy wearing the "I'm With Stupid" t-shirt with the finger pointing at Mike. What a pair. I lean on the truck's horn and use all the strength I have left putting it in gear. I turn the wheels to right, push the accelerator to the floor and release the clutch slowly so not to stall. The tanker jumps forward, smashing into the rear of the white van that pushes it into a black 1963 Buick Riviera. I manage to hit the guardrail at thirty-two miles an hour at such an angle that the trailer behind me leans heavily to the right before rolling over the rail. I climb out the driver's side window and grab what's left of the guardrail as I hear the tanker truck splash into the Rio Grande River below. Too weak to pull myself onto the bridge, my plan is to hang on as long as possible like that Reverend guy, Gene Hackman did in the *Poseidon Adventure*.

Hand over hand, turning the large steam valve closed, allowing the others to escape. Eventually he tires and falls to his death in a pit of flames. Not a very happy ending for Hackman. I'm hanging about fifty feet above the water and see no sign of the truck except for an opened red umbrella floating on the surface. Losing feeling in my fingers, I promise myself I won't let go until after the explosion, which should be any second now. My thoughts begin to drift to Clare when I feel two hands grab me around the forearms and begin pulling me up. Looking up, I see a man with half a moustache, veins popping from his neck and forehead. Just when I think Diego's going to fall in the water with me, an explosion rips below my feet with such force that it violently pushes me up over the rail on top of him. Lying on our backs exhausted, we feel the bridge ripple and twist underneath us before everything gets eerily quiet. Thankful for still having all my limbs still attached, I lean sideways and glance at Diego, lying on his back. Thank God I'm on his good side - side that looks like he has a full moustache.

"Thanks Diego," I say softly.

"How many times I gotta tell ya - I'm too old for this shit," he says.

"Let's make this the last time," I respond.

We sit up against the damaged Black 63 Riviera, listening to all the sirens going off inside Mexico and the US. It's Diego who spots him first.

"Hey Joseph."

"Yeah Diego," I respond.

"Why's Kingman not wearing any pants?"

"Don't know. That's the way I found him, tied up behind the seats in the truck's cab. You'll have to ask him," I say.

"Not me Joseph – no way. I'll just ignore him."

"Good plan Diego. Let's just ignore him and find him something to wear."

As Kingman gets close, wearing only his "Stupid" t-shirt, Diego and I laugh. Thank God the shirt long is enough to cover his tighty whities. Unfortunately, when he lifts his arms and waves at us, that veil of privacy is gone. Deciding not to wave back, I help Diego to his feet, so we can meet Mike and Kingman and get back on land. As we start in their direction, two nearby explosions almost knock us off our feet. My guess is the other two border crossing bridges have been blown up. I get the feeling that what just happened here is minor. That thought passes quickly when I see a white and blue jet airliner that looks like Air Force One, flying slowly towards us. As it gets closer, we see it's missing a large piece of its right wing. Losing altitude, the plane dips to the right and plunges into the river less than a hundred yards from us. I apologize to Diego for breaking my promise as the four of us jump off the bridge into the water, and begin swimming for the floating airliner. Right now, I'm feeling too old for this shit.

CHAPTER 46

Saturday / 12:18 PM
Veterans International Bridge over the Rio Grande River
Border Crossing – Matamoros, Mexico / Brownsville, Texas

I hit the water swimming upstream towards the airliner, I can taste oil in my mouth and notice the floating plane moving in our direction. Doing simple math, I realize that even a one-winged plane will not make it under the buckled Veterans bridge. The others must have realized the same thing as I see them swim away from the airliner drifting towards us. Nearly exhausted and not a great swimmer, I'm unable to move out of the way. I'm close enough now to see people in the cockpit wearing yellow life preservers. I have no choice and brace myself as the remaining wing of the aircraft hits me, knocking the wind out of me. Getting a foothold on one of the pitot tubes found under the remaining wing, I'm able to pull myself onto it. Pitot tubes are normally used to measure airspeed, but work great as a step in an emergency.

I walk carefully towards the fuselage door, hoping not to lose my balance and fall back into the river. As I get about ten feet from the door, it opens and three men and two women in military style uniforms jump onto to the wing. I yell "hang on" and "get down" as the sun disappears and the plane starts to float under the bridge. Knowing the tail section won't make it; I lay flat on the wing. The others see me and do the same. We're back in the sun as the airplane's tail hits the bridge above us. The force knocks everyone into the water, except me. As I watch them float away wearing their yellow life preservers, I scream several times "Where's the President?" I get blank stares from them as several explosions go off on the Mexican side of the border.

The plane has stopped moving, but I can hear its metal tail grinding and pounding against the bridge. Staying in the center of the wing, I walk carefully back to the open door and peer inside. I yell out a "Hello!" and "Is anybody in here?" before going in. I'm standing in knee deep, oily water that sloshes against the walls as the plane twists and turns in the river's current while being held in place by the bridge. The emergency lighting is on, but only adds to the eeriness. The smell of jet fuel is so strong, my eyes begin to water and my throat feels like it's beginning to close up. Pulling my shirt up over my nose and face, I go quickly from room to room, looking for anyone left behind.

Remembering a book I read recently, Air Force One has about 4000 square feet of living space. Larger than most houses built today. With the floor below me flooded, I finish searching the immediate area and head up the stairs. Looking out through the cockpit window, I count three Navy Sikorsky Seahawk helicopters flying search and rescue patterns along the Rio Grande. Off to the side, I see Diego standing on the wing, waving his arms at me. He's yelling something and pointing up in the air behind him – behind the plane. Seconds later, I see him run to the end of the wing and belly flop into the water. Wow, that's gonna leave a mark.

I quickly leave the cockpit and head for the stairs, and then hear a loud crash on the airplane's roof, followed by the front lifting out of the water. Losing my balance, I slip down the stairs and fall into the oily water below. The airplane is now inverted about sixty degrees, so that I have to climb up and over furniture to get to the door. With the floor at such a drastic angle, I'm forced to wedge myself into the opening to keep from falling back inside. Looking out towards the tail, I see why we're sticking out of the water. The bridge collapsed on the back of Air Force One and drove it into the mud forcing us out of the water. I'm about twenty feet above the river and crawling on the wing is no longer an option due to its sharp angle. I notice a section of wing near me where it looks like some rivets have popped opening the skin about 2 feet. I'm hoping I can step out the door, get my feet into that two-foot hole, regain my balance and prepare for a swan dive that even Mark Spitz would be proud of.

Instead, my thought of being an Olympian Diver goes wrong when I slip on the oil covered wing, hit my head on the fuselage and fall into the water sideways. Floating on my back, gazing into the sun, I realize how tired I am. It's a struggle to move my arms and legs, but I manage to kick and paddle away from the President's inverted airplane. Deciding I've done enough, I float on my back, listening to sirens blaring on land from both countries. To block out the noise, I think of Clare and the time we spent together. Unfortunately, most of it revolved around chaos – always my fault. The best thing for her would be if I floated down the Rio Grande and into the Gulf of Mexico. Left for dead or maybe picked up by pirates, which eventually would lead to more chaos – my fault. Made to walk the plank, only to be saved by Captain Nemo.

As I plan my days, 2000 Leagues under the Sea, I'm awakened from my death bed stupor by the familiar thumping noise of two General Electric T7000 Engines attached to a Seahawk helicopter. The air from the rotors whips up the water as I see someone in bright red shorts jump out the door. As the body hits the water, I see another person jump out the same door. This person has long hair and a woman's shape. Listening to voices getting closer, I hear a man's voice, Mike's I think. The voice I recognize right away is Clare's. I smell strawberries as she places a tube or something under my arms. I feel her kiss my cheek, holding my hand as my body starts to lift out of the water towards the rotor blades whirling above my head.

I look around me and see smoke pouring out throughout the neighborhoods of both Matamoros and Brownsville. Lights flashing and fires burning. Looking down, I see the strange sight of Air Force One, sticking out of the Rio Grande, the Veterans International Bridge broken in two, lying on the tail section of the President's airplane. I've seen enough for today and close my eyes, only to open them when I get to the helicopter's door. I hear a familiar voice – loud and ringing over the thunderous noise of the Seahawk. My vision becomes cloudy as tears begin to fill my eyes. Her gloved hand reaches the cable and pulls me inside the chopper and hugs me like any mother would. She whispers softly in my ear.

"Joey honey, you had us worried sick. You can't do this to us – ya know. Disappearing, chasing bad guys – trying to save the world. Ya know Joey, sometimes the world doesn't wanna be saved. Most people know the consequences, but still act like assholes anyway. You know sweetie, get with the wrong people. Try to navigate through life the easy way. Can't do it Joey – just can't do it," she says.

"You're right Stella. I know you're right," I say as I slide along the floor, feeling dog tired.

I'm awakened as the smell of strawberries fills the cabin arousing my senses. Opening my eyes, I see Mike standing by the door in his bright red shorts and a faded "IT WAS AN ACCIDENT" NRBQ concert t-shirt. Clare sits next to me, wearing a bathing suit top that reminds me how good it is to be alive. She wraps a blanket around us, saying nothing. We lean against the back cabin wall facing the cockpit. I look to the right and see Mike give me the thumbs up sign. Glance to the left and make eye contact with Stella – she smiles. Looking straight ahead into the cockpit, the pilot turns slowly around and mouths, "I love you." After the shock passes, I say back "I love you too." My mother turns her head back towards the front and I look at Clare who says, "who knew?"

Mike passes out Bose Headphones so we can communicate with each other. Of course the first voice I hear is Diego's telling us to "hang on" as we jolt forward. In less than two minutes, we're over land, flying a few hundred feet above Brownsville. I hear Diego and Mom talking about landing in a parking lot. Within several minutes, we're circling a white two story building with a cement parking lot. In the middle, a man is holding a red umbrella. He waves and runs off to the side near the building. Thank God he's wearing pants. As mom lands the Sikorsky, I read the name off the front of the building – Saint Jerome's School.

CHAPTER 47

Saturday / 3:00 PM
Saint Jerome's School / Brownsville, Texas

Sitting in the opening of the helicopter's door with my arm around Clare, I realize I know very little about Brownsville, Texas. My limited knowledge includes one of my favorite Bob Dylan songs – Brownsville Girl. All I can remember from that song is some guy named Henry Porter, a pompadour and a man with no alibi. I hear Clare take a deep breath and turn towards me.

"Pedro's gone," she says softly. "Left this morning with relatives. Drove down yesterday from Austin. They seemed very loving, you know – nice. Pedro even remembered them from a visit they made to Mexico last year."

"I'm sorry, Clare," I say.

"He wanted to stay Joe, you know, to say goodbye," Clare says while wiping the tears from her eyes. "But we didn't know where you were, when you'd get here. Pedro's relatives had to get home; one of them had to get back to work on Monday. Maria maybe, I don't remember. Anyway, at least they managed to leave before the chaos."

"Clare, once this mess gets cleaned up and things get back to normal, we'll take a drive to Austin and visit," I say, my voice barely above a whisper. As those words leave my lips, I realize what I started.

"Normal Joe, really? What's normal? I'm not sure what that means anymore. I think it's been years since I knew. Working at Holy Spirit Mission, before I met you, children died in my arms from diseases I thought no longer existed. Mothers and fathers would drop off their babies to us for the day, and guess what Joe – many never came back! Thank God for John and Sharon Hammond, here at Jerome's, they'd help us find good and safe homes for these abandoned children."

"Clare, I'm sorry I didn't get a chance to say goodbye to Pedro. I promise, we'll go see him once this is over. We'll have a nice long visit."

"Joe, you don't get it. I'm happy that Pedro is back with family in the United States. He'll have new brothers and sisters to play with, tell him bedtime stories and walk him to school. He won't have to sneak into garbage dumps looking for food or wear shoes from someone around his age who recently died. I'm happy for him Joe, I really am," Clare finishes.

Our conversation ends as quickly as it began. I watch her as she carefully steps down from the helicopter and onto the lined cement parking lot. She pulls down the top of her wetsuit to her waist and adjusts her red bikini top. I watch her sit down, stretch her legs out in front of her, lean back and tilt her head towards the sun. Clare catches me staring at her, smiles and closes her eyes. I jump down to the ground, sidle up against her on the ground and feel the warm sun on my face.

I quickly doze off and find myself running into a room with bloody body parts scattered along the floor. Strapped into a dentist like chair is a woman I know. She has dark hair, is terribly thin with veins protruding from her arms. Her shirt is ripped open and I can see a thick electrical band wrapped around her chest, attached to the band are two heavy wires that terminate to a box of car batteries under the chair. An obese, sweaty old man with very few teeth looks over at me as he's about to inject some yellowish green fluid into her arm. I fire my weapon and hit him directly in the forehead. He smiles at me before hitting the floor dead. As I remove the wires and straps holding the woman to the chair, her name quickly comes to mind – Abby. Her eyes begin to open slowly and I hear her whisper "thank you."

I wake up in a lawn chair in the Texas sun, with my heart pounding and hands shaking. The Sikorsky Seahawk is still in the parking lot, doors wide open with no one in sight. I feel myself beginning to relax with my head bobbing until my eyes finally close, transporting me back to the torture room. Abby is trying to stand. I see Diego walk out of an adjacent room hunched over and upset. I move quickly past him into the room lit by one yellow bulb dangling from the ceiling. In the corner, near a metal sink, I see a bed frame with someone lying in the middle. As I get closer, I see the hands and legs are tied down, burn marks all over the naked body and blood oozing from open cuts. The yellow light begins to flicker and goes out. Feeling the stray light on my back from the other room, I lean in towards the body; move the long blond hair away from her face. Realizing I'm too late, I gently kiss Clare on the forehead. Her skin is cold. I take off my jacket and lay it across her. Knowing her death is my fault, an infinite sadness begins creeping into every part of me. I can't speak – say I'm sorry. My vision becomes blurry. I feel my throat tighten with bile permeating the inside of my mouth. As I'm about to throw up, the overhead light comes on, illuminating the twisted and burned body lying on the bed. This time something's different. The pale yellow light weakly brightens the facial features of Abby, not Clare. An acute feelings of déjà vu rips through my body as I wake up dry heaving, hands violently shaking.

Hearing a gentle voice and feeling an arm resting on my shoulders, I turn to see my mother sitting next to me. The pain etched into her face tells me that things are going to get a lot worse before they get better.

CHAPTER 48

Saturday / 6:30 PM
Saint Jerome's School / Brownsville, Texas

Alone and lying in bed, I stare up at the whirling ceiling fan that reminds me of rotor blades on a helicopter. I stand up gingerly, let my dizziness pass and walk over to a window. Focusing my eyes on the parking lot, I see several people in overalls and Navy caps clambering all over the Seahawk helicopter. The fact that it's still here reminds me of the governmental power my mother has, including skills I never knew, like flying a helicopter.

Beyond the lot, I see black smoke blanketing the neighborhoods. Hearing the water going off in the next room reminds me of Mike and Diego stripping off my clothes and holding me up under the cold shower a few hours ago. The bathroom door opens and I turn to see Clare wrapped in a thick red towel walking towards me. She opens her mouth to say something, stops and then tries again.

"Are you feeling better, Joe?" she asks, barely above a whisper. "The crisis, bombings, we couldn't find, any doctors to help you. The color, it's back in your face," she says moving closer.

"I feel good, I just need to brush my teeth with a wire brush and gargle with some mouthwash. I warn you to stay back."

I rush past her, into the bathroom and I find several boxes of sealed toothbrushes and toothpaste. I tear them open and begin a cleaning ritual that helps lift my mood and promises people won't make twisted faces when they're near me.

"We're going to war," Clare says leaning against the bathroom door looking away from me. "It's a mess Joe. Your mom says the President can't be found; he's missing. Does that mean he's dead, kidnapped, what?

167

Nobody seems to know. Tell me," yells Clare, "how does the President of the United States go missing? Every bridge connecting Mexico to the US has been blown up – all impassable. Including the one you were on. Mike said that even though you drove," Clare stops for a second. "I'm sorry, drove that truck over the railing into the water. Mike says the explosion buckled the supports underwater – and now it can hold just foot traffic only. Joe, why do you keep doing this? Taking chances that don't, I don't know, won't make a difference."

Her voice goes silent as she moves away from the door, back into the bedroom. Since I don't have an answer or even a witty comeback, I stay quiet. I rinse and spit for the final time and take a seat on the toilet lid. After listening to Clare rustling around in the other room for a few minutes, I hear a door open and close – no goodbye. A real sense of dread begins to settle in – deep down, wrapping itself around my soul. Feeling like a sumo wrestler is sitting on my chest; I drag myself over to the open window and take several deep breaths. I look out into the empty lot, this time I see the Sikorsky helicopter, door closed and void of any Navy personnel. What really catches my attention are two people standing in the far corner near a leafless tree under a red umbrella. I see Kingman's lips moving a mile a minute while the other person just stands there with hands moving around his head. The man is adjusting the mask that covers the side of his face.

I don't know if I should wave or let this moment pass. I decide to save this father/son moment for another time, get dressed and leave the room to look for Clare. I head down a brightly lit stairwell to the first floor. Stepping out into the hallway, I hear Mike's loud voice telling everyone: "Be quiet, the Vice President's about to speak." The volume on the television goes up as the voices go silent. I stop short of the room, lean up against the wall and slide to the ground. I feel my body tense up, then relax as I hear James Carlone, Deputy Director of the DEA, introduce the Vice President of the United States.

CHAPTER 49

Saturday / 8:00PM
Prime Time Vice Presidential Address

"Good Evening. At approximately 12:00 this afternoon, Central Standard Time, a series of coordinated bombings took place along the US – Mexican border. Over forty bridge crossings have been destroyed or deemed structurally impassable. The crossings include vehicular, railroad and foot bridges. The latest report puts the death toll at over six thousand, with close to ten thousand injured. I am confirming that an undetonated dirty bomb was found in the San Diego – Tijuana area. Several federal agencies headed by Homeland Security are on location, working to determine who was responsible and the best method for disposal. The latest report shows radiation levels are normal.

I regret to inform you that at approximately 12:30 this afternoon, Central Standard Time, the President of the United States was kidnapped at a small airport outside Brownsville, Texas. Early reports had stated the President was killed aboard Air Force One when it crashed into the Rio Grande River. This is untrue. We believe those who kidnapped the President are the same responsible for the coordinated bombings along the border. We also believe that everything points the responsibility for today's atrocities to the drug cartels. I'm sad to announce that our State Department has confirmed that Mexican President Arroyo was assassinated while getting into his car after making a speech in Matamoros Mexico. President Arroyo was a great friend and partner with the United States. God rest his soul.

I stand here before you tonight to let you know that the cartels have declared war on the good people of Mexico and United States. This will not stand! Every law agency on both sides of the border is now hunting down these murderous criminals to bring them to justice. We will not rest until our President is found safe and those responsible for killing Mexican President Arroyo are brought to justice.

I have asked our Secretary of State to submit a plan to me tomorrow, by ten o'clock Eastern Standard Time, that will bring close to fifty-thousand service men and women back home to the US to fight a war that's been simmering along our southern border for the last forty years. Speaking as the Vice President of the United States, I believe we can no longer be the police force for the entire world. We can no longer allow ourselves to be the paid mercenaries that in our own hearts, we detest. We need to take care of our own business, first and foremost.

As of six o'clock tonight, I have ordered the mobilization of our National Guard and Reserve in all fifty states. Along with our military and twenty-thousand border patrol agents, they will help secure our two-thousand-mile border with Mexico.

I want to make it very clear that we are not at war with the country of Mexico or its people. Our fight is with the drug cartels throughout Mexico, Central and South America. In hunting down these criminals, the United States of America does not, will not recognize the borders of any country harboring these terrorists. This is not a declaration of war, but rather a warning to either fully cooperate with us or stay out of our way. The United States has not been this provoked into conflict since December 7, 1941 with the attack on Pearl Harbor and the World Trade Center bombings on 9/11. I assure everyone that we will have the same outcome against our enemies – victory.

I ask those listening to me tonight to pray for the dead and the injured. Please know that we will find our President and bring those responsible for his kidnap to swift and final justice. Tonight, we must all look into our souls as Americans and set a new path forward that shuts down the supply of illegal drugs. Shouting across the aisle at one another has only forced us to take our eye off the ball of what's really important in our country. This afternoon, with strong bi-partisan support, I enacted a Presidential Executive Order to start bringing our soldiers home from around the world to where they are needed – right here.

I have assigned James Carlone, the Deputy Director of the DEA to coordinate all efforts between our federal agencies and military. His group was very instrumental in solving the recent terrorist attack in Washington and I expect him to use every resource possible to locate the President and bring the cartel members responsible to justice.

In closing, I must admit we were caught off guard. Snared in an elaborate trap set in motion and carried out by demons. Knowing that we paid a heavy price for our lack of vigilance, I make a promise that the United States will never again let down its guard against its enemies. I will not rest until we snare these devils and bring every one of them to trial for what they did on this day. May God bless and protect the people of Mexico and the United States of America. Thank you."

CHAPTER 50

Saturday / 8:50 PM
Saint Jerome's School / Brownsville, Texas

I rise to my feet and head towards the TV room, hearing my mother assure everyone that the President will be found – soon. She almost sounds like she knows something the rest of us don't. Was the President actually dead? Maybe the Vice President didn't want to tell the public – fear of panic maybe? I don't know. Thousands of people are dead, including the Mexican President. It's incredibly sad and scary stuff.

I enter the room to find my mom standing in a corner, talking on her cell phone. She looks over and signals me not to go anywhere. Clare is sitting in a bright yellow bean bag chair, rubbing Fina's ears. Mike's standing in a doorway under a red lit EXIT sign, typing something into his smartphone. He stops his slow one finger peck, nods and goes back to typing. I sit next to Clare on the carpeted floor, look at her face and tell she's quite worried - like the rest of us.

"I'm sorry about before," I say quietly. "I know I've turned your world upside down. Everything you had, you knew, is gone because of me. But I have to tell ya, you know be honest, if none of this happened, I'd never have met you. I know it's strange, saying all this, but, but something did come out of this – you. Clare, if you tell me right now it's over – you and me, I'll certainly understand. Just don't be surprised if I still manage a smile, maybe just a small one, but still a smile. That's because I fell in love with you. The first time I saw you at the Mexico City Airport."

"Stop it Joe, please stop," Clare says softly. "I'm scared Joe, really scared."

"We're all scared," I reply. "But what's."

"Stop, quiet, please let me finish," she says. "I know none of this is your fault. Like the Vice President said, this war's been simmering under the surface for a long time. When I came to Mexico a few years back – it was there –you could feel it. But, I chose to ignore it. You know Joe; I told you we took food, clothes, and all kinds of supplies from the cartels. All to keep Holy Spirit Mission going, we had little money coming in. It was a way for us to keep our mouths shut. In this way, I guess, I accepted bribes – blood money."

"Guilt Clare - we all feel it. Unless we stick our head in the sand, we've all done something. Something we're not proud of. I'm racked with guilt about what I put you through – put Mike through."

"We'll get through this. Got our trip to visit Pedro," she says.

Before I have a chance to respond, the power goes out. The air raid horn starts blaring. I scramble for her hand as a powerful explosion is felt outside the building, blowing out the windows in the hallway. The emergency lighting quickly comes on as we pick ourselves up off the floor.

"Everybody ok?" yells Mike, standing crookedly on a flipped couch clicking the safety off his Colt M1911. "Nobody leave the room! They may be waiting outside for us!"

"He's right," yells Mom, as she runs into the room with Diego. "Everybody get down on the floor! I just saw somebody coming in through a hole in the wall."

Pulling the Glock from the small of my back, I fire off two shots at a large man running into the room carrying an Uzi. He hits the ground like a sack of flour. Diego grabs the Uzi lying on the floor, waiting for the assault. Thankfully, it's one and done - lone wolf.

"Everybody listen!" yells Mom. "Grab what you can and meet at the helicopter in thirty minutes. Stella and I have to check on a friend. Hey, where's Kingman? Anybody know where Kingman is?"

"Saw him in the parking lot about an hour ago," I reply. "He was talking to Dad, Tomas, you know the guy with the mask."

Mom and Diego give me a strange look as Clare and I run past them.

"Tomas is here?" says Diego. "How can that be – he's injured. Sure it was him?"

"Yeah Diego, I'm sure."

CHAPTER 51

Saturday / 9:38 PM
Brownsville, Texas

As instructed, we meet in the parking lot by the Seahawk. To my surprise, it's still there and most importantly, in one piece. Mike's inside with Clare. I'm outside, nervously guarding the helicopter waiting for Mom, Stella and Diego. The power's still out and the surrounding area is drenched in thick blackness, made worse by smoke drifting in the wind. The pungent odor reminds me of the death and destruction your eyes can't always see. I'm surprised how quiet it is – peaceful really. Based on what the Vice President said, I thought we'd see signs of the National Guard in the streets. As I climb aboard the chopper behind Fina, my phone begins to vibrate. Checking the screen, I see it's Carlone calling.

"Hello Jim," I say. "Heard you on TV tonight. Mike said that striped shirt you were wearing made you look thinner."

"You guys alright?" he asks.

"I think so Jim – better than many."

"Still in Brownsville?"

"Yeah, still here. The school we were in was bombed, and then attacked by a lone wolf. It was a small battle, but the good guys won and nobody's hurt."

"Joe, Brownsville is not safe. Especially for anybody that looks military."

"Do you think having a Navy helicopter parked in the middle of a parking lot gives us away?" I nervously laugh.

"Caroline needs to fly you out. The Calvary won't be getting there till late tomorrow. Your mom needs to fly you north – away from the border."

"I'll tell her as soon as she gets here," I reply. "Jim, any word on the President?"

"Not yet," he says, sadly. "We last saw him at a private airfield outside Brownsville. Someone on the ground said they saw him being forcibly escorted onto a white Beechcraft King Air. Oh and Joe, guess the logo painted on the tail?"

"It must be that picture I see every time I close my eyes to try and sleep," I say. "White tiger with black stripes and feet?"

"You guessed it! If what's happened so far is not enough, we're expecting the stock market to drop to new lows when it opens on Monday. If the overseas markets are any indication of what's to come, financial panic may be the phrase of the day."

"Didn't know Mexico played such a big role in the world economy," I say.

"It goes way beyond that. Like it or not, the United States of America was attacked by Mexico. This is Pearl Harbor and 9/11 all over again. A sleeping giant caught off guard – that's us buddy – scary stuff. This underground war with the cartels has been going on since the early 1980's. Nobody knows this better than you and your mom. Your grandfather was killed by these bastards in '82 – same day you were born," he says voice trailing off into a dead silence.

"Still there Jim?" I ask, thinking we've been disconnected.

"I'm here Joe – sorry. Just tired I guess."

"Maybe sick and tired. You and I almost got killed several times over the last few months by the cartels. That's bound to put anyone on edge."

"It's more than that. Look at us – the United States. We have some type of military presence in many countries around the world under the guise of protecting our interest overseas. I don't even understand what that means anymore. When you pull out a magnifying glass and read the fine print, it seems like were protecting every else's interest except our own."

"Both sides of the aisle argued for years about bringing troops home," I say. "Unfortunately, it looks like it took the border disaster to make it happen. The Vice President was right to start the process. She made a tough decision, but one that I think most Americans will agree with – especially now."

175

"I've got a call coming in. Get that chopper in the air and head northwest towards San Antonio and Lackland Air Force Base. I'll get you slotted in. Call me when you land. Bye."

I slip the phone back into my pocket and look around the cabin. I see Clare dozing off under a blue Navy blanket and Mike sound asleep in the co-pilot's chair with Fina on his lap. Moving quietly through the cabin, I'm suddenly startled by someone outside banging on the door. Pointing the Glock at the window in my right hand and clicking on the flashlight in my left hand, I see Diego leaning against the door with blood on his face. Sliding the door open, his head falls onto the floor and garbled words pour from his mouth.

"They're go…. gone – taken……. kid………napped," Diego says spitting out blood. Teeth? "We went to check on a friend – Stella's friend, from the roller skating days. Trap, it was a trap. You see, Stella got a call, we went with her. Got to the house, friend's dead on kitchen floor. Several men burst out from another room, grabbed us, and throw us in a white minivan. After a mile or so, they open the door; throw me out while the van's still moving. Ran back here – fast as I could."

"Where's Mom!" I shout. "Where is she?"

"With Stella," Diego shouts while spitting out more blood on the ground. "Sorry Joe, couldn't save them. Tried, but couldn't."

The four of us talk about what to do as Fina runs past me and leaps out of the cabin. We all agree that we must get outta here. Since my limited flight training consists of only takeoffs and not landing in a helicopter, we decide to take a dark green 1973 Buick Riviera parked in the lot under a basketball hoop. Mike finds the keys under the seat and fires it up. The V8 455cc four-barrel carbureted engine reminds us that power is very loud when there's no muffler. Mike shuts it down immediately as we look for another vehicle. As we're about to settle on a black Ford Econoline, My iPhone begins to vibrate. Seeing its Jim Carlone I answer it right away.

"Joe, where's your mother? I received an emergency alert from your mother's phone. The tracking mechanism is telling us she's moving across the river towards Mexico. If she's not in the air, she must be on a boat or something. Don't cross the Rio Grande into Mexico! It's not safe, you must go north!"

"Jim, Mom and Stella have been taken!" I yell into the phone. "We're still on the ground. Going to look for them right now."

I throw the phone to Mike and tell everyone to get in the helicopter right away. I jump in the pilot seat with Mike strapping in next to me.

"Diego, Clare, grab Fina - fasten your seatbelts," I yell as Mike begins to fire up the engines. "According to Jim, Mom just activated the emergency alert on her cell phone. Right now she's crossing the Rio Grande into Mexico."

I smell strawberries as Clare quickly leans over and kisses me on the cheek for "luck." As I wait for her to strap in, I ask Mike a very important question.

"You know how to land this thing, right?" I say, staring at the instrument panel.

"I think so," he says. "It's like riding a bike, except I flunked out due to my daily bout of airsickness. Everybody said, 'you'll get used to it.' Guess what - I didn't."

It's funny how my few lessons in a helicopter were all about taking off. Mike's lessons were landing. I think going forward may be our biggest problem. As Mike is yelling something off a checklist he found in one of the compartments, I see a black Volvo station wagon pull into the lot — lights off. Watching it move closer to the Sikorsky, I unfasten my belts; take the Glock from my bag between the seats and move towards the cabin door. Looking through a cabin window, I see a head pop into view. The face is wearing glasses, overly tan with a Loctite Racing hat on his head. He gives me a wave and I slide the door open with gun in hand.

"Joe, let him in," yells Clare. "That's John, John Hammond, he and his wife Sharon manage the School."

"John," I say pulling him inside. "Sorry about what happened to your building! Somebody was using it for target practice."

"With all that's been going on, I'm just glad you're all okay," he replies.

"John, hey John, where's Sharon?" Clare says loudly over the revving engines.

"She went up to her sister's in Florida a few days ago — missed all this craziness. I was out buying supplies this morning for new arrivals on

177

Monday when the attack happened. Took me close to ten hours to go less than forty miles – road blocks."

"We're heading to Mexico to pick up my mom and her best friend. Might be a bit dangerous," I say quickly.

"I'll stay behind," he says. "I'm expecting 11 children here on Monday. Looks like I need the time to clean up. Anyway, if Sharon comes home to find me missing it might cause a stir."

"John, you sure you'll be alright?" I ask.

"Don't worry about me, I'll be fine," he replies.

"Joe, Mr. Hammond was in the CIA for over twenty years, he's got skills," says Diego, grimacing. "You know – connections. He'll be ok!"

"Okay then John, we'll check on you later." I shoot back – "Be safe!"

"You too," he replies as he steps to the ground, crouching away from the cabin.

"Ok everybody, we're off to Mexico for a little rescue. I'd buckle in real tight if I were you," I shout.

"Our pilots have less than twenty hours of flight instruction between them," Clare says slowly with wide eyes.

"The last time I flew with Joe, we crashed into a river," Diego says smiling at Clare. "That helicopter was much smaller and less sophisticated than this one. Joe rode the severely damaged aircraft over some pretty wild waterfalls."

"You're Joseph Dustan?" Clare asks sarcastically. "Son of Caroline Dustan?"

"Yes ma'am, at your service," I say winking at her. "Sit back and enjoy the ride."

CHAPTER 52

Sunday / 12:10 AM
Skies over Brownsville, Texas

Listening to Mike read take-off instructions in the cockpit was difficult due to all the nervous chatter in the cabin. Clipping a tree with the rotor blades probably didn't help calm any fears. Mike hands me a pair of Bose headphones and we're finally able to communicate without hearing all the "oh no's, he's gonna hit it! This is a bad idea" coming from the crew in the back.

"Okay Joe, I dumped your mom's coordinates from your iPhone into the helicopter's tracking computer, or whatever's it called. See that little red dot blinking at about the three o'clock position – head for it," Mike says, adjusting some important looking knobs. "That's your mom. It's less than twenty miles, I think."

"Thanks buddy; we'll need some sort of a plan."

"Hey Joe, pull up!" Mike screams, causing me to rip off my headphones. "Tell me you see that radio tower!"

"Got it Mike!" I yell unconvincingly. "Just getting use to the controls!"

Flying over Brownsville at night reveals a dying city. As we get closer to the Rio Grande; we see lines of fires stretching along the river banks for miles on both sides of the border. The sight is powerfully sad. The crew is speechless. The rhythmic thumping of rotor blades reinforces the fact that this is not a dream.

"It stopped," says Mike pointing at the computer console. "The blinking red light. Got a plan?"

"Almost – still working on it," I say looking back into the cabin at Clare, her beautiful blue eyes focused outside the cabin window.

179

"Okay it's moving again," says Mike. "According to the GPS, they're on land moving south at about thirty miles an hour."

The Sikorsky Seahawk helicopter breaks out over the Rio Grande at a hundred and fifty miles an hour, rocketing past a half sunken fishing trawler. Somebody on deck fires off a flare gun as I take a hard right around it.

"Stay away from the boat!" Mike yells.

"Got it, just need to come around it," I say loudly pointing at the moving map in front of us. "See that main road going into Matamoros? We were on it yesterday morning heading to Brownsville. I don't remember high electrical poles or obstructions."

"It's running a few miles parallel to the road your mom is on," Mike says.

"I wanna get in front of them – cut 'em off," I say jerking my head back around to check on the crew. Diego picks his head up out of the military issued barf bag long enough to give me a worried smile.

I swing the Seahawk around to the left and align us with the street. We're about thirty feet off the ground, running at over a hundred miles per hour tearing the branches off the trees in this incredible machine. With one eye on the blinking red target, I maneuver the helicopter hard to the left taking us down a dark side road in an effort to intercept our target. The lack of flight training and narrow streets cause me to zig zag my flight pattern.

"In two miles, take a hard right heading south," Mike says. "Five miles down that road is a large shopping center. With any luck, we land this thing in the parking lot and wait a few minutes for Caroline's vehicle to come by."

"Got it Mike," I yell, taking the turn heading for the lot. Before I have a chance to say anything, we hear a loud crashing noise and feel the chopper pitch down in the back.

"Joe," Clare screams from her seat peering out the window. "We have a streetlight following us – I mean attached to us."

I feel extra weight through the controls that moves the Seahawk a bit sideways, before I do my best to straighten it.

"Mike, Joe, Clare's right," yells Diego standing behind our seats. "Some sort of cable was wrapped was around the landing gear, but now it's gone!"

"Sit down Diego!" screams Mike. "Buckle up — we're landing in three minutes.

"Hold on everybody!" I yell at the top of my lungs turning my head to the crew. Clare gives me a calm smile I'll never forget. At this very moment I know one thing for sure. This beautiful woman trusts me just a little too much.

Parking lot in sight, I sloppily slow down the Seahawk, sending a violent shudder through her that only a Sikorsky designed in Connecticut could survive. Feeling a little bit out of control, I swing the bird in several large circles ten feet off the ground.

"Mike, it's all yours," I shout. "Put us on the ground — please!"

He gently takes over the controls, starts a consistent hover while lowering the engine's rpm's. Watching the blinking red dot on the screen get closer, I wipe the beads of sweat from Mike's forehead as he places the Seahawk on the ground without even a bump. Damn show-off.

CHAPTER 53

Sunday / 12:52 AM
Matamoros, Mexico

The decision is made to keep Diego with the chopper to guard it while Mike, Clare and I hit the pavement, trying to intercept the vehicle with Mom and Stella in it. I wanted to keep Clare with Diego in the helicopter, but her protests ate away at precious time. I hand the loaded sawed off shotgun to her and the three us run through the dark parking lot, dodging potholes towards the main road. As we take up positions behind a candy apple red 1963 Chevy Impala, my iPhone starts buzzing in my shirt pocket. Carlone's on the line.

"Joe, just spoke to Diego and he told me you're going to intercept the vehicle –with Caroline and Stella. I wanted to let you know that it's not one vehicle, but two. One of the space satellites snapped close to one hundred pictures. The lead vehicle is white, looks like one of those armored cars, like a Brinks truck. The second vehicle is a red late model Toyota truck, Tundra we think."

"Thanks Jim," I reply. "Hang on - something coming up the road. Only the parking lights are on."

"You got a plan?" Jim says.

"No, but Mike promised to let me know once he had one. Gotta go, call you back," I yell into the phone as Clare grabs my hand.

"Stay behind the car Clare – please," I say letting go of her hand.

"Mike, stay here, I'm gonna cross the street," I say clicking the safety off my Glock.

Dashing out from behind the car, I see the dim lights of the vehicle getting closer. As I'm about to cross the road, I trip on something that stops me in my tracks. Getting up, I start to run, but realize it's too late.

The slowing armored vehicle passes me as I crouch down in an attempt to fire off a few shots – take out a tire or two. I stop at the last second when I see someone standing on the back bumper holding onto the door handle with one hand. In his other hand, he's holding an open red umbrella. While I admit this is truly bizarre, the person I make eye contact with in the second vehicle restores my belief in miracles. We both share a "what the hell minute" before the brakes on the Red Tundra start screeching, bringing the truck to a stop. The driver side door opens and within seconds Ensign Kelly Rogers is standing with us in the middle of the road.

"Kelly!" yells Clare as she runs and hugs her.

"Ensign Rogers, can you fly a helicopter – a Sikorsky Seahawk?" I say.

"Yes sir, went to Navel Flight School right after High School," she replies. "Why you got one?" she says looking around.

"Clare, please take Ensign Rogers to the helicopter," I spurt out. "You can follow us from the air. Mike and I are going after mom and Stella. Oh yeah, and Kingman."

"Okay Joe," Clare replies, "but be careful!"

"I will - love you. Glad you're okay Rogers!"

"Me too Joe, thanks. You all heard about the President."

"Yeah," we all chime in.

"Might be a chance that the armored car we're following could lead us to him," Rogers says.

"Okay, let's go," I shout.

"I'll drive," Mike says climbing into the driver's seat.

Running over to the passenger side of the truck, I see Clare and Rogers moving quickly through the parking lot, talking as they go. It's like they'd been friends all their lives. Mike now has the Toyota going up over a hundred miles an hour down an unlit, poorly paved road. I quickly throw on my seat belt as we slow for an upcoming intersection. Noticing two Matamoros police cars parked off to the side, Mike slows the vehicle down to whatever he thinks the speed limit might be. Unfortunately, his guess is wrong and both cop cars pull a u-turn behind us and begin chase. Mike looks over at me and smiles, pushes the accelerator to the floor, just as the back cabin window is blown out. As we both know, that kind of changes things.

CHAPTER 54

Sunday / 1:33 AM
Matamoros, Mexico

From the air this must look like something you'd see in a movie. A white double axle Brinks truck with a guy holding an umbrella being pursued by a red Toyota truck followed by two police cars with lights flashing and sirens blaring. Even though I can't see it, I hear the Sikorsky helicopter coming up behind us overhead. The wind noise inside the truck is loud due to our missing rear window and speeds close to a hundred. Mike and I can't believe that Kingman is still able to hold on to the loading door of the Brinks truck. At times, the crazy Englishman even manages to wave. The shooting from the police continues behind us. I squeeze off a few rounds in their direction, but it doesn't slow them down.

"What the heck is he doing now?" Mike yells. "Looks like he's waving us off to the side or something."

"I don't know Mike," I shout back. "Aw darn, there goes his umbrella. He dropped his umbrella."

"He dropped it on purpose!" Mike screams. "Now I know why he's waving us off to the side."

Immediately after Kingman lets go of the umbrella, he reaches inside his coat and pulls out a very big shiny gun – 44 Magnum I think.

"Look at Kingman, thinks he's Clint Eastwood in those old Dirty Harry movies," I shout. "Jeez, I love those movies!"

Mike jerks the steering wheel over to the right, almost clipping a parked car. The two police cars behind react too slowly as Kingman fires off several shots, causing the lead car to careen out of control up on two wheels before flipping onto its roof, sliding down the road in a shower of sparks. As the second car regains control, someone leans out the passenger

184

side window and shoots at Kingman, standing on the Brinks bumper. Mike quickly realigns the Tundra behind the Brinks, protecting Kingman from the bullets that are now hitting us. Out of rounds, I climb into the back and search under the seat for something I can use as a weapon. Careful of the shards of glass, I find a few empty bags of fast food, coffee cups, old newspapers, first aid kit and a package of road flares. As I begin to formulate a plan, my phone begins vibrating in my pocket. It's Clare; I answer right away.

"Can you hear me?"

"No!" I scream into the phone. "Talk louder!"

"Joe, it's me – Clare," she blares. "Kelly says pull over on the count of three! Did you get that? On three!"

"Hang on Clare," I yell jumping back into the front seat.

"Mike, when I say pull off to the side, do it!" I shout.

"Got it Joe, tell me when!" he replies quickly.

"Go ahead Clare. Start counting when ready!"

After what seems like a lifetime, I hear Clare yell three. I scream "Now!" and Mike steers quickly off to the side. Within seconds, the police car passes and Mike gives them a thumbs up sign. The Tundra is lit up as a missile whooshes past us into the police car, exploding into a large fireball. Mike pulls back in behind the Brinks truck, and I hear Clare back on the cell phone.

"You guys okay?"

"We're fine, thanks!" I reply.

"Look, Kelly says we need gas for the helicopter. Says there's an aircraft carrier about ten miles off the coast we can refuel at. Will you boys be okay without us for about an hour? We hate to leave you, but we have no choice."

"Okay Clare, we have about three quarters of a tank of gas and we still have no idea where the Brinks is heading or stopping for that matter," I say.

"Be careful - we'll be back soon. Kelly mentioned something about reinforcements. She's been speaking to someone on the ship we're heading to."

"See you soon, then Clare."

The line goes dead and we see the Seahawk's flashing strobes evaporate into the horizon. Nodding at Mike, we notice the Brinks is beginning to slow down in front of us. After five minutes, it stops in the middle of the road. We watch Kingman jump off the back and run towards the front. Mike maneuvers the Tundra around a large pothole and comes to a stop across the street in a dirt parking lot, next to what looks like an old, abandoned railroad station. I grab the flares from the back seat, tuck them into my jacket pocket and we start walking slowly across the street towards the back of the parked Brinks. We drop to the ground when we see two people leap from the cab and begin running in the opposite direction, being pursued by Kingman. Mike and I run over to the truck and peer inside through the small barred, window using the light off my iPhone. I think I see two, maybe three people lying on the floor with bare feet sticking out from under a grey blanket. As I try to open the rear door, Mike reappears and tells me to get away from the truck.

"Joe, the Brinks is parked on railroad tracks" Mike says. "Hear that? I think a train's coming - listen!"

"Can't Mike, can't do it," I reply, pausing a sec to hear the blaring horn of a locomotive. "Mom and Stella may be in back – we need to get them out. You, you go ahead - get away. I need to find the key or something to open this damn door."

"Joe, I'm begging ya," Mike says. "You know as good as I do that those two assholes that jumped from the cab and ran away did so for a specific reason – they knew when the train was coming through town."

Before I have chance to reply, we see Kingman break out of the woods running at full speed towards us, screaming at the top of his lungs.

"Get away from the bloody truck! I see lights – moving fast towards us!"

The sight of his uncoordinated long legs almost tripping over each other catches me off guard. He grabs my right arm and forcefully pulls me away from the truck, dragging me across the roadway. I manage to break free just in time for Mike to pull me back towards the abandoned rail station. When we reach the Tundra, I hear the explosion from the collision and see the Brinks truck lift several feet off the ground and fall back onto the tracks on its side in a ball of flames. The black locomotive is showered

186

in sparks and flames, pushing the Brinks down the tracks at a high rate of speed.

"Watch out!" Mike yells as one of the tires from the Armored Car lands less than ten feet from us. I jump up, chasing the train, hoping for another miracle. A series of high pitched screeching forces me to cover my ears and glance quickly behind me. I thought I'd seen just about everything, but what's happening behind me is something totally new. Knowing now that one miracle won't be enough; I desperately change direction and sprint away from the tracks.

"Joe stop – get your bloody ass back here!" Kingman screams. "Your mom's phone – I have it. You guys tracked me, followed me. She let me use it back at the school!"

CHAPTER 55

Sunday / 2:20 AM
Outside Matamoros, Mexico

The idea of running back to the abandoned rail station and meeting up with Mike and Kingman is dramatically altered when I see an expansive wall of freight cars lifting off the tracks. The cars whipping through the air remind me of toys being hurled with such force they rip away from each other, eventually sliding along the ground taking out anything in their path. I watch in horror as several train cars, still hitched, violently exit the tracks and roll over the wooden and brick constructed train station like it wasn't even there. I see the red hood of the Toyota under a tanker rail car with a large gash on the side, emptying its liquid contents on the ground. The smell of gasoline is so strong; I swear I can taste it. I yell for Mike and Kingman several times before a series of explosions go off, knocking me to the ground.

Face down and feeling the intense heat of the fires, I manage to get up on my knees. I look over to where the train station once was, and see walls of flames ten stories high with thick black smoke that seems to be emanating from everywhere. I cover my mouth with a piece of my jacket and run along the fire perimeter, yelling for my friends. I pull out my iPhone; hit Mike's number - no answer. After several attempts, I try to get hold of Clare – no answer. Trekking up a small hill, I see what looks like miles of derailed train cars burning and scattered throughout the valley.

Navigating through overturned freight cars and ejected cargo, I take out my compact LED flashlight and start searching for the locomotive. My Timex watch beeps to inform me that it's 3:00 in the morning. Walking in near darkness, stepping over open boxes of lettuce, diapers, car alternators and Pepsi soda cans, I feel a severe level of exhaustion kicking in. I plod on towards the front of the train, surprised to see the main locomotive – first engine, still on the track all by itself. No Brinks truck anywhere. I climb up the ladder of the locomotive into the cabin and find no signs of life. Not knowing much about trains, I determine that all power to the engine was shut down. My guess is that the Engineers probably shut it down and bailed out prior to hitting the Brinks.

I scour around inside the locomotive and find a large steel cabinet that has two cases of bottled water, various tools, 2-way radios, bags of Doritos and three Sig Sauer P290 pistols along with several boxes of bullets. I put one of the pistols in my pocket along with a handful of bullets. I stow the other two inside a tool box. Grabbing two bottles of water, I take a cushion off one of the chairs and carefully throw it up on the locomotive's roof. Climbing slowly up the ladder onto the roof, I sit down and drink the two bottles of water. Watching the fires burning in the distance, I lie down and lay my head on the cushion. I'm thankful for the warm night as my mind drifts off to thoughts of Mom and Stella, and now Mike and Kingman. I hear Mom making that great speech at my college graduation. I watch Stella race around the track on eight wheels during her roller derby days. I see them hold each other when Stella finds out her daughter's been murdered. A two-word text from Mike – "We're okay," followed by my own text – "Me too," abruptly ends the rush of adrenalin flowing through my system. It's at this point that I'm overcome with total exhaustion and fall into a deep sleep.

CHAPTER 56
Sunday / 6:35 AM
Outside Matamoros, Mexico

Waking up to the sounds of deep thumping rotor blades seems to be the norm for me lately. Being on the roof of a train's locomotive is not. I look off to the horizon and count six Boeing AH-64 Army Apache helicopters heading south flying a hundred feet over the treetops. Realizing they're flying too fast in the opposite direction to have any interest in me, I reach into my backpack and pull out my cell phone, power it up and view four calls from Clare and two from Mike. I'm relieved to see the last call from Mike was less than an hour ago. I hit the redial, get his voicemail and leave a message. Grabbing a few containers of bottled water, I climb down the ladder of the locomotive. I take a small towel out of my pack and do my best to wash my face, followed by meticulous teeth brushing. Reaching into my pack, I grab the last clean t-shirt, a gift from my mother, Library of Congress written on the front. I think of the many hours I spent with my mom in that place both as a child and adult. Her happiest days are spent working in that library complex. My pleasant memories are cut short when I hear footsteps behind me. Before I have a chance to turn around, a familiar voice blares out the one thing I need to hear.

"She's not dead you know – Stella either. They've been taken alright, but still alive," Kingman says as I turn around. "You heard me say they weren't in the Brinks."

"How do you know?"

"Your father told me, Tomas or whoever that guy with the mask is to you. You see Joe, your mom and Stella were never in that Brinks truck. In the truck were friends, British intelligence officers – like me."

190

"I'm sorry Kingman," I reply sadly. "So you had Mom's phone. It was being tracked by GPS – you were on the boat and the Brinks truck."

"Yeah, I borrowed it back at the school. My friends were already dead, bloody killed prior and thrown in the armored car after landing in Mexico. Shot like animals on the boat. I saw it with my own two eyes, but couldn't do a bloody thing about it. I was hiding on the dock and jumped in the boat at the last second as it pulled away."

"What were you doing riding on the back of the Brinks?"

"Don't think I know. Seemed like a good idea at the time. You know – chums and all."

"Again, sorry about your friends," I say. "Have you seen Mike?"

"Yeah, he's here. We split up looking for you," he says climbing the ladder into the locomotive. "What a beauty. My ole pop would have loved this."

I lose sight of Kingman when he goes inside the cabin. I decide to look for Mike among the overturned rail cars; I leave a message for Clare on her cell phone and yell to Kingman "I'll be right back." Walking through the debris field, I find it's impossible to walk in a straight line for any length of time because I'm either going around or climbing over something to reach a destination point I've picked out in front of me. I see people picking through the railcars, filling sacks with anything found. Coming out from behind one of the cars, I see Mike walking with two small children who also are picking up stuff off the ground. He sees me, waves, and begins heading slowly in my direction with the children close behind. Mike stops every few seconds or so, picks up something off the ground and puts it in a brown sack one of the kids is carrying.

"I'm so glad to see you!" Mike yells across the field. "But, I knew you'd make it – you always do! Did you see Kingman?"

"Yeah, he's on the train – in the locomotive," I reply, pointing down the track.

Mike grabs a few more items off the ground before reaching me. He drops the items in the bag, says something in Spanish to the children and they begin to move in the opposite direction.

"Poor kids," Mike says. "Some of the rail cars rolled over the houses in their neighborhood – including those two. Killed a sister, father missing

191

and the mother told them to go out and scavenge anything from the train. They seem all too used to this kind of stuff. It's sad, ya know?"

"Yeah, unfortunately I do know – from meeting Clare. She was the major caretaker for many children when she worked at Holy Spirit Mission. Clare understood their sadness and tried every day to make them feel special."

"Sorry we got split up earlier this morning," Mike says. "When Kingman and I saw that train derailing and the rail cars heading in our direction, we just ran. I'm sure he told you who was in the back of the Brinks."

"He did."

"Did he tell you about Tomas? What he said?"

"He mentioned that Mom and Stella were kidnapped – not in the Brinks, that's it."

"Listen, Tomas told Kingman they're being held at a monastery in a magic town. Whatever the heck that means."

"Magic town?'" I say.

"Yup, magic town," Mike replies. "That Kingman's a strange guy, but leads an interesting life. He told me he can trace his bloodline back to royalty. Has papers, you know, like a purebred dog or something. Oh and his first name is Charles."

"Sounds like a prince of a guy," I grumble back.

Before Mike gets a chance to reply, we hear a series of loud booms and backfires coming from the tracks ahead. Running back towards the locomotive, we see a large plume of black smoke followed by five long blasts of a horn –a train horn maybe?

"Hey Joe, did Kingman tell you what his dad did for living back in England?" Mike asks breathing heavy.

"No - no idea." I say panting.

"He was an engineer." Mike replies

"What, electrical, mechanical, aerospace?"

"Try train engineer," Mike says. "Working on the railroad type of stuff. Told me he went on train trips with his dad during summer breaks from school. Said it was the best time of his life. Father used to let him drive the train and everything!"

"Can you believe we're boarding a train being driven by Choo Choo Charlie?" I yell back to Mike.

"I'd say there's still good and plenty – to worry about," Mike says busting himself up referring to the old Good and Plenty candy commercials still found on YouTube.

We leap onto the slow-moving train, make our way up the ladder and see Kingman, Choo Choo Charlie, hanging out the window, brandishing a huge smile while wiping the tears from his eyes. I'm not sure if it's from the happy memories of his dad, sad thoughts of his murdered friends, or both. Mike and I climb up on the roof of the mighty locomotive as Kingman continues to increase her speed over the tracks that lead somewhere. We decide to give Kingman his nostalgic moment before we quiz him about our destination. I get the feeling that our next stop will be some place called Magic Town. I don't care where we go as long as it takes me to mom and Stella as quickly as possible. I pull my vibrating iPhone out of my pocket and see Clare's calling.

"Clare – I can't hear you! Can you speak - talk louder," I yell into the phone climbing down the ladder back into the cab. "What? Hang on!"

"Sorry, Clare – back, I'm back," replying in a more normal tone.

"Joe, is that a train's whistle I hear in the background?"

"Oh yeah, that's what it is," I reply quickly watching Kingman adjusting large knobs on some type of control panel. "Don't worry though; Choo Choo Charlie Kingman is at the controls."

"Charlie Choo who?" Clare yells into the phone. "What are you talking about?"

"It's Kingman; he's driving the train – actually just the locomotive. Learned from his dad when he was a kid – or something like that. Tell ya later."

"Can't wait to hear all about it," says Clare.

"Where are you?"

"Getting ready to find you," she replies. "Just refueled the helicopter on a carrier off the coast of Brownsville - almost had to give it up. We called Jim Carlone, explained the situation. He put us on hold for close to an hour – said the chopper was ours for forty-eight hours. Jim told us the

VP – President – whoever had to approve it. Hang on; Kelly's saying something – one sec."

Waiting for Clare, I poke my head outside the cabin window and follow the line of track that turns off to the right about a mile ahead. As we get closer to the bend, I view an expansive bridge that shoots across a deep valley disappearing into the side of a mountain. Seeing spots, I remove my sunglasses and clean them with my shirt. Unfortunately, even with my shades off, the spots are still there and now moving on the tracks in front of us.

"Joe, Joe, are you still there?" Clare's voice booms through the phone. "Turn on the tracker, wait, Kelly says turn on your beacon, sorry, tracker beacon on your cell phone. Can you hear me? Joe are you there? We'll come find you - pick you up"

"Sorry Clare – got it," I reply quickly. "Turning beacon on – now!"

"People on the track! People on the track!" Mike yells from above, hanging upside down, head popping in through the cabin window. "Gotta stop Kingman! You know how to stop this thing?"

"Get in you bloody fool!" Kingman screams back. "Of course I know how to stop this thing. Hang on lads, this is gonna be close!"

Pulling Mike inside the cabin, I watch Kingman's hands moving switches, hitting buttons and talking to himself. I realize he just finished saying a prayer, since his silence is followed by the sign of the cross. I feel the locomotive dip and hear loud rhythmic clacking below us as we break out over the bridge. Looking down, outside the open cabin window, I struggle to find the bottom of the canyon and get a sense of flying. Moving back inside, I feel the train begin to slow and watch Mike sound the horn to alert those ahead walking on the tracks. Our speed continues to dissipate as we get towards the middle of the span – closer to the people running up ahead. Sparks are flying with the heavy smell of something burning surrounding us. As we finally slow to a stop about three quarters of the way across the bridge, bullets begin piercing the front windshield of the locomotive. Mike gives me that "I can't believe this" look as Kingman works feverously to get the train in reverse. Having another shootout with strangers is certainly something to be concerned about. But, what's really bothering me now, at this very moment is the sight of another train popping out of a tunnel – heading in our direction. Mike sees the train coming straight for us and looks over at me. This time I send him "I can't believe this" look as we both tumble to the cabin floor when our locomotive bolts into reverse. Kingman looks down at us, smiles and begins talking to himself again. I figure we all must do a little praying right about now.

CHAPTER 57

Careening down the tracks in a locomotive that must weigh close to a few hundred tons and riding over a narrow bridge so high you can't see the bottom is one thing. Going backwards at speeds close to sixty miles per hour is another. The fact that five men wearing black masks are climbing up the front of the locomotive, moving towards us tells me we have even bigger problems. They must have jumped on when we came to a stop before Choo Choo Charlie reversed our direction. The good news is the train in front of us has slowed down, eliminating the possibility of a collision. We decide the best course of action at this time is to get inside the cab with Kingman and lock the door. Just as I bolt the door closed, a haze of bullets shatters the glass of the cab's side window, forcing us to the floor. One of the ricocheting bullets hits Kingman in the left calf, causing him to use one of his ultra-white hankies to staunch the flow of blood. I hand Mike one of two loaded Sig P290's and a gun battle quickly ensues. Since the P290's only holds six bullets at a time, the shootout rapidly becomes one sided.

Watching Kingman hobble inside the car turning switches, adjusting levers and slamming down red buttons is a sight to see – especially during the gun battle. He seems relatively calm and at home, except for when he screams for us to "get down!" From my position, I see we're getting closer to solid ground as the canyon walls begin to appear behind us.

"Load your guns boys!" yells Kingman glancing at his watch. "Get ready, hang on, not yet, okay, another bloody second! Hold on to something!"

As the last word leaves his lips, the locomotive abruptly slows down, causing it to move slightly sideways before regaining its traction on the rails. During this well-planned maneuver, I see three of the five masked men go quickly by the windows with arms flailing heading towards the front of the locomotive. Judging by their screams seconds later, I would have to say that they'll soon know what the bottom of the canyon looks like. Mike gives Kingman a "Bloody well done!" in the worst English accent I ever heard. The quieting clacking sound below us tells me that we are off the bridge and back on land. Thinking we still have two men on board and a train heading in our direction, Mike and I cautiously crawl along the cab floor and out the door to look for them, and leave the train stuff to Choo Choo Charlie Kingman.

We find no one on the locomotive, and figure that either all five went over the side when the train engine slowed dramatically, or two jumped off when we got back over land. We go back into the cab to check on Kingman, who's making the sign of the cross - again. He hears us behinds him, turns and speaks.

"I'm allowing the train in front of us to get all their cars off the bridge. I remember a turn off just before the bridge," he says calmly. "Need to get this baby off the main track."

"Nice job Kingman – thank you." I say.

"Yeah thanks - you saved our butts!" Mike chimes in. "Your dad, he'd be proud – real proud."

"Leg okay?" I ask.

"It's fine," he replies. "Just a nick. Hurt myself worse shaving."

"You do have nice clean legs," I shoot back. "Noticed the day you weren't wearing any pants."

"I shave my face, you bloody fool – not my legs!"

"Oops – sorry. I guess I just assumed based on the lack of hair."

"I think his bikini wax might have gone a little too low," Mike blurts out.

All three of us break out in laughter. I don't think any of us know what we're laughing about. It's probably the fact that somehow we're still alive. It's barely noontime and we're all exhausted.

CHAPTER 58
Sunday / 12:00 PM

With both trains stopped, nose-to-nose, Kingman walks over to meet the Engineer to talk about "siding" our locomotive. According to Kingman, this means getting our locomotive off the main track and onto a side-track that's not being used. Mike pulls out a map to find our location. When I make a comment about him reading it upside down, he wads it up and uses the GPS function in his smart phone. I give Clare a call and catch her on the first ring.

"We're on our way Joe," Clare says loudly, over the sound of the rotors. "Kelly says we'll be at your location in less than, hang on, got it, less than ten minutes. We have some information on your mother and Stella – the President too. Hang on Joe, be right back. Diego needs a word."

"Joe, it's me – Diego. Looks like my brother, Tomas, may be right about all three being held somewhere in Real de Catorce. Kelly says it's about 150 miles from your present location. It's what they call a Magic Town, a small village really, built into the side of a mountain. Close to 10,000 feet above sea level."

"Did you say 'Magic Town' Diego, or something else?"

"Yeah Joe, it's a Mexican cultural thing – tell you about it later. The last time I visited – think maybe 2001 - I saw Miss Julia Roberts and Mr. Brad Pitt filming a movie there. The mountainous terrain and abandoned silver mines makes it a great place to hide somebody. Hey Joe, coming up on your position – I see the railroad cars scattered along the ground. Kelly wants to know where you want us."

"I'm looking at a great landing spot about fifty yards off the railroad tracks. No trees, obstructions of any kind. Just keep an eye out for wandering children," I reply.

"Did you just say wandering children? Wandering Children?" Diego asks.

"Yeah, Mike says about seventy-five."

"What are seventy-five children doing out in the middle of nowhere?"

"Not sure, they were on a train we almost collided with."

"I can't wait to hear about this one," Diego says loudly over Fina's barking.

"Try to stay out of trouble till we at least get there."

I climb back up the ladder into the train, grab a bottled water and park myself on the cab's roof. It's amazing that Tomas knows where my mom and Stella are. How, I'm not sure, but he always seems to be one step ahead of me. As I listen and wait for the Seahawk helicopter, I read an incoming text from Carlone. "Air and Ground war has begun against cartels in Mexico, Central and South America. Fifty thousand military personnel crossing border. Mexican government is falling – coup possible – US trying to stabilize. President held in Nicaragua? Rendezvous with your team at 1800 hours. Details to follow – JL Carlone."

What team? We have a team? Maybe Carlone's bringing a team – that's gotta be it. Yeah, he's got a team. He must know we need help. My thoughts get scrambled when I hear our locomotive start up, sending a series of heavy vibrations through my body. Lowering myself from the roof into the cab, I hear Kingman yelling over the engine noise and pointing out the smashed window. He says something about a "ground frame" and "mechanical levers," which I think I understand. What really throws me is when he screams something about finding "Annett's key." Feeling this may be important, I jump in and ask "Who's Annett? What does the key look like and where was it lost?"

"You bloody idiot," Kingman replies laughing. "The Annett's key is a device used to unlock the levers in the ground frame. In simpler terms, the levers allow us to move the track so we can side the locomotive – move it off the main track."

"Okay, okay, I get it. But let's not tell him just yet," I say pointing to Mike crawling along the ground, looking for something.

Kingman and I share a quick laugh as the helicopter passes slowly overhead. I leap to the ground, jump over Mike on his hands and knees and begin sprinting towards the Seahawk, which lands in an open field adjacent to the tracks. I slow down my run to watch at least a dozen vapor trails lining the sky behind military jets on their way to somewhere. We're truly at war with the cartels.

I approach the helicopter cautiously as the engines are being shut down. The cabin door opens and Diego yells out "Hello!" and gives me a wave. Fina jumps to the ground and runs full speed in my direction. At the last minute, she sees something in the tall weeds and changes course. I stop and watch Diego help Clare to the ground. Her blonde hair is tucked under her Boston Red Sox cap, and she's wearing a button down light blue sweater and faded jeans. She knows I'm checking her out and just smiles. If she wasn't carrying an opened, sawed-off, double-barreled shotgun in her right hand, I might have forgotten – for a short time that this team, as Carlone calls us, is about to embark on a dangerous mission. Finding Mom and Stella in a small village by the name of Real de Catorce. Or as Diego calls it – "Magic town." All this in the middle of a war. Let's hope that Real de Catorce still has some magic left when we get there.

CHAPTER 59

Sunday / 2:08 PM
Outside Linares, Nuevo Leon, Mexico

After about an hour of messing around with Annett's key, mechanical levers in the ground frame, Kingman is able to move the locomotive off the main track. Mike and I were a little nervous since Choo Choo Charlie Kingman seemed to know more than the full-time engineer from the other train. We learned that the occupants from the other train are mainly orphaned children, ages three to seventeen. They're on their way to a monastery located in a city named Montemorelos, which is approximately thirty miles north of Linares. Clare says it's an old monastery built in the early 1700's converted to a home for children in the late 1980's.

"I think it's known as Kuiama Los Niño's En Casa – Kuiama Children's Home," Clare tells us. "Went there over a year ago to help with a flu outbreak that hit this area pretty hard. I remember meeting a beautiful Vietnamese woman, probably late forties who owned and ran the home. She had long silky black hair that the young girls loved to braid when we sat out in the yard at the end of day. The children just adored her. They called her Miss Kui, short for Kuiama. She told me she came to Mexico as a child with her parents in the early 1970's after the Vietnam war. Kuiama loved Mexico and told me she'd never leave."

"Sounds like a remarkable woman," I say.

"She was – is, we should try to visit her after we find your mom and Stella. You know, when things get back to normal, or least something close to normal."

"I think that's a good idea, let's plan on it," I reply softly.

I try to imagine what it must be like for all those heroes coming home from the wars in Iraq and Afghanistan. After all they've been through, how do they ever get back to normal? I guess living with the horrors of war just becomes part of you – the new normal. Our one-sided conversation comes to a stop when Rogers comes over to talk with us.

"Tell me something Joe, honestly," she says. "Is all that stuff that happened off and on the train real? Or, was your buddy Mike making it all up?"

Clare gives me a wanting to know more look. "Come on Rogers, you must know Mike by now – he has a tendency to exaggerate," I reply quickly.

"Okay, so a train two miles long didn't derail, setting a small town on fire – during which time you went missing," Rogers says.

"Hardly, temporarily separated – yes," I reply looking at Clare. "There was an incident – sure - let's call it a derailment."

"How about a near collision, with this other train right there," she says pointing. "Mike said the bridge was so high off the ground, you couldn't see the bottom of the canyon."

"It was too foggy to see the bottom," I say. "Anyway, Kingman knows a lot about running trains – he knew what he was doing."

"Mike said Kingman was so afraid, he almost peed his pants," Ensign Rogers says with a smirk on her face.

"I don't know anything about that," I say glancing at Clare. "The man was shot in the calf. A ricocheting bullet hit a water bottle. Anyhow, we can talk about this later - let's get outta here. We gotta find Stella and Mom - and the President too."

"Got it Joe, I'll start the preflight on the helicopter," she says disappearing in the tall weeds.

Clare grabs my hand and we hurry off to round up the team. We find Mike and Diego saying goodbye to some of the children on the train. Clare and I break out in laughter as Kingman steps down from the locomotive wearing a pair of farmer jeans, straps and everything. The problem is they're very large in the waist and the length stops a few inches above his ankles. I think kids still call them high waters. He gives us a smile and heads for the chopper. Of course Mike has to have the last word. "The rumor is he peed his pants," he says loud enough for all to hear.

Our laughter gets drowned out by the noise of the two General Electric T700 engines being fired up on the Sikorsky. We're quickly jolted back to reality. I see the pain in Diego's face and realize for the first time that he is truly in love with my mother. I let go of Clare's hand, give him a big hug and whisper to him. "We'll find her Diego. My mother's a fighter and can survive anything. Stella's a big time derby professional roller skater. Who's gonna mess with her? Just make sure you have your Swiss Army Knife ready – we may need it."

CHAPTER 60
Sunday / 4:00 PM

We store our gear in the chopper and strap ourselves into our seats. In the cockpit, Kelly's in the pilot seat with Mike in the co-pilot's chair. Clare, Diego, Kingman and I are in back. Fina has buried herself under a pile of blankets she found in a corner. Our team of five will be meeting Jim Carlone somewhere along the way, based on GPS coordinates given to Kelly. She says it's in the middle of nowhere outside the village of El Leoncito on our way to Real de Catorce. If all goes to plan, we should arrive before dark. The first problem we have is what to do with the Seahawk since we can't just chopper in and blow the element of surprise. We'll figure something out once we pick up Carlone. The latest Intel from Tomas says that Mom and Stella are being held at either a church or cantina. According to him, the President is not being held with Mom, but in the area. Diego is expecting an update from Tomas within the hour once he gets to Real de Catorce. Again, he's one step ahead of us.

After being airborne for only a few minutes, I notice Clare has lost the battle trying to keep her eyes open. Diego's staring at the cabin's ceiling and Kingman is reading some sort of manual he found in one of the storage cabinets. I decide this would be a good time to surf the internet and see what I can find out about the town we're heading to – Real de Catorce.

Real de Catorce is located near the top of one of the highest plateaus in Mexico, close to ten thousand feet. The story goes that in the late 1700's a traveling musician was camping out in the area and discovered silver. Spain was running Mexico at the time, and since the King received a fixed percentage of all claims, prospectors were encouraged to search for new silver veins. The silver boom lasted for many years through a civil war, slave labor, peasant revolts and various technical setbacks. According to several websites, silver is still being mined in Real de Catorce.

One of the more interesting things I learn is that to get into town by ground, you must go through a one lane passageway known as the Ogarrio Tunnel. It's one and a half miles long, and has a small chapel named Capilla de Nuestra Señora de los Delores, just inside the entrance. The Chapel of our Lady of Sorrows. Diego is correct in saying that several movies were filmed there, including *The Mexican* with Brad Pitt and Julia Roberts, as well as *The Treasure of The Sierra Madre* starring Humphrey Bogart. The town's population has less than a thousand full time inhabitants. I'm praying we can get in and out without disturbing the peace.

I insert my Bose ear buds and plug the other end into my iPhone. Thumbing through my playlist, I stop at *Derek & The Dominos* and begin listening to *Layla*. In the middle of the piano movement, the Seahawk begins to slow, followed by an abrupt turn to the left. Looking out the cabin window, I see a familiar airplane pass below us with someone in the front seat, waving his arms while the pilot is standing in the back. The thing that really catches my eye is that the propeller is stopped. Looks like our "bud" ran out of gas. Knew I'd see him again – and his Waltzing Matilda.

CHAPTER 61

Sunday / 5:17 PM

Near Palo Blanco, Mexico – 15 Miles NE of Real de Catorce

I watch the 1932 Brunner Winkle Bird CK biplane turn its nose into the breeze and touch gently down on a dry river bed. Captain Rogers banks the Seahawk away from the Matilda in search of a landing zone in which the GE engines will suck in the least amount of dirt. After a soft landing, Mike appears in the cabin doorway.

"Joe, did you see Carlone in the front seat of the biplane waving his arms around? What'd ya think that was all about?" he says smirking.

"Looked like he was trying to communicate with pilot Bob."

"Communicate? It looked more like panic to me," Diego chimes in.

"Yeah – I agree!" Mike says. "And tell me why Pilot Bob was standing on his seat. Shouldn't he be doing something else, like flying the airplane, maybe?"

Our conversation comes to a screeching halt when Diego's cell phone starts ringing. He steps down to the ground to take the call. The rest of us pile out behind him. Mike chocks the wheels while I conduct a quick inspection of the fuselage. Clare walks down a small hill to meet Carlone when a loud, familiar voice breaks the stillness of the moment.

"Hey buds, told you we'd meet again real soon," say pilot Bob coming over to us, carrying something in his hand. "Your friend there, Carlone, he's a real nervous flyer isn't he? I'd rather fly with you two babies any day."

As he gets closer, I'm finally able to see what he's carrying. "Nice to see you pilot Bob," I say. "But if you don't mind me asking, why are you walking around with a snake."

"Aw dang, this thing," he responds quickly, while throwing the snake at Mike.

"What the heck is that?" Mike screams as he jumps out of the way, causing the snake to hit the ground emitting a rattle noise. "Did you just throw a rattlesnake at me?" He says grabbing his Colt 1911 from his holster.

"Hang on there bud!" yells Bob. "No need to get all crazy on that snake! Put away that water pistol."

"That thing could've bitten me you crazy fool!" shouts Mike.

"I don't know about you, but I've never heard of a plastic reptile biting anybody," he replies with a big smile on his face. "My business partner Jute must have put it in the Bird CK before I took off this morning – just a little joke. Heck, your buddy Carlone thought it was real too."

Our little group goes quiet as Fina the wonder dog runs by, grabs the snake in her mouth and begins violently shaking it. "At least I'm not the only one who thought was real," says Mike sounding vindicated.

"Sure thing Mike," I say, "but I've seen Fina do the same thing with a Frisbee."

CHAPTER 62

Sunday / 6:00 PM

Near Palo Blanco – 15 Miles NE of Real de Catorce

Pilot Bob tells us the Matilda ran out of gas just after the wheels hit the ground – "perfect timing." Even though no one said anything, I think a few of us saw that the Winkle Bird CK dropped out of a drifting cloud bank with a still propeller. After all that happened between Mike and Bob, I was happy that no argument ensued over the sketchiness of the facts. When we too ran out of gas on the bird, I remembered how peaceful it was. This gives me an idea of how we might initially get into Real de Catorce without being noticed. I decide to have a chat with Bob while he transfers gasoline from a five-gallon container into the Bird's tank.

"Excuse me, Pilot Bob; can we talk for a minute?"

"Sure bud, what can I do for you?" he says.

"Have you ever been to Real de Catorce?"

"Why heck yeah, bud!" he yells. "Have you ever heard of a guy named Pitt, Brad Pitt? You know – big Hollywood actor type – good looking, once married to the long dark-haired woman with those beautiful lips. You know bud, they have all those kids!"

"Yeah, I know Brad Pitt. Well, don't know him, but saw many of his movies. And his ex-wife is Angelina Jolie."

"Alright Joe, guess you don't know him like I do," Pilot Bob fires back. "Anyway, I flew Mr. Brad Pitt and his PR guy, Steve, Sam, somebody to Real de Catorce from Mexico City. It was back in 2000, maybe 2001, don't exactly remember. But, let me tell you, the studio people were pissed that Mr. Pitt missed his ride that was supposed to take him and a few other actors into Catorce. Can I tell ya something Joe?" he asks, leaning in my direction.

"Sure Bob, what is it?" I say, as he moves within twelve inches of my face.

"The CIA, you know – Central Intelligence Agency – they called me," Bob says whispering. "Had a job for ole Pilot Bob Roe – wanted to know if I was interested. Somebody in the NSA – ya know – National Security Agency- told them about a drop off I just did. They knew I was still at the Mexico City Airport."

Fully amazed that Pilot Bob knows how to whisper, I move in closer to make sure I don't miss anything.

"They said they had a job for me – an important job. Said it'd take the rest of the day. Said I was to meet with two men on the tarmac near the Philips 66 hangar. They'd be in a dark limo, parked near the two white fuel tanks adjacent to the repair facility," he says pausing and then staring at the sky.

"Pilot Bob, you okay?" I asked.

"Did I say Mobil or Philips 66?" he says slowly.

"Philips, not Mobil," I reply.

"Good. It was Philips. Okay, so listen, here I am in a Mexico City Airport bar, finishing up a non-alcoholic beer – hate that crap – after talking to the CIA. Two men in Mexican Army uniforms come up beside me. They say a few words to the bartender in Spanish and before I know it, they're lifting me out of my stool. Joe, they lifted me, told me in perfect English to "hurry." Next, we're hustling down a locked stairway that leads to double doors that open out onto the taxiway. Less than two hundred feet in front of me, I see the two white fuel tanks, the Mobil, not the Philips 66 sign sitting on top of a grey steel hangar. Parked off to the side is a black limo with the back doors wide open. Well Bud, this must be some high-level VIP, you know, very important person."

"Got it," I reply while glancing at my watch.

"Well guess what Bud?" he shouts.

"What?" Mike yells back overhearing our conversation. "Get to the punch line!"

"It was Brad Pitt – the actor! That was the VIP – very important person." He says loud enough for everyone to hear. "So yes Joe, long story made short, I've flown into Real de Catorce with a big time Hollywood

209

actor," he bellows proudly. "Please, I even got his autograph!" he booms out. "Said I'd fly him back to Mexico City if needed – not necessary though. Said a chopper was picking him up in a few days to take him to California. Hang on, got his autograph, in my wallet."

Clare looks over at me, gives me a wink because she knows what I'm thinking.

Mike's standing there, wheels turning in his head, waiting for me to speak. Kelly and Diego are standing next to each other, turn in my direction and give a salute. Kingman begins to slowly flap his arms as I can see the excitement building in his face.

"I got it!" shouts Pilot Bob. "Why didn't you just ask me to fly you into Real de Catorce?"

"I thought I did - sorry," I say.

"Bud, you asked me if I've ever flown into Catorce. Not if I'd fly you there," Pilot Bob says slowly emphasizing each word. "Either way, I don't care, I love telling that Brad Pitt story," he says.

"Really?" Mike shoots back. "I couldn't tell."

"Yes sir, you're right. I need you to fly me into Real de Catorce." I say.

"Joe and I need to get in the air as soon as possible. No time for long stories – no more waiting. Can you do it?" asks Clare.

"Certainly I can do it!" he shouts back to Clare. "I'll take ya!"

Needless to say, I'm caught off guard as Clare jumps in to get her seat on the Brunner CK. In a crazy way, it actually makes some sense.

"Wait a minute!" Pilot Bob screams out. "Due to some recent modifications we'll be able to squeeze in a third person. But, they'd have to be skinny enough to fit in the area where I keep the spare fuel tanks. They'd have to be long enough to help balance our weight correctly. Lastly, they can't be afraid of tight, dark places," Bob finishes looking over at Mike.

My attention is drawn to coughing fits coming from under a small dead tree - lanky sort leaning off to one side. I see a smiling Kingman with his umbrella opened. I think we found our skinny person, unafraid of dark, tight places.

CHAPTER 63

Sunday / 7:10 PM

Near Palo Blanco – 15 Miles NE of Real de Catorce

After ten minutes of spirited discussion, two teams are agreed upon. Clare, Kingman and I will pile into the Brunner CK with Pilot Bob – destination Real de Catorce. Once we unloaded all the junk from the airplane, siphoned out a few gallons of gas, Pilot Bob was quite sure that he could get the Bird off the ground. Due to the weight and balance limitations, each of us was only allowed a handgun and one spare clip. Because Real de Catorce is tucked into the side of a mountain at over 10,000 feet above sea level, at that altitude the air is less dense, so the Brunner Winkle's engine will require less fuel flowing through the carburetor. Most modern airplanes have a mechanism for leaning out the fuel mixture at higher altitudes – either manual or automatic. Pilot Bob assures us that he can lean out the engine via a simple cable assembly that goes from the carb to inside the cockpit. Looking for myself, I see a round black knob that says "CHOKE." It looks like something you'd find on a lawn mower. Well, if Brad Pitt can fly in this bird to Real de Catorce, so can we.

Diego was quite angry that he would not be going with us in the Brunner. He felt Clare should stay behind with the second team – told us so. He did start to calm down during our weight and balance calculations, knowing that he was close to a hundred pounds heavier than Clare. Mike knew the deal – it made sense to him and Carlone. The first team is the scouts. The second is the Calvary.

With daylight quickly fading, I lay out the plan that may work.

211

"At this point, we assume Tomas is somewhere inside Real de Catorce. He may know the whereabouts of Mom and Stella. Finding him may prove difficult, but he seems to have the knack for finding us," I say.

"Joe, I will call you when I hear from my brother," Diego quickly replies. "Just tried him – no luck. But you're right, he should be in Catorce."

"Thanks Diego," I reply.

"We're on our own," says Carlone staring "I can't raise anybody – anywhere, Washington, Texas, or Mexico. The last report I got was over a damn hour ago, said many of the border towns on both sides of the Rio Grande are still on fire and nearly deserted. Our Vice President has called on our allies in North, Central and South America – told them to get their military on standby. 'We expect your complete cooperation in crushing these drug lords throughout the Americas," says Carlone reading off his iPad.

"Listen you bloody fools!" Kingman jumps in. "That bullshit war on drugs has been slowly killing your United States over the last fifty years. So whether we like it or not, we are now deeply emerged in the real drug war. It's been a long time coming – believe me! Let's put our plan into motion!"

Kingman's voice gets drowned out by the Kinner's R5 radial engine in the 32 Brunner Winkle starting up. Pilot Bob throttles her up and the engine stalls. We watch him smile, climb out of the cockpit, and walk to the front and begin tinkering with the engine. With darkness quickly approaching, I turn on my flashlight, wink at Clare and join Bob at the front of the airplane.

"Thanks Joe, getting dark," he says. "Just want to make some quick adjustments before we take off."

"Can I help?" I ask.

"Yeah, go inside the cockpit, on the left side of the instrument panel you'll see a black knob that says "CHOKE", white letters I think," he says looking towards the sky. "Yeah white, bought it from a guy who was scrapping out an old John Deere tractor. Bought it for two dollars – it even works," he laughs. "Pull the knob forward about two inches or so. Can you do that?"

Walking back to the cockpit, I reach in and gently pull on the choke knob.

"A little more, pull it out a little more!" shouts Pilot Bob.

Following his instructions, I pull the knob towards me and it breaks off in my hand.

"Too far Joe, too far," he yells. "Guess we won't be using that. Okay, no problem, won't need it anyway," he says turning, facing the group. "It's a short flight and I know my way through the canyons. Grab your stuff and get aboard — let's go! Got about fifteen miles to go, twenty minutes in the air and less than ten minutes of daylight left!"

"Alright, you heard Pilot Bob, load up," I say. "Anyway, if Brad Pitt can fly in this plane all the way from Mexico City to Real de Catorce, we can certainly go twenty minutes in this thing."

"Joe, wait a minute, hold on a sec," says Pilot Bob with a slight snicker. "Please, I never said Brad Pitt flew in the Brunner, never did say that. I think the only way he'd fly in a bird like this is if it were in the movies. Probably have a stunt double — too dangerous for some Hollywood movie star," he says laughing. "Pitt's people insisted on a rented luxury Bell helicopter with all the bells and whistles. He probably thought he was still in his living room for goodness sakes - heard he slept most of the way."

Watching Clare climb into the front compartment of the Winkle Bird as Kingman crawls into the small space in front of the cockpit, I pull aside group two for a quick chat.

"Kelly, when the wheels of the CK leave the ground, go ahead and start the countdown," I say. "The helicopter needs to be in the air, heading to Real de Catorce one hour after we leave."

"Diego, keep trying to reach your brother, Tomas. You know we're flying blindly into Catorce with a plan based on a few hunches."

"Carlone, we're gonna need more help. I'm hoping our kidnappers are using up their manpower guarding the President somewhere, and not my mom and Stella. Try to get a location on the President. We don't want to miss him if he's in Catorce."

"Joe, I can't raise anybody on the cell or on the Seahawk's radio," Jim replies. "I've been trying for over an hour — no luck. Look, let's focus on finding your mom and Stella and I'll keep trying to raise someone on the radios – try to get a fix on the President."

"Agreed– thanks!" I shout over the Brunner's engine's noise. Mike mouths, "Be careful," as I turn to see Clare waving her hand from the passenger compartment. It's my signal to get in the airplane as it slowly moves away. Before I have a chance to run to the Matilda, Diego hugs me from behind and places something in my jacket pocket. "I love you Joseph," he says quickly. "Your mother too," he adds. "Be careful!"

Sprinting towards to the moving airplane, I see the right tire disappear in the darkness, followed by a popping sound. The Brunner Bird turns quickly to the right before it comes to an abrupt stop off the side of the road, causing a mini dust storm. We run down the embankment to make sure everyone's alright, as the engine comes to a stop. I help Clare climb down to the ground with Kingman close behind.

"Sorry everybody!" shouts Pilot Bob from the cockpit. "I checked the road for holes, must have missed one."

"Nobody's hurt except the Brunner," I say looking at the semi-flat tire and slightly bent axle.

"I can fix it, don't worry! Can get us in the air in less than thirty minutes," he replies. "Gotta be used to this stuff happening working and living in Mexico. Heck, it's like being a bush pilot in Alaska for darn sakes. Anyway, she ain't flat, just need a little Fix-A-Flat!"

The air goes suddenly quiet with Clare and I standing close together. I feel her take my hand and give it a squeeze.

"Okay everyone!" I yell. "It's on to Plan B! So much for sneaking into Real de Catorce! Captain Rogers, please fire up the GE engines on the Sikorsky so this rescue team can do some rescuing."

Kelly, Clare, and Carlone move off together to the helicopter while Mike, Diego, Kingman and I help Pilot Bob prop the right wheel assembly off the ground using three large stones we find in the area. He insists on staying to repair the Brunner and says he'll come by later to "save all our butts." After we make sure that Pilot Bob has everything he needs, we say our goodbyes and head towards the booming sound of the Seahawk helicopter warming up. The four of us walk through the darkness and discuss what a Plan B might look like. We share a little laugh when we discover that Plan B looks a lot like Plan A. Not much there and mostly made up as we go. Our bout of humor quickly disappears when we hear the helicopter's engine's go up to full power and it begins lifting off the ground into the night sky. Small arms fire breaks out all around us as we watch the Seahawk disappear from sight into a bellow of dimly lit clouds.

"I think we need a Plan C!" screams Mike hitting the ground while reaching for his Colt 1911.

With bullets whizzing over our heads, I grab my cell phone in an attempt to reach Clare in the chopper. No luck. Crawling along the ground and down a small embankment, I see a Coleman lantern, lit to full brightness under the right wing of the Brunner CK. I see Pilot Bob pumping up its tire using an old fashion bicycle pump, not bothered by anything going on around us. I think I even hear him whistling.

CHAPTER 64

Sunday / 8:17 PM
On the move – 15 Miles NE of Real de Catorce

The thumping rotor blades of the Seahawk helicopter pounding overhead does little to stop the errant shooting happening on the ground all around us. Pilot Bob finally decides the tire has enough air and shuts down the lantern after waving us over. With barely enough light to see, we run towards the Brunner and slip down the dirt embankment to find Bob holding a small flashlight under his chin, lighting his face.

"Boo!" he yells. "Look, we got a problem here. Some bastards hiding in the bush are firing at you guys – somebody's gonna get hurt. Oh, and your ride to Real de Catorce left without you – what just happened there?" he says smirking.

"Not quite sure," I reply loudly. "My guess is Rogers heard the gunfire, needed to get the chopper in the air – out of danger!"

"It's in the area – just heard it," says Mike.

"Look, it's getting too hot," says Pilot Bob. "I'm getting out of here! I can fit two of you in front – we leave now!"

I take a second before I blurt out my response. "Diego, Kingman get in the airplane. Bob, get these two to Catorce – no nonsense, no stops – they're on a critical rescue mission."

Bob points to Diego and Kingman – "Get in the plane. Joe, here, take the lantern, and run as fast as you can down the road and after thirty seconds, stop and re-light it." He then reaches to the ground and sticks his hand inside a dirty brown duffle bag. "Mike, take this!" he says handing him a small Uzi. "You know how to use this thing?"

"Sure do," Mike says, smiling.

"Good, now go and hold back those shooters so we can take off," Bob says, winking at Mike.

Without a word, Pilot Bob, Kingman and Diego climb into the Brunner as Mike disappears into the darkness towards the gunfire. I pick up the Coleman lantern, check my Timex and begin running down the dark, deserted road. Within a few seconds, I hear the airplane's engine fire up. At thirty-three seconds, I move to the side of the road and light the lantern. The helicopter is buzzing somewhere overhead. In less than a minute, the Brunner slips by me with the wheels a few feet off the ground. As they pass, Kingman smiles and gives me the thumbs up sign. Diego waves, yelling into his cell phone. Pilot Bob gives me the two-fingered peace sign before I lose sight of him in the darkness. I quickly turn off the lantern and listen to the Uzi being fired in the distance. As the shooting begins to wane, I feel my iPhone vibrating in my jacket pocket. It's Clare.

"Joe, did Pilot Bob just leave?" Clare asks.

"Yeah," I reply. "Are you okay? What happened?"

"Not sure," she says. "We're waiting for you guys in the helicopter and next thing we know someone starts shooting at us. Jim's sitting, feet hanging out the door and a bullet grazes his leg. He jumps in and tells Kelly to take off – said we'd come back to pick you up."

"Carlone okay?"

"He's fine. I didn't even see any blood. But Joe, he wrapped his calf with so many bandages he had to slit the bottom of his pants. Hang on, one sec!" Clare says. "Here's Jim."

"Joe, listen, we're coming back around to pick you up," says Carlone. "Hey, we see what looks like somebody still firing on the ground."

"That would be Mike," I say. "Pilot Bob gave him an Uzi and he's been testing it on whoever's shooting at us."

"I'm only picking up two bodies on the ground," Carlone says. "Where's Kingman and Diego?"

"Gone to Real de Catorce – left a few minutes ago. Mike and I stayed on the ground to hold off whoever was using us for target practice. Knew you'd come back sooner or later to pick us up."

"Joe, tell Mike to stop shooting – the area's clear," I hear Rogers yelling in the background.

217

"We're dropping in Joe – Kelly's gonna flash the lights," says Carlone. "There's a landing zone – about a quarter a mile east down the road from where you're standing right now. Get Mike and hurry – we don't want our friends to come back."

Mike ends up finding me and we start to jog down the dirt road lit only by stars and a half moon. We hear the Sikorsky buzz over our heads with its lights flashing, illuminating the area around us. In less than two minutes, we're climbing inside the helicopter and on our way to Catorce. The seven-minute flight gives me enough time to get reacquainted with Clare while Mike harasses Carlone about his near fatal war injury. "I'm personally gonna fill out the paperwork for both a Purple Heart and Medal of Honor for you," he says. "Tell me how it happened again?"

Still believing we might have the element of surprise on our side, I ask Rogers to land about a mile from the main entrance outside the canyon town of Real de Catorce – a mile from the Ogarrio tunnel. "Hang on Mom and Stella – we're coming," I whisper.

"Amen," replies Clare squeezing my hand.

CHAPTER 65

Sunday / 9:20 PM
Ogarrio Tunnel Entrance – Real de Catorce

The flickering, single yellow light bulb barely throws enough lumens to read the name carved into the solid rock above the one lane road. It's the entrance to the 1.5 mile Ogarrio Tunnel that was built through the mountain around 1900. Our erratic breathing reminds us that Real De Catorce is almost 10,000 feet above sea level. When dropped off, the chopper's altimeter read 9600 feet. We thought it best that Clare and I go alone, looking like lost hikers getting back late. Rogers, Mike, Carlone and the wonder dog will stay with the Seahawk to manage communications and rescue us when called. We see no one on our walk from the helicopter, and find the tunnel entrance deserted. We've yet to hear anything from Pilot Bob or his crew – not surprised.

Off to the right of the tunnel entrance is a small parking lot with an old yellow windowless school bus. Parked next to it are three cars – all missing at least one wheel, some glass and even a few doors. Checking the inside, it looks like none of the three vehicles have been operational for quite some time. A large white dog sleeping in the backseat of one certainly doesn't surprise me. His eyes open momentarily when Clare calls out my name with a distinct echo.

"Joe, Joe, where are you? Come here – look what I found!"

I find her kneeling on a rock laid floor, just inside the tunnel, hands clasped together and lips moving in silence. As she completes her prayer with the Father, Son and Holy Spirit gesture, I try and read the sign above the makeshift Altar. It's decorated with beautiful violet and blue flowers surrounded by at least fifty lit candles, scattering shadows along the walls. Embarrassed by my lack of knowledge of the Spanish language, I say

219

Capilla de Nuestra Señora los Delores to myself. Unfortunately, Clare sees my lips moving, which causes me to stop and look the other way.

"It says Capilla de Nuestra Señora los Delores," Clare states in beautiful Spanish. "In English it means Chapel of our Lady of Sorrows," says Clare.

"It was on the tip of my tongue," I shoot back.

"Sure Joe. I'll let you get the next one," she says, smiling. "Anyway, the Chapel was built to honor the memory of all those who died mining in this area."

"Thank you Clare and yes, please allow me to get the next one. Remember, nobody likes a showoff."

"Look who's talking about showing off?" she replies, sarcastically.

"Hang on! Do you see what I see?" I say pointing off to the left side behind the altar.

"Yes, I sure do — let's go!"

We grab the two bikes leaning against the tunnel's wall, check the tires for air, throw our packs over our shoulders and begin to pedal on our 1.5 mile journey through a barely lit cavern that smells of cold, wet dirt and rock. As we get closer to the end of the tunnel, we actually see light as well as hear faint music.

Clare and I bike slowly out of the tunnel veering off to the right on a dirt path, stopping under a large tree. My Timex watch beep tells me it's 10:00 PM, but the town of Real de Catorce is far from going to sleep. Standing under the oak, a hundred feet from the Ogarrio's exit, it's easy to see why they call this a Magic Town.

"Isn't this just beautiful?" Clare says. "The way the valley's carved through the mountaintop, with the town built into the rock on both sides. The air is so clean and refreshing. It's different from the air we were breathing on the other side of the tunnel."

"You're right," I say.

Taking a moment to look down the valley with all the twinkling lights strung out over the roadways and houses, I hear a familiar non-rhythmic sputtering sound overhead, that's not part of the distant music.

"Can you hear that?" Clare says, looking up at the sky.

"Yeah, I hear it."

Before I have a chance to say another word, the Brunner Bird CK floats a hundred feet over our head before the engine finally goes silent. Clare and I look at each other when we hear Pilot Bob's booming voice break through the relative calm of the area before we lose his voice in the music. The colorful blue and yellow tail of the airplane gets absorbed in the night's darkness as it glides away from our position. Clare and I grab our packs off the ground, throw them over our shoulders and give chase. Unfortunately, we don't get very far when a man in a uniform jumps in our way, pointing a gun and tells us to "Parada," stop. Before I have a chance to react, Clare does some type of karate move in which she knocks the gun from his hand. She executes a rabbit punch to the side of his neck, causing his legs to weaken. With barely a sound, he falls to the ground.

"What was that?" I say, shocked.

"Just a reaction," she replies.

"Reaction my butt, I'm impressed. Really, what was that?"

"Maybe Tae Bo or something I saw on TV. Anyway, he'll be out for a while - let's move him," Clare says, pointing to a nearby row of bushes.

"Yes Ma'am," I reply with a mock salute. "You got it, right away!"

CHAPTER 66

Sunday / 10:15 PM
Real de Catorce

Since we lost sight of the airplane, we determine it must have landed somewhere north of us, in the valley. Pilot Bob said he knew the area well and we're confident we'll join up again soon. Clare and I decide to walk through the neighborhoods, acting like tourists in love, holding hands and enjoying a late evening stroll. The streets are nearly deserted, and those we see pay little attention to us. As we walk past a place named Quinta Puesta del Sol Hotel, my phone vibrates with a text. I pull it from my pocket and bump heads with Clare as we both read the message. "In Real de Catorce? Meet us at the corner of Constitution and Zaragoza – across from Plaza Hidalgo – Hotel San Juan –Diego." I send a reply back to Diego. "Here – will find you – Joe."

Before I have time to finish my text back to Diego, Clare runs out into the street and stops a stooped over, dark-haired woman carrying a baby. The woman smiles, hands the baby to Clare and starts whispering in Spanish, using arm gestures to reaffirm directions. The only words I can make out are Jolie Roberts, Brad Bit and San Juan. After several "gracias" and hugs, Clare finally gives back the baby to the friendly woman and we start running down a dirt road that goes through the center of town. The colorful, twinkling lights strung along the houses and storefronts provide enough light to see Clare in front of me. She quickly comes to a stop, does a complete 360, before dashing off to the left down a blackened narrow alleyway forcing us into a slow walk. She grabs my hand as we carefully navigate around families and neighbors congregating next to small fires emanating from earthen colored clay pots. The smell of cigarettes, beer and smoke penetrate our nostrils, causing Clare to go into a sneezing fit as we continue our way through the alley. Many of the people say "Dios le Bendice" as we pass with Clare hoarsely replying "gracias." I'm relieved to find out they're saying, "God bless you" and not "get your guns."

After a few minutes, the alley opens up to a well-lit road where we go right up a small hill. Running to the top, we see a faded white sign, dangling off the side of a cream colored building above an open doorway. It reads "Hotel San Juan." The sight of a tall, lanky man, wearing a wrinkled three-piece suit and leaning on a closed umbrella tells me that we found the right place. We can also hear Diego's loud voice coming from inside the door of the hotel. I notice a medium built man, dressed in black appear at the door and start speaking with Kingman. It forces me to squeeze the blood out of Clare's right hand. She gives me a calm down look, followed by a "Relax Joseph" when we stop less than fifty feet from them. The two men turn and Kingman gives us a genuine toothy smile. It's hard to tell what type of look we're getting from the other man, since the right side of his face is covered by a frosty white mask. He's the same guy I saw several months ago, floating on his back down the Usumacinta River in southeast Mexico. Oh yeah, that was a few minutes after he saved my life. To this day, I still believe he would have rescued me, whether I was his son or not. Anyway, we'll save that stuff for family therapy.

Before we have a chance to talk, a group of heavily armed men come running out of the stone building across from the Hotel San Juan and quickly surround Kingman and Tomas and forcibly throw them to the ground. Clare and I look in the opposite direction, pretending not to notice the skirmish and begin running. We take a quick left and find ourselves back in the people friendly alleyway. Unfortunately, this time it's eerily empty. Just black smoke rising from fire pots, with no signs of human or animal life. The music dissipates into the quiet night as we break out onto the main road and see the twinkling lights begin to go off throughout the area. The music is replaced by the sounds of crickets and the occasional baby crying. It's 11:00 PM and Real del Catorce is shutting down. And, so is Clare.

CHAPTER 67

Monday / 12:02 AM
Real de Catorce

Clare stirs to the clanging of church bells off in the distance. She's lying wrapped in two jackets, using her pack as a pillow and smiles as she sits upright. After all the recent commotion, we decided to hide out behind several old ore cars that were piled up near a ten-foot stone wall. They provide natural cover and help absorb our voices as we plan our next move.

"Feeling any better?" I ask her.

"Yeah, thanks," she replies rubbing her eyes. "Sorry I nodded off. How long was I out?"

"About fifteen minutes."

"Sorry Joe, felt like I hit a wall. Just needed a quick break."

"I'm surprised you've gone this far. Anyway, let me tell you what I found out."

"Sure, go ahead," Clare says, laying her head back down on the pack.

"Diego texted me – he's safe" I say. "He did see Kingman and Tomas being escorted, both walking under their own power, but with guns at their backs. Diego thinks Mom and Stella are somewhere in that hotel."

"They're in the hotel? Is he sure?"

"No, but he's connected – and so is his brother Tomas. Anyway, he's going to meet us back at the hotel at one. Says he's got some friends in the area willing to help. We also have to find Kingman and Tomas – thank God this is a small town."

Before heading out to meet Diego, I call Carlone and give him an update. I realize things have gone from bad to worse when he answers, yelling over the alarms going off in the cockpit.

"Hang on a sec Joe - wait a minute! Kelly – fire on the ground – three o'clock – hundred yards! Joe, can't talk now," he says. "Somebody's shooting at us - again, had to take off, we're in the middle of heavy maneuvers – call you back! Turn on your beacon – smartphone. Mike's on his way to find you. Oh and Joe, there's a caravan – approximately 30 vehicles, looks military – not ours - about five miles, heading towards Magic Town. It's too dangerous here – we're bugging out! Call ya back!"

"Be safe!"

The line goes dead and my body is now pumping heavy amounts of adrenaline.

"Let's go Clare. Rogers and Carlone had to move the chopper due to ground fire. Mike's here - searching for us. Mexican military vehicles are coming to town."

"Mexican Military?"

"Yeah, Carlone said five miles out," I reply as we cross through an old cemetery.

"Mike's here?"

"According to Carlone – yes - somewhere."

We're back out on the main road and see the Hotel San Juan in front of us. It's after one in the morning, but music continues to seep out onto the streets through its partially opened windows. A familiar Santana song penetrates the alleyways, increasing in volume every time the main door is opened. I hear Clare humming the song behind me as we approach the entrance. Walking inside the dimly lit bar, all heads turn in our direction. Once the men are done checking out Clare, they go back to whatever they were doing. The few women in the room barely give notice. Off towards the back, we hear music and see flashing lights coming from an open door. Clare grabs my arm when we see someone, five yards in front, walking towards us carrying a sawed-off shotgun. I automatically reach for my Sig tucked into the small of my back – we stop. Seeing no one else in the immediate area, and standing in the middle of what looks like an old dance floor, I step in front of Clare and squeeze off a quick shot at the only light hanging off the ceiling. The fixture shatters, with sparks lighting up a familiar figure standing behind the bar. The room goes dark as bullets start flying in our direction. This causes massive panic and the patrons begin fleeing towards the exits – in our direction. Clare and I scramble behind the bar as the throngs of screaming shadows storm out the door and into the street. Feeling we're not alone, I whisper to Clare "don't move" and edge slowly down the bar wall, using my hands as guides in near darkness when I hear a voice.

"Is that you? Who's there? Is that you Joe?" the woman's voice says loudly over Santana's guitar solo.

"It's me," I yell back, reaching clumsily for her hand in the darkness. "It's me Mom."

Before our reunion has a chance to start, the music cuts out, replaced by high pitched whistles and the sound of heavy footsteps. Sounds like the cops have arrived. Since they're probably not feeling too good about Americans right now, I grab hold of Clare's hand and we follow Mom through a trap door hidden inside the bar's structure. We climb down a rickety ladder with a few missing rungs towards a beaming flashlight below. I hear Stella's voice telling us to "be careful." She never had a quiet voice or could whisper, but right now I could care less. I hit the ground last and find Clare, Stella and Mom in a group hug. They quickly pull me in and we say nothing. This would have gone on for a long time if several lit flares weren't being dropped from above and landing at our feet. With the area lit, I count four bodies lying on the ground – hog tied and gagged. Mom looks at me and smiles.

"Joey honey, you know me – I can only be pushed so far," Stella says. "When they started threatening to hurt Caroline I had to use some illegal roller derby moves on them. Dang Joey, those tough guys were almost crying like babies."

"Actually, two of them were," Mom chimes in.

Echoing Spanish voices and ear deafening whistles pierce the rancid air, forcing us to move deeper into the tunnel. We start looking over our heads for a way back to the street. I shine the light on Clare and notice she's starting to look a little woozy. The last time Clare was underground in Mexico she was tortured and almost killed. I manage to catch her before she stumbles and start carrying her. Mom understands the need to get above ground and whispers, "Follow me" soft enough so not to be heard by those coming up behind us. Stella turns, winks at me, and says, "Come on honey – we've got a way to the street."

CHAPTER 68

Monday / 1:35 AM
Real de Catorce

I notice the air getting fresher as we begin our trek up a slight incline. Clare's now back on her feet, following Stella with Mom in the lead. We get about a hundred yards further and stop at an opening in the ground - ten feet above our head. A yellow climber's rope hangs in the center and a man's voice echoes loudly down to us.

"Let's go ladies, hurry now – we've been discovered! Let's go!"

"Clare, you go first!" Mom yells. "Quickly, put your foot in the loop – grab the rope! They'll pull you up. Don't worry honey, just hang on," Mom says calmly.

I give her a quick kiss and help get her shaking foot into the loop.

"Go Diego – bring her up!" screams Mom. "You're next Stella!"

Clare is quickly pulled up and disappears above us. In less than a minute, the yellow rope is dangling in front of Stella. She places her foot inside the loop and yells towards the opening.

"You gonna need to use all your strength, the both of you to pull me up. I ain't no skinny girl like Clare," she says. "Don't forget, I'm a retired roller derby queen who may have put on a few pounds since I hung up my skates!"

"Don't worry, angel. You're in bloody good hands with us!" an unseen Kingman says from above.

You can hear Stella reciting the Lord's Prayer as she's pulled up into the darkness that ends in an ear-deafening scream. The rope falls to the ground at our feet. Behind us, an explosion goes off, pelting us with dirt and stones - knocking Mom and I to the ground. We quickly get back on our feet and begin to run as fast as we can up a sharp incline in order to beat the walls caving in behind us. Our one flashlight brightens the way through a maze of abandoned silver mine tunnels that once fueled the prosperity in Real de Catorce. I read somewhere it's empty of silver, but full of miner's souls, wandering the tunnels still hoping to strike it rich.

"Mom, I think we covered more than a mile," I say spitting out a glob of dirt on the ground.

"I know Joseph. The good news is we've been going up instead of down. Improves our chances of getting out – I think."

"Sounds right," I say staring at my iPhone. "No service – nothing."

"I'm sorry Joseph, bringing you into this mess. My job, life in the federal government, Diego and Tomas. People gone missing, tortured or killed. People I love," Mom says, her voice breaking. "Mexico and the United States at war with each other. How'd that happen?"

"Look Mom, none of this is your fault! Think of all the lives you saved – wars you prevented. This battle we're in started a long time ago. It's between the Cartels and us - the American people who support these worldwide illegal drug networks. Today, they, we must pick a side," I say. "Until we do, more lives will be wasted, families torn apart and bodies tossed into unmarked mass graves, all victims of the war on drugs. The guilty and the innocent, side by side in death."

Our conversation ends when we see what looks like moving shadows of people huddled around a fire flickering out of an old oil drum. As we get nearer, I see they're actually standing outside the tunnel entrance. The rising smoke from the fire gives the stars a hazy appearance, fading in and out of the early morning sky. We crawl towards the tunnel opening and encounter a group of Spanish-speaking men. If it weren't for the assault weapons strapped against their chests, I might have introduced myself. Seeing the President of the United States with a bloody bandage wrapped around his head covering one eye and sitting inside an old ore car, tells me we'd never get along anyway. As I turn to whisper something to my mother, I see she's gone. She was always friendlier than me.

I click on the homing signal on my smartphone, stand up and fall behind my mother. Doing some quick math, I see we're outnumbered twelve to two, three including the President. Based on his situation, I think I'll leave him out of the equation, at least for now. We move towards them and they begin to encircle us, with weapons pointing in our direction. My mom has the Sig in her right hand resting at her side. That leaves me with only Diego's Swiss Army knife tucked into my boot. She walks through the circle of armed men and over to the President, gently touches the bandages, says a few words and turns towards the mob. Before she has a chance to say anything, the Waltzing Matilda flies ten feet over our heads at a very slow speed with Pilot Bob's voice yelling something. We all momentarily stare at the sight over our heads and a few of the men begin to laugh and draw their guns, shooting them in the air. The laughter quickly dies down as the Sikorsky Seahawk flies in right behind the Brunner, lights blazing and guns pointed at our little circle. Now we have a fair fight.

CHAPTER 69
Monday / 4:55 AM
Real de Catorce

The downdraft of the rotor blades forces us to the ground. The swirling rocks and sand pelt us mercilessly as the helicopter swings in a small arc around us, twenty feet off the ground with its flashing strobe lights stopping men in the shadows. I spy my mother lying on the ground behind the ore car, arm reaching up towards the President's hand dangling over the side. Pandemonium breaks out at the make-shift camp as the kidnappers scatter into the desert and fire at the dipping Seahawk as it comes back around. I scramble along the ground to join my mother behind the ore car on the track as bullets ping all around us.

"Mom," I scream! "We gotta get out of here before the chopper starts firing back!" She looks at me with eyes wide open and nods her head in agreement.

"We need to get the President out of here!" she yells, standing and climbing into the car.

When she gets inside and towards the front, I see the car move a few feet along the track and stop. As the Seahawk comes over us on another pass lighting up the area, I notice we're on a small patch of land tucked into the mountainside. This must have been one of the ways the miners moved the silver down into the valley of Real de Catorce. With gunshots and explosions all around us, I make a snap decision. The lighted tail of the Seahawk begins to disappear as it swings once again in our direction. During this maneuver, I send a text to Carlone, who I hope is in the cockpit – "TURN OFF LIGHTS!" When the fast approaching helicopter is about to scream over our heads, all the lights go off and we're thrown into total darkness. I shield my eyes from the flying debris, get up behind the ore car

231

and use every ounce of strength I have left to push. I feel movement in the car and see my mom peer over the side as it finally begins to roll. We only need to move about ten feet before we hit a decline. It might as well be thirty miles as my energy level is fading fast. As my legs are about to give out, I feel someone beside me helping to push the car. Even though it's dark, I recognize a rather familiar face, partially covered by a white mask.

"Get in Joseph," he orders, "now – hurry!"

I feel the ground begin to slope and throw both arms over the wall of the car. A pair of arms grab me and start to pull me in. Tomas falls back onto the tracks and disappears from sight as we begin to pick up speed. Tumbling inside the car, I hear a series of loud explosions behind us that light up the sky with flashes as a shockwave helps push our car down the track. Several of the waning flashes momentarily light up the inside of our vehicle.

"I think he's okay Joseph," Mom says over the clacking of the track. "I have a strong pulse and hear him breathing. Can you hear me Mr. President?"

"Mom, we need to get some help, or none of us will make it out of the valley. Are you okay?"

"Yes – fine, a little sore in places, but that's it."

I search all my pockets and I find I must have dropped my smartphone somewhere along the tracks. We're sitting in a moving ore car going down a mountain side, picking up speed with no brakes. The safety of the President of the United States, who's barely conscious, forces me to clear my head and start thinking of a way out of this. I stare over at my mom and notice her eyes begin to flutter. Her head dips slowly to her neck and jolts back, eyes wide open. At first, I think it's exhaustion. What she's been through, both mentally and physically would have killed me days ago. It's the red stain on her jacket, near her shoulder that makes me think otherwise.

"Mom, you're hurt – there's blood – on your shoulder?" I say clutching her hand.

"Joe, Joe, Joseph, I'm tired", she whispers. "Hold my hand, please, where's your hand?"

"Here Mom, right here, I've got you. Rest - you're tired. I'll be right here"

"Few minutes, I'll rest. Just need a minute," she says before drifting off.

I check her shoulder and determine a bullet went clean through leaving a small hole that continues to drip blood. Wiping the tears from my eyes, I feel a hand gently touch my arm.

"Here son, let me put some pressure on the wound. I've known your mother for many years; a bullet through the shoulder will barely slow her down," the President says in a steady voice.

"Thank you Mr. President."

"Sam, it's Sam, not Mr. President. Okay Joe? I heard so much about you I feel like we're best of friends. Your mom has saved the world more times than I can count. It's your sixth sense I tell her, some gift she has for moving us in the right direction. Cutting through the crap, details that lead us down the correct path," he says while shifting his position in the car. "Unfortunately, even the correct path sometimes brings death and destruction, followed by great sadness."

We share a few moments of silence as the ore car comes slowly to a stop. There is a faint glimmer of light as the sun begins to rise in the east. I check my mom's wound to see that the blood loss is down to a trickle. She says my name a few times with a couple of "Diego's" mixed in. I watch the President stand up and gently place his legs over the side of the car and back onto solid ground.

"How're you feeling?" I say as he struggles to stand up. "You look like you need to sit down."

"I'm good," he replies. "Just a little beat up I guess, but okay."

"Good. I need to get my mom to a hospital right away. Any ideas?"

"Hand her out to me Joe, so I can lay her on the ground in a more comfortable position. Keep light pressure on the shoulder."

I gently pick her up and transfer her into the arms of the President. He lowers mom to the ground onto the coat he was wearing. I hear her stir and say my name.

"I'm here, Mom," I say loudly, hoping to penetrate the coma-like state she's in. "Right here."

Before climbing out myself, I search the bottom of the car and find my fully loaded Sig and best of all, my phone. I see that it still has half its battery life. Clicking on the GPS icon, a signal goes out to identify our position. Hoping someone's on the receiving end of the signal, I feel a second wind in me as I climb out of the car. When I hear the distinct sound of the Kinner R5 Radial engine overhead, I feel our luck is about to change. The 1932 Brunner Winkle Bird CK makes a wide swing a hundred feet above ground before it comes in for a smooth landing on the desert floor.

"Pilot Bob to the rescue!" I holler.

CHAPTER 70

Monday / 6:15 AM

Outside Real de Catorce

The Winkle Bird comes to a stop fifty feet from us. Bob climbs out of the cockpit with his booming voice, yelling, "Hey Buds. Look, I brought your sissy friend with me." Behind him, stepping to the ground from the front passenger seat is Mike. Pilot Bob wraps his arms around the President and lifts him off his feet. It's not until I hear a few "Buds" and laughter do I start to calm down.

"Joe, I'd like you to meet one of my oldest and dearest friends – Bob Roe," the President says proudly. "We met at Mardi Gras over twenty years ago, told me he worked for some glue company. Today, I'm the President of the United States and I'm still not sure what he does or doesn't do."

"Please Sam - Mr. President, I've met Joe and he knows I run a reputable transportation company with my buddy Jute."

"Joe, we followed you down the mountain," Mike says, walking towards us.

"That chopper was clogging up the airspace – had to get out of there. Anyway, Mike was the one who spotted you pushing the car," Bob says. "With that guy wearing a mask."

The mood turns serious when they see me hunched over Mom, lying on the ground.

"What happened?" Bob says leaning down placing his hand on her forehead.

"Shot - through the shoulder - lost a lot of blood," I reply. "We need to get her to a hospital!"

"Sam, under my seat in the cockpit, grab the first aid kit," Bob orders. "Need to clean and dress this wound before we move her. Hurry up Sam!

Mike, get that damn chopper on the phone right away. Joe, don't worry – she's a strong woman – your mom," he says softly. "You probably don't know this, but I first met your mother in Peru – thinking it was 1999 – yeah 99. Found her with the Uros, Uru-Iruitos people living on the lake – Titicaca - on those islands they make using reeds of some sort."

"She was trying to return something to the Peruvian government, but was set up," I say. "She mentioned a helicopter crash and being carried off by a group of locals. Mom says she doesn't remember what happened after that – ended up on a train in Lima two days later."

"Yep, that's what happened. Put her on that train myself," Bob replies as the President hands him the first aid kit. "Thanks Sam."

"You put her on the train?" I ask.

"Yeah, but she doesn't know it. Anyway, we'll talk later."

Watching Bob, I can tell this is not the first time he's dressed a wound. In less than five minutes, he's done and Mom begins speaking coherently.

"You alright Joe, you look tired?" she asks.

I laugh. "I want to ask you the same thing since you're the one who got shot."

"I guess I'm a little tired - thirsty too."

I open one of the bottles of water found in the bottom of the ore car and help get it to her lips. "Slowly Mom, drink slowly."

Between sips, she begins asking questions. Most I don't know the answers to.

"Where is the rest of our group? Oh my God - Stella?"

"Stella's fine. She's with everyone else in the Helicopter. Mike's working on their location right now."

"Is the President okay?"

"Yes, banged up, but alright. He's here – with us."

"Oh that's good. Is the United States at war with Mexico?"

"Not sure. Definitely at war with the Cartels."

"Can we get out of here?"

"Yes – at least you and the President, thanks to Pilot Bob."

"Who's Pilot Bob?"

"Someone you need to talk to once you're well. He might be able fill in some of the blanks from your time in Peru back in 99. Anyway, he's been friends with Sam – the President – for twenty years. He's your ride to a hospital – most likely in Tampico."

"That's nice Joseph. It's been quite a while since I've been in Tampa – Redskins game against the Buccaneers I think, or maybe a convention." She begins drifting off to sleep. Says something about having Diego or Stella take her to Washington Medical. I was glad she was sleeping so I wouldn't have to tell her that we're in the middle of Mexico. Hearing footsteps behind me, I turn to find Mike, the President and Bob ready to discuss a plan.

"The chopper's down," Mike says. "No one's hurt, but they're about thirty miles from here. Rogers says a bullet or something nicked one of the hydraulic lines – tail rotor problem. They're attempting repairs – Rogers thinks she can fix it. But she's unsure how long it will take."

"Clare and Stella okay?" I ask.

"Yeah, everybody's fine. Spoke to Clare, said it was a normal landing."

"Good – thanks," I say, relieved.

"The bad news is that neither of us is able to contact anybody in the outside world. It's eerie – like radio silence. Rogers is unable to raise a soul – not even the carrier group. Said the last she knew; the group was heading south."

"Okay so we move on," Bob says. "In speaking with Sam."

"Who?" Mike asks.

"Sam – the President for God's sake – pay attention. Anyway, here's what we know. Almost ten hours ago, the United States was forced to go to war with the drug cartels. As a result, the country of Mexico became involved. One dirty bomb that we know of was found undetonated on the border – San Diego area, I believe. This man, right here," Bob says pointing, "was kidnapped by members of the cartels. The Vice President is now in charge."

"She is more than capable to make the right decisions to get us out of this mess," the President chimes in. "But right now, getting Caroline out of here is our top priority!"

"I agree. The last time I had contact with the outside world, maybe three hours ago, the border towns were on fire and deserted," says Pilot Bob. "Joe, we're on our own and need to get your mother to a doctor. With the chopper unavailable, I'll fly to Linares – to the northeast - about 125 miles. I'll get in touch with my partner Jute to get a weather briefing and make contact with our friends in that area."

"Yeah, it's our best and only option - I like it – thank you," I reply. "You take Mom and the President. Mike and I will go back into Real de Catorce and find our way from there. Let's hope Rogers gets the chopper back in the air. If she does, we'll find you."

"Hang on, just spoke to Rogers – they're still grounded," Mike jumps in. "Got a better fix on their location – it's closer than I originally thought. Depending on our groundspeed, we should meet up with them in one, maybe two hours, depending on terrain."

Mom insists on sitting up for at least some of the trip on the Waltzing Matilda. She said she never flew in an open cockpit airplane before and was excited about the experience. "Joseph, the wind on my face. Oh and Joseph look, the President of the United States sitting beside me. Blue sky above and the beautiful Mexican countryside below." Pilot Bob found a pair of "aviator goggles" for Mom to wear, which looked more like eyewear you'd see on a ski slope. Mike did the final seatbelt check to make sure both were snug and secure. We say our goodbyes and within five minutes, Pilot Bob and company defy gravity taking off in the Brunner Bird CK. As I watch the plane's tail vanish into the horizon, I feel a momentary chill shake my whole body. I am hit with an inescapable feeling of dread thinking I will never see Mom again.

A vehicle approaches us from the north. As it gets closer, I'm able to see that it's an old Toyota Land Cruiser. It has no top or doors, but it does have a skinny man standing on the passenger seat looking over the cracked windshield in our direction. As the vehicle slows, he gives us the one finger salute and tells us to get in. At the same time, Mike and I yell "stranger danger" and don't know if we should get in or run. Kingman certainly has that effect on people. Oh well. I'm just glad he's on our side.

CHAPTER 71

Monday / 7:45 AM

Outside Matehuala, San Luis Potosi, Mexico

After I explain to Diego what happened to my mother, we pile into the "borrowed" Land Cruiser and head east to Matehuala to do some shopping – for helicopter parts. It's about a fifteen mile ride through the desert on washed-out roads. Kingman is in the backseat bending Mike's ear about being held as prisoner back in Magic Town by a guy who looked like the Hulk. Not the green superhero, but the wrestler. Mike has that look on his face, letting me know he is about to jump out of the moving vehicle.

"Joe what happened?" Diego yells over the wind noise.

"During the shootout, she got hit in the shoulder – clean through. I didn't notice it till we got to the bottom of the canyon. I don't think Mom even knew she was shot. She was too busy worrying about the President."

"That's your mother alright – concerned about everyone else!" Diego says, shaking his head.

"Hey, look Diego, she's on her way to get proper medical attention – in Linares – thanks to Bob Roe," I stutter. "She'll get the help she needs. They're probably there by now."

"I hope so," say Diego. "This Bob – Pilot Bob ran out of gas two times since I've known him. And how long have I known him – two days?"

"Stop Diego!" Mike shouts from the back. "Don't worry, she'll be fine. We had to get them out of Catorce – had no choice at the time!"

"Mike's right, it was our only option," I say. "Take a look around – we're in the middle of nowhere."

"They're right," Kingman chimes in. "I'll wager a bet that she's safer than we are right now. So please - stop your whining and let's get on with it!"

239

Diego stares straight ahead, attempting to keep the Cruiser from hitting any large holes. Clare, Rogers, Carlone and the wonder dog are on the ground several miles east of Matehuala in a deep canyon off route 62. After texting back and forth with Clare, I learn that the problem with the helicopter is not with the tail rotor itself, but rather a wiring harness that controls its movement. Based on Clare's description, it sounds like stray bullets caused a short circuit and small electrical fire. Carlone and Rogers have been able to bypass some of the burned circuitry with minimal results, but are confident they can fly. Our job is to go into town, find an electrical type of distributor and pick up a few spare items. Two Americans, one Englishman and a Mexican riding in a "borrowed" Toyota Land Cruiser with no top or doors is sure to get some attention.

CHAPTER 72

Monday / 10:10 AM
Matehuala, San Luis Potosi, Mexico

Following coordinates taken from Carlone's email, our GPS leads us north on Route 57 right through the center of the city. The roads are quite busy since it's the middle of the morning. People take notice of us, but show little interest. Diego displays a friendly wave or two, while the rest of us slump down in our seats.

"Diego, merge left off 57," Mike says from the back seat. "We need to get over to Ponciano Arriaga – street, avenue, boulevard – something or other. There's a split ahead – stay left."

"See it," replies Diego.

Off the main road and onto a side street, we pass the Oficinas de la Policia Federal on our left. We see several heavily armed people walking in front of the white glassed building dressed in military style uniforms. Two of the soldiers turn their heads in our direction as we drive by. No one thinks to wave. Unsure about what to expect from the close encounter, my spirits are lifted when we pass under a cement arch with a sign that says "Bienvenidos Matehuala." It's like a smaller version of the Gateway Arch in St. Louis Missouri.

"Next left – Cipres," Mike yells from the back. "Go to the end – right on Juan Sarabia. Guys, once we make the turn look for Applied Industrial Technologies. They should have the stuff we need for the chopper."

"Bad news gentlemen," Kingman says. "We have two motorcycles about a quarter mile behind us – ridden by police. They just put on the flashing lights. Suppose it's us they're after?"

"Knew we should have waved," I reply.

241

"Applied coming up on the right," Diego says.

"Pass it," I shout.

"Motorcycle cops slowing up behind us – looks like traffic issues," Mike says.

"Diego, you and Kingman go in – pull over," I say. I'll take over the driving – Mike, you're with me."

"Okay," Diego replies. "Kingman's got the list?"

"I dandy well do!"

"Listen you guys; we'll let them to chase us around town. When you're ready, text us and we'll come back to pick you up."

"Let's be careful!" Mike chimes in.

Speeding away from the curve, Mike informs me that they made it into the store.

"I'll try to circle the block – stay close," I say.

"I don't think so," Mike replies. "We have two, no three motorcycle cops closing in behind us. Must be looking for us?"

"Agree – especially since we have two police cars heading towards us."

"Take the next left!" Mike yells. "Before they block us in!"

I take the turn early and hit a curb that sends the Land Cruiser up on two wheels crashing down into a wooden bench. I manage to get the vehicle back onto the narrow road when my smartphone begins vibrating.

"Mike, read this text," I yell handing him the phone.

"Watch the road – donkey – ass – horse looking animal, ahead on right!"

"I see it!" I reply, slowing the Toyota. She's in front of the police roadblock."

"Oh yeah – I see that too."

"Our friends on the motorcycles are right behind us," I add.

"Joe, text's from Clare – they got the chopper working. Says they're coming to pick us up."

"Tell them to stay on the ground – wait to hear from us," I say, grinding the Land Cruiser into four-wheel drive.

We're now off the road and literally driving through neighborhoods. I guess I must be doing something right because my best friend next to me is wearing a smile from ear-to-ear. My ego suddenly deflates when two motorcycles pass on the right leading us into an alley. A smile quickly comes to my face as the riders on one bike wave to us. One's wearing a three-piece suit clutching an umbrella and the other has an Applied bag sticking out of his shirt. On the other motorcycle, the driver's wearing a white mask covering the right side of his face, looking straight ahead.

CHAPTER 73

Monday / 10:35 AM
Matehuala, San Luis Potosi, Mexico

"Joe – behind us," Mike says. "Motorcycle cops – the real ones."

"See 'em," I reply. "Hang on – quick left!"

The Land Cruiser bounces down a small hill before crashing through a rickety homemade picket fence and goes into an empty dirt parking lot. With no motorcycles or police in sight, I slow the Toyota down to thirty miles per hour before coming to a dead stop in front of the muddy soccer field.

"Are we stopping for a reason?" Mike says. "Game hasn't started yet."

"Yeah we are," I reply. "Time to go home."

"I'm ready to go. This action adventure stuff is great, but Joanne needs me at home. You know she has a hard time when I'm gone."

"I do Mike. I'm sure a lot of people miss you when you're gone."

"I think so," he replies. "But they know that even when I'm not around, I'm always thinking about them – no matter where I am."

"Okay buddy, let's go home. Get Clare on the cell and tell her to get the chopper in the air to pick us up. They can zero in on our signal, but just in case, tell her X marks the spot!"

I slowly drive the Toyota Land Cruiser onto the soccer field and stop. Mike finishes his conversation with Clare, looks over at me and smiles.

"Now I get it," he says. "And I'll tell Diego to get over here right away."

I throw the Cruiser's gearshift into four-wheel drive low. After several attempts, it finally locks into place. I begin to slowly move the vehicle diagonally across the field. The wheels on the Toyota dig into the mud, making deep impressions on the field as we go. I stop on the opposite side,

244

take the transmission out of four-wheel drive low and make a hard left. When I think I've gone far enough, I stop and put the transmission back in low. We head off in the opposite direction of our first trek across the field and head to the other side. Our two impressions meet in the middle of the field just as the parking lot starts filling up with police and military style vehicles.

"Looks like they're waiting for us," Mike says. "Think they know what we're doing?"

"Don't think so – has to be seen from the air."

When we get to the other side, I stop and take the Land Cruiser out of low. Several vehicles move towards us as a single motorcycle rips down the center between them. I start to move the Toyota when the motorcycle pulls alongside. Kingman is the driver, with Diego the passenger who looks like he's about to be sick. We both stop.

"Guys, the chopper is on its way!" I yell.

"Should be here in 6 minutes," Mike says looking at his watch.

"Where?" shouts Diego.

"Here – right here!" replies Mike.

"Looks a little too busy – don't you think?" Says Kingman.

"It won't be," I snap back.

"You two take that motorcycle back into the neighborhoods – wait for the chopper to arrive. Mike and I will take the Federales on a little sightseeing tour around town."

"Got it – bloody good idea," says Kingman. "So we'll see you in 6 minutes then."

We split up in opposite directions as the police come within a hundred feet of us.

"They look mad," Mike says.

"Now why would that be?" I reply.

"Simple – you destroyed their soccer field. Sign said game tonight at echo - eight," Mike laughs.

"No game tonight – too muddy," I say. "Anyway, call Clare again – tell her we're leaving the area. Get a fix on our position now. Oh, and tell them to look for the X."

We've lost sight of Kingman and Diego on the motorcycle. Looks like most of the police vehicles are chasing us. Knowing that the Land Cruiser will never be able to outrun them, I tell Mike to hang on as we once again head for the cover of the neighborhoods just as the shooting starts. I tell Mike to relax – "I'll put the top up." He laughs as I drive into a blind alleyway with a police barricade waiting for us at the end. I slam on the brakes and throw the Cruiser into reverse. Unfortunately, police cars are blocking us in from behind. We roll to a stop and I'm thinking OK Corral – not good.

CHAPTER 74

Monday / 10:55 AM

Matehuala, San Luis Potosi, Mexico

"We've been lucky for way too long," I say, looking over at Mike. "Blocked in a narrow alley with nowhere to go – except maybe to jail."

"Listen, I've been in a Mexican jail and believe me, we don't want to go there," Mike replies. "At least they're not shooting at us."

"Yeah, but they're moving in closer from both ends," I add. "Getting out of here in this vehicle is not an option."

"On foot won't work either," Mike says.

The police cars stop and their doors fly open. A man in a military uniform takes up a position behind the passenger side door, shouts through a bullhorn using broken English. He tells us to "Get our arms over" and "Live our car." He could speak in any language and we'd surely get the message. As we're about to comply, a garage door opens on our right side, causing a momentary state of confusion.

"Mike go - run!" I yell.

He quickly disappears inside the dark garage as I throw the Toyota into first thinking I might be able to squeeze it through the door. I end up slamming the right side of the car into the outside wall. Knowing I'm not gonna get inside, I put the Cruiser in reverse and move it from the wall and stop. In the rearview mirror, I can see the two police officers moving in behind me with guns drawn. The officer in front is back on the bullhorn telling me "We not hurt you – get our arms over." His verbal warning begins to get drowned out by the sound of an approaching helicopter. The cops behind me stop and look up to the sky. It's at that very moment that I glimpse Mike in my rearview jump in their car as he rolls it out of the alley in reverse with tires squealing. The distraction is enough for me to slam the

247

shifter into reverse and back out of the alley. The police behind me start firing wildly as they sprint to get out of my way. I roll the Toyota onto the main street, slam on the brakes and jam the shifter into first. I see Mike up ahead in the police car, waving his arm out the window. Looks like I'll be getting a police escort back to the soccer field – how special.

CHAPTER 75

Matehuala, San Luis Potosi, Mexico

Mike is having the time of his life with the siren blaring and lights flashing on the Mexican police vehicle. Racing down Benito Juarez at 70 miles per hour on our way to the soccer field, the damaged right fender on the Toyota comes loose and bounces off the hood. It crashes onto the road behind me and gets wedged under a white GM Hummer that was following a little too close. A dark shadow quickly crosses the road as the Sikorsky Seahawk flies over the street at tree top level. We take a left on Juarez and immediately I have a motorcycle on my tail. If the driver wasn't wearing a three-piece suit and his passenger clutching an umbrella, I might have started to worry. As they fly past me, Diego stills has the gumption to give me the one finger salute as they get in behind Mike.

We take a fast right onto Leona Vicario and a line of five Mexican police vehicles fall in behind me. With traffic heavy and knowing that our final turn into the soccer stadium is quickly approaching, I begin to slow down. I allow several vehicles to turn in front of me before finally losing sight of Mike's flashing police car and that strange pair on the motorcycle. On my right side, I can see the Seahawk slowing above the houses and hovering over what must be the field. I purposely stay straight and miss the turn that leads to the field. With luck still on my side, the five police cars follow me past the turn. I step on the gas and bring the Toyota back up to sixty, weaving in and out of traffic. In an effort to get back to the stadium, I take a fast right into a parking lot, avoid hitting several pedestrians and disappear down an alley. I stop the vehicle and watch the Mexican police cars speed by, realizing I finally need to make this call. I pull my cell from my pocket and hit speed dial.

"Joe, where are you?" Clare screams. "We've landed – we're on the field!"

"I'm running late Clare – sorry. How about the others – did they make it?"

"Yeah, Kingman, Mike and Diego just got aboard. No you!"

"I love you Clare – on my way."

"Hurry Joe – please," she cries. "Rogers says we barely have enough fuel to make it back to the coast. And she also finally made contact with the Carrier Group. Where are you Joe? I'm scared."

"Don't worry, I'll see you soon." I reply as I put the Toyota in gear and begin moving down the alley. "Clare, honey – please pass the phone to Carlone."

"Joe, I'm scared you're not gonna make it – really am. I love you,"

"Love you too – I'll make it - don't worry."

I hear the cell drop and Clare crying in the background.

"Joe, where are you?" Carlone asks.

"Too far away to catch this ride," I reply. "You gotta get out of here – don't wait. It's too dangerous and you have a fuel problem."

"Joe, we're not leaving without you – no way!" Carlone fires back.

"Listen, you have no choice. You must get the chopper in the air and get everyone outta here – you, more than anyone know it's not safe!"

"Joe, the Navy is sending a few jets our way to provide some cover."

"That's great, but it won't solve your fuel problem."

"Ten minutes – you got ten minutes to get your ass to this field. This area is going to be getting hot very soon. We're gonna take off, circle the town and come back for you in ten minutes. Got that!"

"Listen Jim, I'll do my best, but you gotta promise me that if I don't make it, you won't land and get outta here."

"Agreed," Carlone replies. "Hey, its eleven o'clock now – be safe."

"Okay – see you in ten."

The line goes dead as I approach the end of the alleyway and ease back into light traffic on the main road. With no cops in sight, I begin to relax thinking, I might have a chance. I can hear the thumping of helicopter blades overhead. Unfortunately, my moment of Zen quickly vanishes as the road ahead begins to get congested. It's stop and go. I read a text from

250

Clare reminding me that they'll be back at the field in six minutes and that I'd better be there – "love you."

Moving at a snail's pace, I think I finally see the cause of the backup. That white Hummer that was behind me when the Toyota's fender fell off is parked on the side of the road. Being too hemmed in by other vehicles, I have no choice but to pass it. As I get closer, I see a motorcycle lying in the middle of the road and a shirtless man standing with his back to me, handcuffed to the passenger's side door handle. While twisting his body to avoid people spitting on him, I notice his back is red and thickly scarred with a white tiger tattoo on his neck. Thinking now might be a good time to repay some favors. I reach under the seat and retrieve my fully loaded Sig. As I pull alongside the Hummer, the timer on my iPhone goes off letting me know that ten minutes have passed. I turn off the alarm and stop the Toyota.

CHAPTER 76

Monday / 11:10 AM
Matehuala, San Luis Potosi, Mexico

As soon as I get out of my vehicle, horns start beeping and the angry drivers begin yelling at me. I doubt they're saying anything nice, but I smile anyway. With gun in hand, I walk slowly to the back of the Hummer. I fire off two shots that instantly flatten the tires. I walk around to the front and do the same. I finally make eye contact with the man handcuffed to the door – he smiles.

"Tomas," I yell over the noise of the horns. "Pull your arm away from the door handle."

He nods and I fire a shot that breaks the chain, freeing him from the door.

"Gracias," he says.

"Get in – we're late," I reply.

He slides into the passenger seat and I walk to the back of the Toyota. I reach into my surf bag and pull out a tee shirt and toss it to him. As I'm about to get in, my eye catches something white under the Hummer. I reach down, pick it up and wipe it as clean as I can with my shirt. I hand it to Tomas.

"Gracias again – Joe."

"You're welcome – Tomas."

He slips the mask over the right side of his face as I slip the car into gear and we start to move forward. Needless to say, I caused quite a commotion and sirens can be heard coming from all directions. I manage to get the Cruiser up on the sidewalk, over a bed of flowers, through a crowd of onlookers and onto a side street. Moving along at a high speed, it's hard to make any conversation with Tomas due to the Seahawk flying 100 feet over our head.

My smile quickly fades as a police car crashes into the rear of the Toyota, trying to force us off the road. I take a hard left breaking us free, but am forced to drive down a rocky ravine, which causes one of our rear tires to blow. We begin to tilt before the Toyota finally rolls onto its side. When we come to a stop, looking through the front windshield, I notice three things. The soccer field is in front of us. Tomas is lying on the sideline still strapped into his seat. And, we're surrounded by an army of police.

CHAPTER 77

The Mexican police drag me out of the car, throw me into the mud on my stomach and zip tie my hands behind my back. I hear Tomas moaning as they cut him out of the seat and push him to the ground. They rip the mask off his face and toss it on the ground. He looks over at me as they force him to his feet and shove him into the back of one of their vehicles and slam the door. Two cops get in the front seat and drive slowly away as a heavy-set man in a military uniform walks over to me.

"Señor Joseph Dustan, get to your feet," he says over the sound of the approaching helicopter. "We've been looking for you."

"Well, you found me – congratulations," I reply, as I struggle to my feet. "Look, I'm sorry about damaging your soccer field, but I will pay to fix it."

"Yes, Señor Dustan, you're right – you will pay. But before we discuss your reparation, you need to contact your chopper and tell them to leave this area and the Mexican airspace immediately. Or we'll be forced to shoot it down."

He pulls wire cutters from his pocket, walks behind me, and snips the zip ties from around my wrists as the Seahawk circles a few hundred feet above the stadium. I pull the ringing cell from my pocket while watching several soldiers place portable Stinger missile launchers on their shoulders.

"You see Señor Dustan, our two countries are at war," he says. "Who's at fault is not my concern. But people who enter my country illegally causing death and destruction are. Call your helicopter now or we'll be forced to protect our homeland."

"Excuse me – your name?" I ask. "Before you start your own personal war, I want you to know that the helicopter is fully armed. Enough firepower to level this town."

"Martinez – Jose is my name. It's not wise to threaten me."

"No threat Martinez – I just want you to know what you're up against."

"Oh, in that case, thank you," he replies pulling a handgun from his coat pocket. "Now make the call Señor Dustan, or you will be too dead to see what happens," he yells placing the gun against my temple.

Out of snappy comebacks, I grab the cell from my pocket and hit Clare's number.

"Joe," Clare screams. "Tell those bastards to back off! We're landing to pick you up! Please - tell them to move back."

"Clare - can't do that," I reply. "They have surface-to-air missiles down here and they're threatening to shoot you down."

"Joe, we're landing! Here, talk to Mike! He'll tell you!"

"No Clare, tell Rogers not to land – please."

"Joe, it's Mike, what's the situation?"

"Not good. They have Stingers and I think they'll use 'em if you try to land."

"You sure?"

"Yeah, I'm sure," I reply. "Hey, listen Mike, it's time you all go home. I'll be fine. If they wanted to kill me, they'd have done so. Tell Carlone we don't want to start another international incident – just get out of here. Oh and Mike – tell Clare I love her and will see her soon. Take care of everyone – see you soon – bye."

I hang up the phone and drop it in the muddy water at my feet. Through the murky film, I see ripples breaking the surface as the phone begins to vibrate. Knowing who it's from, I pull myself together and start walking away.

"Señor Dustan, where do you think you're going?" Martinez asks.

"I did what you requested – now I need to take a walk."

"You'll have plenty of time to walk in the yard of a Mexican prison," he replies.

I look up into the sky and watch the Sikorsky Seahawk Helicopter circle the area one more time before it heads east towards the coast. I am relieved. I say a quick prayer that they will be safe. I end it speaking aloud - "Father, Son and Holy Spirit – Amen." I look at the soldiers around me, take a deep breath and start walking. I hear the rumble of jets and then see two Navy Super Hornets fly above the tree tops. I smile, knowing that my recent prayer was answered. A navy escort for the helicopter. Go Navy!

I walk on, pick up the white mask and tuck it into my shirt. Trailed by a group of Mexican cops, I stop; look up in the sky hoping for one last miracle, which quickly fades along with the jet's vapor trails.

CHAPTER 78
Monday / 9:30 PM
Aboard the USS Harry Truman / Gulf of Mexico

Dear Joe,

Stella said I was in shock on the flight back to the Carrier Group. I remember her holding my hand and mumbling that, "Things we'll be alright – you'll see." I was aware that we landed shortly after leaving you – stranded in Matehuala. I heard someone say Magic Town after Mike and Diego got off the helicopter. Diego used his Swiss Army Knife to shave off the rest of his mustache. Said it was all your fault after I stopped laughing.

Kelly Rogers said we barely had enough fuel to make it back. Stepping out onto the flight deck of the aircraft carrier reminded me how much I hate boats. But seeing the Waltzing Matilda tied down next to a Navy Jet did bring a smile to my face.

Even though I'm exhausted, I don't think I'll be able to sleep as long as you're away. Sounds foolish I know, but I have to believe that we'll find you – alive. You'll come back to us. War or no war. And somehow we'll find a way to start over.

Joe, I'm going to take a hot shower, put on some clean clothes and visit your mother in sickbay. Jim said she's recovering nicely and should be back on her feet in a week or two. I heard the President is already on his way back to Washington. Jim told me the buzz on the ship is not about the President, but Pilot Bob – Bob Roe. He said Bob was followed by Mexican airplanes and had no choice but make a run for the Truman. Whether the part about his plane running out of gas as he touched down on the flight deck is true or not, I'll leave that for you to decide. Please know that we'll find you very soon.

All my love, Clare.

CHAPTER 79

Tuesday / 8:00 PM EST
Prime Time Presidential Address

"Good Evening. Seven days ago there was a series of tragic events that took place along our border with Mexico. An undetonated dirty bomb was located along the San Diego and Tijuana border. If detonated, thousands of lives would have been lost. Fatalities South of the Border are unknown at this time. The President of Mexico was assassinated and presently the country is in utter chaos. It is unclear who is in charge, but a declaration of war has been posted in the United Nations by Mexico's new ambassador.

Most bridges along the border have been destroyed and needless to say we have restricted all travel into Mexico. At last count, we have close to 70,000 people living and working inside Mexico. All Federal agencies are working together to bring these Americans home. As most of you know, I was kidnapped at the border near Brownsville, Texas and lucky enough to be rescued by a group of people on vacation. It's a story I'll leave for another time.

Approximately fifteen years ago, the heads of the Mexican, Central and South American drug cartels got together and devised a plan code named Snares of the Devil. For those of you who know the Bible, I must mention that the plan had nothing to do with religion. But it was about temptation and price fixing. What we understand up to this point is that the cartels believed that if they conspired together to fix the price of illegal drugs going over the border, they would hook multiple generations. They decided that it would be best to price these drugs artificially low in order to tempt us into buying and using them, thus becoming dependent. This is a similar strategy used by the cigarette industry in the 60's and 70's.

One of the most abhorrent things to come from that meeting was an agreement by all members that if the United States took the Drug War onto

258

Mexican soil and Central America, they would use what was called their doomsday option. Code name – Snares of the Devil. Seven days ago, a snare, trap was set for both countries, celebrating the successes of NAFTA. Using their terminology – "against the devil" – the United States of America.

Thanks to the swift and proper actions of Vice President Jacobs, we have over 50,000 members of our armed services on their way home to help us win this war against the cartels. The Vice President took the courageous stand to let the world know that the United States will no longer be the world's policeman. I must admit, this was a stand I was unable to take based on blind ambition and winning the next round of elections.

Moving forward, the United States will bring home those stranded in Mexico. We will continue to keep the lines of communication open between both our countries. As I said during a recent Presidential address back on February 4th, people are dying in these drug wars, and remember, there is such a thing as guilt by association. We have to eliminate the source, and that is us. As an addendum to that Address, we must remember not only those who have died over the last several days, but the hundreds of thousands who have died because of illegal drugs over the last 25 years.

Thank you and God Bless America."

EPILOGUE
Location Unknown

Sitting in a wooden chair, I'm staring through a fence made of chicken wire. My wrists are chained to a makeshift table with armor shaped grey bugs crawling all over it. On the other side of the wire sits Clare, holding a box on her lap. She's wearing a Red Sox baseball cap and a NY Yankees t-shirt. The single light bulb over our head flashes intermittently, revealing another person. Blinking shadows reveal a white mask covering the right side of his face. His lips are moving rapidly, but I can't hear anything.

"Joe, for your Birthday, I baked you a cake," Clare says, winking.

"Thank you," I reply.

"I'm sorry Joe, but we can't stay long – going to a funeral."

"I – I understand Clare," I stutter. "Who died?"

"You don't know – really Joe? Nobody told you?"

"No, you're my first visitors since I've been here."

"I'll tell you all about it on my next visit. I need to get going – they're waiting."

"Clare, before you leave, remind me how long I've been here. Will you please?"

"Oh Joe – not long. Anyway, you'll be out soon – really."

The light blinks off and on and Clare is standing to leave. The masked man is no longer in the room. I can't help but notice she's wearing a wedding ring. As she walks away, I say her name, but no response. The light goes off and I hear screaming all around me. I find myself lying on a hard dirt floor with pungent odors penetrating my nostrils. With the help of stray light coming from the vent above, I find the box sitting next to me.

Hunger pains rip through my body and I quickly tear the box open. Inside I find a stone about the size of a softball. Moving it close to my face,

I see an image of a man carved into the stone. Could be anybody, I guess. I run my hand under the face and feel what might be writing. Thinking it might be a secret code to get me outta here, I move to the brightest spot in the room. Using my fingers as well as my eyes, I trace out three words. T-R-A-M-P-A-S, no clue. Second word. D-E-L, nothing. Last word. D-I-A-B-L-O, could be devil. Hate puzzles. I drop the stone on the ground and grab what's left of the box. I thought Clare said there was a cake in here. Running my hand along the bottom flap, I feel an object under the tape. After great effort, I manage to release the object from the tape. It's several inches long, about an inch thick. Both sides have a red smooth surface. Moving back to the light, I see it's a Swiss Army knife. I fall to the ground on my back, laughing hysterically, abruptly stopping after what feels like an eternity. I stand up, walk around my tiny cell feeling all four walls from top to bottom. Sinking back to the ground, I realize that I don't have any windows or doors. I crawl along the stinky floor, find the stone and curl up with it. Now I hear screaming – my screaming.

"Joe, wake up – you're dreaming again," shouts a voice from above. "Come on now Joe – wake up."

I feel someone shaking my shoulder as I slowly open my eyes. The stench forces me to start heaving before I finally roll to my side and throw up. I feel the vomit dribble down my cheek.

"It's okay – just a dream," a voice says behind me.

"Nightmare," I reply, still heaving.

Looking through the bars, I see a guy in the next cell hung himself. His skin is wrinkled and grey - eyes bulging from their sockets. A steady flow of bodily fluids drips into a large brown puddle under his feet.

"They'll cut him down," the voice says behind me. "They come every two – three days."

"They – who?" I reply.

"Don't know – military maybe."

"How long have we been here?" I ask.

"We're underground, so it's hard to keep time. A week or two I guess."

I crawl over to the wall and painfully move into a sitting position. It's eerily quiet except for the sound of dogs barking off in the distance. I pull myself up using the cell's bars, and stare at the hanged man. My eye catches a familiar white object lying in a corner.

"Did he do it himself?" I ask.

"No – he had help. Actually, he fought hard against it, even after the bastards beat him with wooden bats."

"Where was I?"

"Passed out – sick most of the time."

"You know his brother always talked highly of him. He saved my life more than once. Rest in peace Tomas. Rest in peace."

"So Joe, I know neither of us is good at making a plan. But, to get out of this shithole, we're gonna need a really good one."

"You're right, this time we'll need a good plan," I reply.

Our cell goes quiet and I listen to the drip, drip, drip. I now realize that I may never find out if Tomas was my father. May never know whose side he was really on. I do know that he was good to me, and to Clare. That's enough for me now.

"Hey Mike?"

"Yeah."

"I'm sorry you never got home."

"Yeah, me too. But somebody had to save your sorry ass. Diego and I knew no one else would. Look at you, throwing up all over yourself. Don't expect us to be roomies ever again."

"Thanks buddy," I say.

"You're welcome. Hey, but anyways, I was surprised Carlone let Rogers drop Diego and I off to look for you. Pilot Bob had an idea where they might be holding you, and he was right. Of course, I got caught and now we're cellmates. Hey, don't forget, Diego's still in the area looking for us."

"I won't forget. Anyway, he's now the main character in our escape plan," I say.

"Yeah right – he's the only character."

"Let's hope nothing happens to him."

"Oh Joe, I almost forgot. When Tomas was brought in, he asked me to give this to you," Mike says, pulling a Swiss Army Knife from his pocket and tossing it to me. "Said your father wanted you to have it."

I clasp my fingers around the knife and pull out the large blade. Not too surprised by what I see, I close my eyes to think about how I got here. How I dragged the people I love down with me. People dying around me, sometimes by my own hand. The sadness of knowing that the world is not a safe place, believing that evil and deep seeded hatred is the root of most problems. Sadly, this is what I've learned to be true. It wasn't until I met Clare that hope existed. "Good Night Clare," I whisper in the dark.

"Good night Joe," Mike replies.

I wake up to the sound of men's voices and the roar of jet engines somewhere overhead. It's hard to make out what's being said over the machine gun sound of Mike's snoring. I look over and see Tomas's shadow still hanging in his makeshift noose. It's the open red umbrella I see hanging on our cell door that gives me hope. As I fall back into blackness, a distinctive dog howling somewhere on the outside forces me to pinch myself hard to make sure I'm not dreaming – "ouch."

The End

FATHER, SON AND HOLY SPIRIT – BOOK 1

A terrorist attack on Inauguration Day stuns Washington.

US security groups turn to one person who might be able to piece it together; a librarian with ties to the White House. Her son Joe, ex-military, goes undercover as a DEA operative racing against the clock to find the terrorists and a missing friend, all without losing Sister Clare.

Throw in an ex-roller derby queen, a priest, nuns, the phantom of the opera, and you have colorful characters with skills.

Get on the roller coaster with Joe as he careens through Mexico hunting down suspects. Who he finds along the way causes him to question his own gene pool.

Can a deadly terrorist attack in DC lead to a unique family reunion?

Find the answers inside the pages of *Father, Son and Holy Spirit.*

Available at Amazon.com

COMING SPRING 2019

The final installment in the Drug War Trilogy with a colorful cast of characters finally brings it all together to answer all questions that have been keeping you up at night. Mark your calendars and keep an eye out for *It is Finished,* the last book in this series.

www.ingramcontent.com/pod-product-compliance
Lightning Source LLC
Chambersburg PA
CBHW061949170626
46813CB00006B/2584